SECRETS RISING

Sally Berneathy

Of course I know right from wrong.
Wrong is the fun one.

Sally Berneathy

This book is a work of fiction. The names, characters, places and incidents are products of the writer's imagination or have been used fictitiously and are not to be construed as real. Any resemblance to persons, living or dead, or to actual events, locales or organizations is entirely coincidental.

Secrets Rising
Copyright ©2012 Sally Berneathy

Original cover art by Alicia Hope
http://www.aliciahopeauthor.blogspot.com/

Prologue

"The world lost a couple of great people when your parents died. But I reckon you know that." George Flanders and his wife, Dorothy, wearing their best black clothes, smelling faintly of mothballs and funeral flowers, were the last of the mourners.

Rebecca Patterson nodded and gave them a shaky smile. "I do know that."

"You call us if you need anything," Dorothy said.

Rebecca hugged her. "I will. Thank you both for coming."

George stepped forward awkwardly, and Rebecca gave the tall, lanky man a warm embrace.

She walked outside with them, onto her parents' front porch, into the heat of Texas in June, and watched them drive away. As their old blue Ford dwindled into the distance, Rebecca turned back to the silent, empty house.

It was a mess, paper plates and cups everywhere, the kitchen full of half-eaten food that should be refrigerated. She'd clean it up later. Right now none of it seemed important. Her parents weren't coming back whether the place was messy or clean.

She walked over to her father's ancient brown recliner and ran her fingers over the soft, faded material. A faint whiff of cherry scented pipe tobacco lingered, and she half expected her father to ease out of the chair, smile and wink, enfold her in a bear hug, tease her about a nonexistent freckle or her naturally blond hair that he jokingly accused his brunette wife of bleaching from the time Rebecca was a baby.

Any minute now her effervescent mother would rush into the room and embrace her, introduce her to the latest guest or guests, ask her to stay for dinner, to spend the night in her old room...if nobody else was using it at the moment.

The three-bedroom, ranch-style home in Plano, a suburb of Dallas, had always been filled with people. Her parents had drawn them like magnets...entertained them, helped them, cared for them.

Since the automobile accident three days ago that had taken the lives of her mother and father, the house had been filled with friends day and night, even more than when her parents were alive. When she was young Rebecca had sometimes wanted the constant stream of people to stop, had wanted the house to be quiet and her parents to belong only to her.

Now she had half that wish. The house was quiet and everyone was gone.

And she'd give everything she had or ever would have to bring back the noise, to have her parents again even if she had to share them with twice as many people.

She retrieved a couple of half-full paper cups from the battered coffee table and almost smiled at the rings they left, at the thought that a few more stains wouldn't matter. The family restaurant had always provided a decent income. Rebecca had never lacked essentials as she grew up, but her parents hadn't believed in luxuries for themselves when others needed necessities.

She'd have to find something to do with all of it...the furniture, the pots and pans, the mismatched dishes, their clothing...

She turned down the hallway to the bedrooms, hesitated at the entrance to her parents' room. Their answering machine rested on a desk in there. She'd been in and out several times the last three days, checking messages, but every trip still felt like an invasion of their privacy.

Numbly she walked over and sat in the desk chair. Instead of listening to more sympathy calls, however, she hit the button to hear the outgoing message, to hear her mother's voice.

"Hi! This is Brenda Patterson. Jerry and I are busy right now, but if you'll leave us a message, we'll get right back to you. I promise!"

The voice that always had a smile in it. Only a voice now, a whisper of the once-vital person. Yet, like the smell of pipe tobacco from her dad's recliner, the voice on the answering machine brought with it a wisp of that person.

Tears obscured her vision so that she had to move the machine closer in order to find the button again.

As she listened to her mother's voice one more time, she noticed a small key where the answering machine had rested. It must have been shoved under the machine and forgotten.

She picked it up and yanked on the top desk drawer to open it, to toss the key inside.

The drawer was locked.

Impossible.

Her open-hearted parents had no secrets, never locked anything.

She studied the key more closely then slowly inserted it into the locked drawer.

It fit.

And turned.

So maybe the drawer had been accidentally locked and the key lost under the answering machine.

Only...how did you accidentally lock a drawer?

Maybe her parents had secrets after all.

Holding her breath, not sure what she expected to find, she slid the drawer open. It contained two items—a square of folded blue fabric and a letter with "To Brenda and Jerry Patterson" written in faded blue ink.

She unfolded the fabric. A dress in a fashion reminiscent of the eighties, small like a child or teenager would wear, but the style more mature. Had her mother, a woman of average height and weight, once been that tiny? Had she worn this dress? Why had she saved it in a locked drawer?

She picked up the envelope, withdrew the single sheet of paper and unfolded it.

Dear Brenda and Jerry, the note read. *I'm going to miss both of you more than I can say. I can't begin to tell you how much I appreciate everything you've done for me...*

Another grateful recipient of the Pattersons' big hearts. Tears threatened to overflow again. Her parents had been special people. She'd been lucky to have them no matter how many people she had to share them with.

...everything you've done for me and for my baby, taking in a stranger, giving me a job and a place to live. But most of all, with my whole heart, I thank you for what you're doing for Rebecca.

Rebecca? Her eyes stopped on her name.

Don't be silly, she chided herself. So the writer of this letter named her baby after her benefactors' child.

It was a perfectly logical explanation, but a chill settled over the room. Suddenly she didn't want to continue reading. She had to force her eyes to move on to the next word, the next sentence.

I know you'll give her a good home and loving family, all the things I can't. But please, please remember your promise and never tell her or anyone else about me. If she ever finds out you're not her birth parents, you must not, under any circumstances, let her try to find me.

The room spun around Rebecca, out of focus, out of control.

Her fingers clutched the paper so tightly her thumb went white.

The letter couldn't have said what she thought it said. She was confused, in a state of shock over the loss of her parents. She'd misread the note, misconstrued it, misunderstood.

She read it again.

And again.

And a deep abyss opened up and swallowed her as her whole world slid away, taking the people she'd believed to be her parents, the lie she'd believed to be her life.

She grabbed at the desk for support, her fingers clutching the answering machine, accidentally pushing a button.

"Hi! This is Brenda Patterson. Jerry and I are busy right now, but if you'll leave a message, we'll get right back to you. I promise!"

The voice of a stranger.

It wouldn't matter whether or not she cleaned out the house and got rid of everything in it.

All remnants of the parents who'd raised her had just disappeared. Her identity, her whole life had vanished...stolen by a few words written in faded blue ink on a sheet of paper hidden in a locked drawer.

Chapter 1

Rebecca pulled into the parking lot of the office building in North Dallas, the address for the private detective she'd contacted. Her hands on the steering wheel of her Volvo were sweaty. Not because the July temperatures were in the triple digits. She'd run her air conditioner on high all the way over, keeping the car cool, even a little chilly.

No, her palms were sweaty because they, like everything else in her life, had gone completely out of her control.

From the seat beside her, she picked up her purse and briefcase then opened the car door.

Heavy heat slapped her in the face, trying to push her backward as if it would stop her forward movement, return her forcibly to a past that no longer existed, a past when she'd thought she had a mother and father, when she'd thought she knew who she was.

As she stepped out, more heat rose from the concrete around her, through the soles of her snakeskin shoes with their three-inch heels. She'd chosen the shoes deliberately. Being tall had always given her a sense of confidence in dealing with people, and today she needed all the external sources of confidence she could find. Her internal source had gone a little shaky.

Cars zipped past on the busy streets behind her. Cars filled with people going from one destination to another, people who knew who they were, where they'd been, where they were headed.

She turned to look at the square, ordinary, brick office building. So what had she expected? A low-rent district, signs hanging askew, strange characters skulking around?

Nothing.

She no longer expected anything.

She crossed the parking lot and entered the air conditioned lobby then took the elevator to the third floor. It was all so mundane. Tan, industrial carpet down the hallway. A brass plaque on the door that identified the offices of *Thornton and Associates, Licensed Private Investigators*.

Her whole world had fallen apart and somehow it didn't seem right that the agency she'd chosen to help her put it back together should be so ordinary. How could anyone in ordinary circumstances understand her extraordinary ones?

She smoothed her wilted linen suit, took a deep breath and sent up a silent prayer that she looked more normal than she felt, then opened the door.

"Can I help you?" the perky receptionist asked.

Rebecca straightened her shoulders. "Yes," she said. "I'm Rebecca Patterson. I have an appointment with Jake Thornton at 3:00."

"He's on the phone right now. If you'd like to have a seat, I'll let him know you're here."

Rebecca moved to the corner of the room, to one of the half dozen anonymous tan chairs grouped meticulously around the walls. This urge to hide in the corner wasn't like her. She'd always been at the front, taking the lead.

Until six weeks ago.

"Ms. Patterson."

Rebecca shot up from the chair at the sound of the deep, quiet voice speaking her name. The man seemed to tower, filling the doorway.

In spite of her stilted shoes and sophisticated designer suit, Rebecca felt unaccountably small and helpless.

Nevertheless, she strode toward Jake Thornton, extending her hand and making an effort to appear confident, like the woman she had been before the death of her parents, before she found the note. "I'm Rebecca Patterson."

He wore a black knit shirt and matching jeans instead of the rumpled suit of movie detectives, but the square set of his jaw, the intensity of his black— no, midnight blue—eyes reassured her. His dark hair was a little too long and shaggy in a careless way, as though he hadn't taken time for a haircut lately.

"Jake Thornton." He enclosed her hand in a solid shake. Please come in." He stepped back to permit her to enter.

She moved past him, vaguely surprised that he was only a little taller than her 5'8" plus her three inch heels. That put him over six feet, but not the giant of her first impression.

His inner office was like the reception area...nondescript, ordinary. A filing cabinet in one corner. A large desk in the middle holding scattered folders and a computer. Not much different from her own office at the Wingate Hotel where she was the Director of Human Resources.

Except Jake Thornton had no pictures of family sitting on his desk.

Actually, she didn't have any on her desk, either. Not really.

"Have a seat." He slouched into the big, black leather chair behind the desk.

She perched on the edge of another tan chair then made herself slide back, set the briefcase on the floor beside her and attempt to appear composed.

"So Elaine Gaither gave you my name?" he asked.

"Yes. You handled a matter for her about a year ago."

He nodded noncommittally. "I remember."

She liked that, the fact that he didn't elaborate, didn't comment by word or expression on the nasty divorce that ensued when Elaine gained proof of her husband's infidelity. She needed someone who would keep her confidences and wouldn't pass judgment.

"So what can I do for you today, Ms. Patterson? My receptionist said you refused to give details on the phone."

"This is a very personal matter."

His gaze shifted to her hands where they clutched her purse in her lap. Checking for a wedding ring?

"No," she said. "It's not like that. I'm not married. I'm not...anything."

Rebecca bit her lip. She hadn't meant to say that. "I just found out I'm adopted." She spoke the words evenly and without inflection as if they were a statement of fact, nothing more.

Jake leaned back, crossing tan, muscular arms over his wide chest, distancing himself from her, shutting her out. "And you want me to find your real parents," he said noncommittally.

"That's right."

"There are several agencies out there you can register with."

"I've done that."

"So your parents aren't trying to find you."

"No. I don't think so. I'm certain they aren't." But she didn't like his reminding her.

"Is this some sort of medical emergency?"

"No."

"If they're not looking for you, are you sure you want to find them?"

She clutched her purse more tightly. She hadn't expected to be given the third degree. "I wouldn't be here if I wasn't sure. It's important that I find them."

He picked up a pencil and slid it through his fingers from end to end to end, his eyes never leaving hers. "It's important." Neither agreement nor a question, merely an expression of disbelief.

She had no more emotional energy left for arguing. She rose and looked down at him. "It would seem I've made a mistake. Apparently you're not interested in taking my case. My apologies for wasting your time."

He motioned her to sit. "Relax. I didn't say I wasn't interested. I just want you to be positive you really want me to find your parents. I've been in this business for several years, and I gotta warn you, not all reunions are happy. If your parents aren't looking for you, they may not be thrilled to be found."

Rebecca sank back into the chair, her legs suddenly shaky. "I know that."

She retrieved the briefcase, opened it in her lap and withdrew the note. Wordlessly she handed it to him, gave her deepest secret into the keeping of this man who seemed completely unconcerned with her problems. That detachment was the element that gave her the courage to do it.

Jake Thornton accepted the folded piece of paper from the attractive, nervous woman seated across from him. She was a strange mix of fragility and determination. A lot of his individual clients had that same *I've got to know but really don't want to* frantic confusion when they came in. That's why he was devoting more and more of his time to his corporate clients. Impersonal. Unemotional. Safe.

Even when he had to deal with individuals, he reminded himself it was still business, still impersonal. His job was to find out what they wanted to know. Why they wanted that knowledge, what they did with it, how it affected their lives, that had nothing to do with him.

But this one was different somehow.

He couldn't quite put his finger on it. There was something about her that made him uncomfortable, something vulnerable and needy that reached inside him and touched places he didn't want touched, places he hadn't realized still existed.

She sat stiffly erect during their entire interview, that small chin lifted just a little, long blond hair perfectly smooth and pushed away from her face. All the while her slim fingers had gripped first her purse and then a leather briefcase so tightly her knuckles were white. Her green or blue eyes—he couldn't tell the shade for sure—widened then narrowed with conflicting emotions.

And he had the strangest urge to loosen those tense fingers, smooth her brow, dig up loving biological parents for her, make everything all right.

Dumb.

He, of all people, knew the likelihood of Ozzie and Harriet parents.

He unfolded the paper. The handwriting was neat and meticulous. Rebecca Patterson with her neat, meticulous appearance and bearing could have written it, but the paper was yellowed and the ink faded.

To Brenda and Jerry Patterson, the note read. *I can never thank you enough for everything you've done for me and for my baby...Please take care of her and never let her try to find me,* it concluded.

He read the note through twice. "All right if make a copy of this?"

She nodded. He dialed Noreen's extension and asked her to make the copy for him. Normally he'd do it himself, but the copy machine was down the hall and he was reluctant to leave Rebecca alone even for the necessary couple of minutes. She seemed so fragile, he had an irrational fear that she'd shatter into a thousand pieces if he left her right then.

Noreen returned with the copy, and he handed the original back to Rebecca. "Just offhand, I'd say you're right. Your mother isn't going to try to find you. She's probably not going to be thrilled to have you show up on her doorstep, either."

Rebecca flinched almost imperceptibly as though he'd struck her a physical blow. Well, damn it, she'd come to him to find the truth and that's what he was trying to give her.

"I realize all that, Mr. Thornton. Nevertheless, I have to find out who wrote this note. Who my mother is. Who I am."

Jake leaned back in his chair and propped his feet on his desk. This woman was just asking to get knocked to the ground, and he wasn't sure she had the strength to get back up again.

Not that it was his place to worry about that.

"Brenda and Jerry Patterson, obviously they adopted you."

"They did."

"Have they been good parents to you? Make you eat your vegetables? Send you to school? Take care of you when you're sick?"

Pain filled her eyes and put a slight tremor in her voice when she spoke. "They were wonderful parents. Nobody could have had better parents."

"Then maybe you ought to go see them, take your mom some roses, your dad a bottle of brandy, spend the weekend with them, be glad you have somebody who loves you and forget about finding this woman who ran out on you."

In amazement, he listened to himself trying to throw this case away. What the hell was the matter with him? Rebecca wanted information, and he had the resources to get it for her. That's what he did. He was a P.I., not a shrink.

Her eyes glistened, and for a moment he thought she might cry, but when she spoke, her voice was surprisingly firm. "I'd love to do exactly that, Mr. Thornton, but it's no longer possible. My parents were killed in an automobile accident two weeks ago."

Jake ducked his head and plowed his fingers through his hair. So much for his misguided efforts to be a shrink. He should definitely stick to investigating. "I'm sorry. I didn't realize."

"It doesn't matter. Will you find my real parents or not?"

Real parents. The phrase stuck him as odd. The people who'd raised her and given her their name were dead, and the people who'd given her life didn't want to be found. Will the *real parents* please stand up and claim Rebecca Patterson?

Not likely.

Jake's feet thudded to the floor. He straightened in his chair, opened a drawer, withdrew a contract and slid it across the desk toward her. "Read that."

"Elaine showed me hers. I'm agreeable to all the terms, and I'm ready to write you a check for the retainer."

So what if the woman wanted to pay for her own grief? That was her business, wasn't it?

He picked up a pen and positioned a notepad in front of him.

"Name, address and phone number."

She gave him the information. "If you call me at work and I'm not available, please don't leave a message. I have an answering machine at home which I'll check frequently. You can be completely open with any message you leave there. I live alone."

"Got it. Now, tell me everything you know about the woman who wrote that note."

"I'm afraid it's not much. I do have one other item." She opened the briefcase again and withdrew a carefully folded blue dress. "I assume this was hers. It was with the note. I found them in a locked drawer of my dad's desk after my parents died." She lifted her hands then let them flutter down aimlessly. "They must have planned to tell me eventually or they wouldn't have saved this stuff. They didn't know they were going to die like this."

"So they never really told you that you were adopted. You just deduced it from this note."

"No, I didn't just deduce it, though that note is pretty strong evidence. I talked to their lawyer after I found this note. He drew up the adoption papers."

Jake nodded and picked up the dress. "She must have been tiny."

He studied the garment carefully. He could almost see the petite blond woman with Rebecca's features who must have worn it. The label was frayed, washed many times, but the embroidered script was still legible. "Sharise's Shoppe. Ever hear of the place?"

Rebecca shook her head. "No. I've made inquiries around Dallas, but nobody's ever heard of it. I asked my parents' lawyer. He said all he knew was that the woman...my mother...had worked as a waitress for Mom and Dad. They owned a small restaurant in Plano."

"What about records from the restaurant?"

"I've been through what records they still have and found nothing. They sold the land a few years ago to a developer and got enough money to retire."

"But they'd have had to have a name and social security number for all employees."

Rebecca shook her head again. "According to their lawyer, she worked for tips, room and board. If my parents paid her...and, knowing them, they did...they paid her in cash. She used the name Jane Clark, but I'd be very surprised if that was her real name."

"Probably not, but the Jane part may be right. People frequently keep their first names, especially if they're common ones. Anything else? A physical description?"

"Only a few of Mom and Dad's friends even remember her. They all agreed that she was small, had short, dark brown hair and wore glasses. Very nondescript. She just appeared one day and started working. Mom and Dad wouldn't talk about her, so they must have known something."

"Most people wouldn't give a job and home to a stranger off the streets, even help her hide her identity. Is it possible your parents knew her?"

"It's possible, but they were the type people who would take in a stranger. They did it all the time. Most of my life we had at least one stray person living with us. They were very generous. I was a little surprised when they didn't give away all the money they got from selling the restaurant."

Rebecca was so transparent, Jake could almost read her mind. After finding she was adopted, she felt she was just one more of those strays her parents had taken in, and she had the stupid notion that finding a blood relative would change things. Well, he'd tried to talk her out of it. He'd done his good deed for the month.

"So you've discussed this with your parents' old friends, and none of them knew who she was?"

"None. She showed up out of nowhere. Pretty soon it was apparent she was pregnant. She worked as a waitress, gave birth and disappeared." Rebecca smiled wryly...or grimaced. Jake couldn't be sure which. "All we have to prove my mother ever existed is this note and her dress."

"And you."

She looked down at herself then lifted one hand to the side of her face as if testing to be sure she really did exist.

"And me," she finally said.

He wanted to shake her, tell her to get on with her life, force her to realize that what happened all those years ago had no bearing on her now. But no one could have convinced him of that truth until he learned it for himself. Anyway, his last attempt to give her advice hadn't turned out so great.

"Okay," he said instead, "just a few more questions."

He obtained from Rebecca Patterson all the information she had. It wasn't a lot, but it would probably be enough. This case shouldn't be too difficult. Disappointing to the client, he suspected, but not difficult to resolve.

He followed her to the door, walking behind her, inhaling the scent of summer flowers that trailed after her, watching the play of light and shadows in the silky strands of her hair.

He'd heard the term willowy applied to women before but hadn't known exactly what it meant. Now he did. This woman reminded him of the branches of a willow tree...slim, graceful, moving with every breeze.

With his hand on the door knob, ready to open it, usher her out and get back to work, he hesitated.

"You know," he said, wondering what the hell he thought he was doing even as he spoke, "you were pretty damn lucky. Born to somebody who wouldn't—couldn't—keep you but left you with somebody who wanted you. By your own admission, your parents were great. You had a good life with them, and now they're gone. I understand that you want them back, but you can't have that. No matter what I find for you, no matter who I dig up, it's not going to be that family. Maybe you should just go home, gather up your good memories and be happy you had them. Find a husband, make babies, raise your own family."

She gazed up at him, her eyes the color of the blue grass he'd seen in Kentucky. Deep green but with hints of the sky in their depths. Looking into those eyes, he knew she wasn't going to take his advice. Right now this woman who wore her designer suit so elegantly, this Director of Human Resources who was undoubtedly accustomed to being in control, was feeling very lost.

"I appreciate your advice, Mr. Thornton, but you're wrong about my motives. I know I can't replace my parents. My real mother may not want me, and that's fine. I may not want her either. But at least I'll know who I am. At least then I'll have an identity."

Jake didn't believe that brave pronouncement for one minute, but he nodded and opened the door. "I'll let you know as soon as I find anything."

"Thank you."

She left, but her scent lingered behind. Or maybe it only lingered in his mind.

Summer flowers. Now where the heck had he come up with that description? What did winter flowers smell like?

He went over to the window and looked out at the parking lot, watched her exit the building. A willow blowing aimlessly with every gust of the hot summer wind.

And she thought finding a mother who'd specified she must never be found would somehow fix everything, give her life direction.

Though the sun shone brightly, a shadow seemed to overtake and surround Rebecca as she walked across the parking lot. Probably an optical illusion caused by the tinted glass of his office window.

Nevertheless, a black chill zagged down his spine. His own projections or the sixth sense he'd developed for survival in his years on the police force?

She got in her silver Volvo and drove away, and Jake returned to his desk. He flopped into his chair, picked up the notes he'd made on his new client Patterson and studied them then laid them back down.

After six years in uniform for the city and five in private practice, any remnants of optimism that might have survived his erratic youth had certainly been destroyed.

Rebecca Patterson was an attractive woman by most standards, but his taste in women ran to the assertive, confident variety. Women who didn't need anything. Women who wouldn't shatter when it was time for everybody to go their separate ways. Rebecca Patterson was already shattered.

He couldn't possibly be attracted to her. That wasn't the explanation for his strange reaction, his peculiar urge to loosen those tense fingers, smooth her brow, dig up loving parents for her, make everything all right.

Maybe the moon was full. That made people do strange things.

He picked up his notes again, balancing them in the palm of his hand as if weighing the information there.

He'd probably be wise to turn this over to one of his associates. He had plenty of other cases to work on right now.

But he made no move to reach for the phone.

She wouldn't like that. She hadn't even wanted to tell the receptionist about her situation. She certainly wouldn't want to be passed around the office to someone else.

He should handle this matter himself. Handle it and treat it like any other case that came across his desk. That's all it was. Just another case. And she was just another client.

But the uneasy feeling continued to dart around the edges of his thoughts, refusing to go away, whispering to him that Rebecca Patterson shouldn't be so eager to find her mother.

Chapter 2

August 9, 1979, Edgewater, Texas

Mary Jordan lifted the lid of her Crock-Pot and poked the roast inside with a long fork.

Almost done. By the time Ben got home and took a quick shower, it would be perfect.

She replaced the lid and leaned back against the counter, taking a long drink from her glass of iced tea. Not that there was much ice left in the tea, but at least it was wet. The big attic fan pulled air through the house, and the kitchen was well-ventilated with windows on two sides and a screen door on the other. Even so, it was unbearably hot. The air moving past her was warm and muggy and didn't feel the least bit cool.

She lifted her heavy blond hair off her neck and briefly considered returning it to the pony tail she wore during the day. But Ben liked it down.

She smiled to herself.

And she liked Ben. Loved Ben. After a year of marriage, she still marveled that he loved her. When he'd left their small town to join the Army, she'd been the skinny kid next door with a crush on the teen-age boy who sometimes pushed her in the swing in the park but most often ignored her.

Then he'd returned with his strange friend, Charles, and they'd both gone to work for the

Edgewater Police Department. And she'd been all grown up, and Ben had noticed her. Dated her. Loved her. Married her.

A blue jay squawked outside the kitchen window, the sound familiar and warm, recalling happy summer days when she was a kid, when her father was still alive and her mother was still...her mother, not lost in some strange land, unable to deal with losing her husband, soon following him into death.

But all the bad was in the past now, over and done with. Happiness was hers again. She had a husband who loved her and a home. A small one, true, an old house with no air conditioning, but it belonged to them. Well, them and the mortgage company.

The yard was huge, large enough to add on to the house later and still have a big yard with a swing set and tree houses and plenty of room for their kids to play. That was all she and Ben needed to complete their family. Babies. Lots of babies. And the way they loved every night, that shouldn't be too far in the future.

She opened the refrigerator, took out two more ice cubes and plopped them into her warm tea, then reached for another. Leaning her head back, eyes closed, she ran the third ice cube around her neck, under her hair then in front, letting the cool liquid trickle between her breasts. Thank goodness for the fashion of shorts with halter tops and no bra!

A knock on the screen door brought her upright.

A uniformed police officer stood on the back step.

"Charles? What are you doing here?" She dropped the remaining ice into the sink. She no longer needed it. A cold chill spread over her, sending goose bumps down her spine.

Without being invited, her husband's partner and best friend opened the screen door and came in.

"Where's Ben?" A sudden fear struck her, the fear that all wives of policemen lived with constantly. "Oh, God! He's not—"

Charles shook his head. "Ben's fine. He got tied up with paperwork at the station and wanted me to come by and tell you."

Relief washed over Mary in huge waves. "Thank goodness!" She smiled, restraining the urge to laugh giddily.

Charles returned the smile, but his was unctuous. Mary looked away from him, lifting the lid and checking the roast again though it didn't need to be checked. Charles affected her like that, made her nervous, apprehensive...made her skin crawl just by the way he looked at her sometimes, and this was one of those times.

"Why didn't Ben call me?" she asked.

Charles didn't answer.

Against her will, she turned back toward him.

His pale eyes stroked down her body, making her wish she had on something more than the halter top and frayed cutoffs she'd been blessing only a few seconds before. If she'd known Charles was coming, she'd have worn an overcoat even in the heat.

Ben said she was imagining things, that Charles respected her and loved her like a sister. He got irritated when she mentioned her reservations about Charles, the man who'd saved his life in battle and was now his partner on the police force. No man could resist ogling his beautiful wife, Ben said, teasing her, but making it clear he thought she was overreacting to Charles' friendliness.

Charles shrugged. "Ben knows I pass right by here on my way home. I told him I'd be glad to stop and tell you in person."

"Well, then, thank you." She forced herself to walk toward him, to place one hand on the wooden door, indicating she was ready for him to leave, ready to close the door behind him as soon as he was gone. And she was. Even with the attic fan laboring mightily to pull in a breath of the sultry air, she'd close the door and lean against it, suffer the heat just to know the solid wood separated her from Charles.

He ignored her action, pulled off his cap and raked an arm across his brow. "These new uniforms get awful damn hot in the summer. I sure could use a drink of cold water."

Mary stood stock still for a long moment, her mind racing frantically to come up with some excuse, some reason to get this man out of her house, to deny him even a drink of water.

Her husband's best friend. His partner. Without him she wouldn't have Ben. He'd be lying dead in a jungle halfway around the world.

"Of course." She turned away and opened the refrigerator.

Behind her she heard the wooden door close.

She tried to ignore the uneasy feeling that crept up from the pit of her stomach and spread over her chest, making it hard to breathe. She tried to reassure herself. He was closing the door because he'd seen her start to do it and assumed that was what she wanted.

To lock him outside, not inside with her!

She took down a plastic glass and filled it with cold water from the pitcher. "Take it with you," she said, handing it to him. "You can bring it back next time you come by."

His fingers closed over hers. "What if I forget?" His voice was strangely husky. He stood so close she could smell the cloyingly sweet cologne he always wore as well as the dark, slightly musty scent he never seemed quite able to cover up no matter how much cologne he wore.

He was too close.

She tugged her hand loose. "It's an old glass. I don't care."

Her voice sounded breathless to her own ears.

Frightened.

That was absurd. Charles might disgust her, but he would never harm Ben's wife.

He raised the water to his lips and she turned away, again checking the roast. "Thank goodness for Crock-Pots," she babbled. "I couldn't bear to turn on the oven in this heat."

His hand slid under her hair, over the bare skin on her back.

"Don't," she whispered. "Please don't."

He lifted her hair and pressed his lips to her neck.

She whirled on him, brandishing the fork she'd used to turn the roast. "Stay away from me!"

Laughing, he grabbed both her wrists and pushed her against the counter. "Don't give me that. You've been taunting me ever since I met you, swinging that sexy ass in front of me, wearing those little tops and no bra so I can see your big nipples."

She strained against his hold, surprised at his strength. He wasn't as tall as Ben, but he was stocky and strong.

He pinned her to the counter, his body hard and aroused.

"Charles, you don't want to do this." She tried to sound calm as she twisted sideways, seeking to escape the wild look in his eyes, fighting the panic that threatened to overwhelm her.

"Oh, yes, I do. And you want me to." His mouth descended on hers and she felt bile rise in her throat.

***

Mary huddled in the corner, sobbing quietly, her body and soul bruised and aching. Charles' dark, sickly sweet scent clung to her, nauseating her.

From behind her she heard the sound of a zipper.

"You better go clean up before your husband gets home," Charles said, his voice perfectly normal, as if they were discussing a spilled glass of water. "I think we should keep this our little secret, don't you?"

His hand came down, clamped on her chin and forced her to look up at him. "Don't you?"

She jerked away from the slime of his touch.

"If you want to keep your husband, I'd suggest you don't force him to choose between the man who saved his life, his partner and best friend, and the whore who seduced that best friend."

She curled into a ball again with her back toward him, biting her lip to stifle the sobs, praying he'd leave, praying Ben would come home, praying she'd wake from this nightmare. No man except Ben had ever touched her. Now a monster had invaded and desecrated the private, sacred acts she and Ben alone had shared.

She heard Charles open the door. Thank God! She had to get upstairs, take a bath, scrub every inch of her body, rid herself of his vile touch.

She had to talk to Ben. Only Ben could ever make her feel right and clean again.

"One word to Ben, and some evening he won't come home." His voice was quiet and hard with a cushioned quality, like the sound of a gun firing through a silencer. "I'm his partner. His life is in my hands every day, just like it was in the war. I had the power to choose whether he lived or died over there. I still have that power."

The door closed, but the foul scent of him clung to her nostrils, her body, everywhere.

She grabbed her torn clothes and held them against her while, with trembling fingers, she locked the kitchen door then did the same to the front. Even so, as she ran upstairs to the bathroom, her heart pounded erratically with fear that he'd return, that he'd touch her again, violate her again.

Leaning over the toilet stool, she vomited again and again as if she could somehow purge herself of the feel of him, of the horror of what he'd done to her.

When nothing more would come, she turned the shower on full force and stood under it, sobbing uncontrollably, her face upturned, letting the water splash over her, blending with her tears.

It wasn't enough.

She took the bar of soap from the dish and scrubbed every inch of her body frantically, scrubbed until her skin felt raw. But it still wasn't enough.

She'd never be able to wash away the feel of his hands on her, of what he'd done to her. She'd never be the same.

She sank to the floor of the shower, crying again…or still.

How could this have happened? How could this horrible thing have intruded into her world? Ben's love should have made her safe.

But it hadn't.

No more than her mother's love for her father had made him safe or her love for her mother had kept her sane or safe.

Some evening he won't come home.

A new terror clutched at her heart as the full implication of Charles' threats came home to her.

She wasn't safe. Ben wasn't safe. Love couldn't keep anybody safe. She'd been wrong to think her life could be different.

Slowly she pushed herself to her feet and turned off the water.

Like a robot she shoved aside the plastic curtain and stepped out.

Charles had taken something from her, but it was over. Nothing Ben could do to him would ever change things, would ever erase what Charles had done.

She couldn't let him take anything else from her. She couldn't let him take Ben.

Some evening he won't come home.

Was Charles capable of that? He'd saved Ben's life once.

But after today she no longer believed he'd saved her husband's life because it was the right thing to do. He'd seen it as an exercise in power. The power to give or take a life.

Charles was capable of anything. He was insane. She'd seen it in his eyes.

She took down a towel and began slowly, deliberately, to dry herself. Somehow she had to pull herself together before Ben came home.

Somehow she had to keep Ben safe.

Chapter 3

Rebecca knocked on the door of room 103 at the Sleep Tite Motel in Edgewater, Texas, then clenched her hands so tightly her nails bit into her palms while she waited for Jake to answer.

I'm in the only motel in a little town about a hundred and fifty miles southeast of Dallas called Edgewater, Texas, and I think I may have found Sharise's Shoppe.

She'd picked up Jake's message when she'd checked her voice mail during her lunch break. Without hesitation or question, she'd asked for and received two weeks of vacation, time to come to the town where her mother might have lived...might still live. Staying in Dallas and waiting patiently, trusting a stranger to do the right things with her unfolding past, had been impossible. That's what she'd unwittingly done all her life, let others have control while she passively accepted. This time she was going to exert some influence on the outcome of events.

Though the evening was decidedly warm, a shiver darted up her spine, along her neck, prickling her scalp.

From nerves? Anticipation? Fear?

All of the above.

The door opened and Jake stood squinting into the still-bright afternoon sun. Obviously he hadn't been expecting company. His shaggy hair was even more tousled than the first time she'd met him. A day's growth of beard shadowed his angular cheeks. He wore faded jeans and nothing else. Dark hair sprang from his broad chest, tapering over a taut stomach and disappearing into the jeans.

Which were unsnapped.

"Rebecca?"

His surprised exclamation brought her gaze back to his face. She swallowed hard and tried to find her voice. "I'm sorry. I didn't...I should have called first." Until that moment she hadn't thought of Jake as a real person who slept and ate and relaxed at the end of the day, a man who might even have a guest in his motel room. Until that moment she'd been totally, obsessively focused on her own goals, on his role in helping her achieve those goals.

"What are you doing here?" His tone was somewhere between irritation and confusion.

"I got your message. I had to come."

"Why?"

His scowl wilted her excitement but not her determination. She straightened her shoulders. "Because you found a clue to my life, and I want to be there when you talk to the woman who owns that dress shop."

He expelled a long sigh as he ran a hand through his hair. The muscles in his arm bulged as he raised it.

A bare chest. An uplifted arm. Nothing she wouldn't see at a swimming pool or in a gymnasium, but somehow this bare chest and arm seemed more personal, more exposed.

"Come on in." He stepped back, permitting her to enter.

Although she'd driven over a hundred miles to meet with Jake Thornton, she hesitated. Going into a motel room with this virile, half-dressed male wasn't the same thing as going into an office with a private detective in a business suit.

That was ridiculous, she chided herself. Of course it was the same thing.

She strode past him into his room. This was his temporary office. After all, she worked in a hotel every day. Business was business, and an office was an office.

Except for a shirt tossed onto the bed, shoes lying next to it and papers strewn over the top of the small desk, it was identical to the room she'd rented next door. Same nondescript picture on the wall, same flowered spread on the—she noted with relief—unrumpled bed. And no one else was in the room. At least she hadn't interrupted something.

"Have a seat." He indicated the single chair beside the desk.

"Thank you." As soon as she sat, he sank onto the bed. Well, it was the only other choice. Where did she expect him to sit?

Nevertheless, unwelcome awareness danced along every nerve in her body, awareness of this half-naked, barefoot man slouched on the bed only a few feet away.

He looked at her intently for a long moment, his dark gaze seeming to penetrate to her innermost secrets, then he ran a hand over his hair in a futile effort to smooth it. "There's no point in your being here. I don't have anything new to report and may not for several days. Like I told you last week, I found your original birth certificate which showed your mother's name as Jane Clark, father unknown. I spent today checking records here in Edgewater under that name and the date listed for Jane Clark's birth and came up with zilch."

Rebecca nodded, biting her lip and squelching her disappointment. "I knew from the beginning the name was probably phony. Jane Clark. It's only one step up from Jane Doe."

"I found no Clarks here at all, though that's not necessarily bad. If Jane Clark came from this town and was trying to hide her identity, she would logically have taken a name that didn't belong to anybody she knew."

"I see." If it wasn't bad, neither was it good. "But you found the dress shop. That's definitely progress."

"Yes, I found the dress shop, or at least where the dress shop used to be. I think you may be expecting too much too soon. An elderly lady named Doris Jordan owned that store for twenty-five years, and it's been closed for ten. The odds of her remembering somebody who bought one blue dress almost thirty years ago are pretty slim. We're not even positive that this is the same Sharise's Shoppe."

"I know all that." She laced her fingers, glanced down at them, then unlaced them. "I know all that," she repeated. "And I know this whole thing is just a job as far as you're concerned, but it's a little more than that to me. Do you have any idea what it's like to suddenly lose your identity? My whole life has been a lie, and the people I loved and trusted most were the ones who created that lie."

He folded his arms across the dark hair on his chest. "So now you don't trust anybody, and you had to come help me do the job you hired me to do."

She wanted to deny his accusation. Even though it was true, it sounded brutal the way he put it.

"It's not that. Not completely, anyway. It's just that I feel like everything's spinning out of control. People have been making decisions for me all my life, and I didn't even know it. My birth mother gave me away. Mom and Dad adopted me but never told me the truth, never gave me any choices. Then they died, and I had no more power to stop that than I've had to manage my own life. I just couldn't stay in the comfortable world where I used to live when I had an identity. When I thought I had an identity. I couldn't sit and wait for someone else to provide me with answers."

Jake's left eyebrow quirked upward in a gesture of incomprehension. Of course he didn't understand. How could he? Two months ago she wouldn't have understood.

Jake Thornton possessed an air of supreme confidence. He was a man who knew exactly who he was and where he was going, much like the person she'd been before the death of her parents.

She bit her lower lip and amended her thoughts. No, she'd never been as completely confident as Jake was. Underneath she'd always felt a hint of shakiness, as if somehow she'd known that she had no real foundation on which to base her life.

"Then why did you hire me?" Jake asked quietly, his tone cool and impersonal with only a hint of the irritation she knew he must be feeling at her intrusion.

"I hired you because I need you," she replied.

The muscles in his chiseled jawline tightened almost imperceptibly, but before he could respond, a knock sounded at the door.

Rebecca released a breath, welcoming the interruption to a conversation that wasn't going well.

Jake shot her an accusatory glance as though this new intruder was somehow related to her presence then went to answer the door.

"Jake Thornton?" The masculine voice had a scratchy quality, as if the speaker had smoked for many years and the inside of his throat resembled sandpaper.

"Yeah, I'm Jake Thornton. What can I do for you?"

"I'm Charles Morton, mayor of this little town. Mind if I come in?"

"Why not? You might as well join the party."

Jake swung the door wide and an older man in a business suit walked in. He was tall, though not as tall as Jake, and big without being fat. His white hair was immaculately cut and styled, and his starched white shirt, tucked rigidly into the pants of his suit, betrayed no hint of a bulging stomach.

The man stopped when he saw her, and his pale blue eyes narrowed, focusing on her with a probing intensity. "I didn't know you had company." His words were addressed to Jake, but his unsettling gaze remained on her.

"Rebecca Patterson, Charles Morton. Mayor Charles Morton. Sorry I can't offer you a seat, Mayor. This room isn't set up for entertaining."

"No problem. I just came by to welcome you to our town and see if there's anything I can do to help you."

Jake moved over to the dresser and angled one hip on it in a half-sitting stance. "That's real nice of you, Mayor. I'll keep your offer in mind if I run into any problems."

Morton shifted his gaze to Jake, and Rebecca sagged in her chair as a captured butterfly suddenly released from its impaling pin.

"This the young lady who's trying to find her mother?"

If Jake was surprised at the mayor's knowledge, he didn't show it. "This is Rebecca Patterson," he said smoothly, noncommittally.

Again Morton's gaze raked over her. "Doris Jordan's in her seventies. Hasn't been the same since her son died in '79. Then her husband passed away seven years back, and she completely lost it. She's pretty senile, probably not going to be able to tell you much."

"Probably not," Jake drawled. "So where would you suggest I start looking?"

"I'm afraid I can't help you there. Wish I could. But you know, more than likely the poor girl who bought that dress was just passing through on her way to the big city."

"Just passing through," Jake repeated. "Could be. But maybe not. You're twenty miles off the main highway."

Morton smiled thinly. "You'd be surprised at the number of vagrants we get through here. What year were you born, Rebecca?"

Rebecca flinched at the sudden focus of Morton's attention on her, his gaze a sharp pin that once again impaled her to the chair. She didn't want to tell him when she was born or anything else about herself.

And that made no sense. If she expected to find her mother, people would have to know when she was born. This was the mayor, a city official, offering to help, and she didn't want to tell him something as innocuous as her date of birth. That made no sense.

He probably already knew. He seemed to know everything else.

She forced herself to reveal her birth date to this man she had no reason to dislike.

He nodded slowly. "Any idea what your mother looked like?"

"Nothing like me." For some reason it seemed important that he know that, important that she assure him he wasn't looking at a carbon copy of her mother. "She was petite, probably around five feet, and she had short, dark brown hair."

"Were your mother's eyes blue-green like yours?"

Though Morton's words were innocuous, something in his voice sent chills through Rebecca. She glanced in Jake's direction, but he gave no indication of noticing anything awry. Likely she was being too sensitive. She'd done a lot of that lately. "We don't know her eye color," she said. "It was all so long ago. The people I talked to said she wore glasses and rarely looked up from her work."

"Doesn't sound like anybody from here, and I'd know if it was. This is a small town and I've been here most of my life. I know everybody, even people that left years ago. I think you folks are wasting your time, but, like I said, anything you need, give me a call. I'll do my best to open any doors I can for you."

Jake eased upright from his half-sitting stance. "We do appreciate that, Mayor. We'll be sure to let you know."

He clapped a hand on Morton's back in simulated good-old-boy camaraderie, guided the mayor out the door and closed it behind him.

Yes, Jake Thornton was a man in control of his world and anyone who infringed on that world.

Including her.

She pushed up from the chair, forcing herself to face him. "How did he find out about you?" she demanded, channeling her uneasiness about the whole situation into anger. "Have you told the whole world I'm looking for the mother who dumped me? I thought this was supposed to be private!"

Jake stood in the middle of the floor, arms again folded across his chest, legs planted wide apart, his expression implacable. "I've just spent the day going through public records at the courthouse and talking to people. When you start asking questions, those people want to know why. I had to tell them I have a client who wants to find her birth mother. But nobody would have known who you are if you hadn't come down here and jumped into the middle of things."

Rebecca sank back into the chair. "Okay, you're right. I apologize for snapping at you. This whole business is making me crazy."

Jake scowled. "You can't let it do that."

"That's easy enough for you to say when all this means to you is a job." She was only too aware that she wasn't maintaining her professional demeanor, but she had to make him understand how important this was to her. "It's a little more than that to me. When I lost my parents...lost them completely, I mean, not just to death...it was like I ceased to exist. You have no idea what something like that does to a person. You couldn't possibly know since it hasn't happened to you. Everything's different. Everything's wrong." She spread her arms helplessly. "Somehow I have to get things right again."

He regarded her for a long, speculative moment, then walked over and placed both hands on her shoulders. "Grieve for your parents. Try to find your real mother if that's what you have to do. But don't let this interfere with your life. Families come, families go...real families, stepfamilies, half families, whole families. In the long run, you're all you've got."

Jake's deep voice resonated through her, his words echoing with a loneliness completely out of character for him. Was she filtering what he said through her own loneliness or did Jake...the man who'd answered her knock tonight, not the private investigator she'd met in Dallas, the man who'd so effortlessly ushered Charles Morton out the door...did he have his own pain, his own losses to deal with?

She lifted her gaze to his, searching for answers, and found instead a thousand questions as his lids lowered halfway and a smoky haze washed over the sharp blue-black stone of his eyes. In the sudden silence, she heard her own quick intake of breath, her own blood racing past her ears. She was excruciatingly, wonderfully, frighteningly aware of Jake's hands on her shoulders.

His nearness blurred the edges of her thoughts so she couldn't remember what it was she'd wanted to ask him. His spearmint scented breath wisped past her, and his chest was so close she could have touched it...wanted to touch it, to take in the warmth of his skin, to press the hairs and feel them spring back beneath her fingers.

His hands slid from her shoulders down her arms and he moved closer, so close his tingling warmth reached her skin through her cotton blouse.

Abruptly he turned away, leaving her arms cold where he no longer touched them and her face hot with embarrassment that she could have responded so hungrily to an incidental contact. Was she so desperate to find a family, someone to belong to, that the first stranger she met was a candidate?

He flopped back onto the bed. "You're paying the bills," he said, his tone deliberately nonchalant but with an underlying huskiness as if he hadn't been totally unaffected by the strange encounter. "If this town is where you want to spend your vacation, go for it. I'll deliver a daily report every night, but you're not going with me to question Doris Jordan or anywhere else I have to go. Do you let other people sit in when you're doing whatever it is Directors of Human Resources at big hotels do?"

"My boss sits in whenever he chooses to."

"Lady, you may be paying for my services, but you're not my boss."

Humiliated, angry with Jake and even angrier with herself, Rebecca drew in a deep breath and lifted her chin. "There's no point in getting into semantics. You've agreed to perform a service for me, but that doesn't preclude my working separately on my own behalf."

"It does preclude your hindering me in performing that service."

Jake's tone, his exclusion of her, bothered her, but she refused to back down. She couldn't back down, couldn't let her life continue to spiral out of control. She had to take charge somehow on some level. "How do you think my presence is going to hinder you?"

His gaze burned across the room with that same smoky intensity as a few minutes before, but his voice was cold when he spoke. "I can give you a good example. If you hadn't been here when Mayor Morton paid a call, I might have been able to get some information out of him."

"I don't recall anything that would indicate he knows something."

"That's because it's my job to notice things that you don't. That's why you hired me. Why'd the man come around at all? Why was he so interested in what I might find? Why is he so anxious to get us out of town? Why did he tell us Doris Jordan is senile? She sounded fine when I talked to her on the phone this morning."

"You think he knows who my mother is?"

"Maybe. He'd have been a young man when you were born. He might remember some high school girl leaving town for a few months, his buddy's sister, his buddy's girlfriend."

A chill clutched Rebecca's chest. "*His* girlfriend?" She choked as she put the thought into words.

"Maybe. But probably not. He didn't look at you in a fatherly way."

Jake had noticed too.

"He made me feel very uncomfortable."

"Why? You're a beautiful woman. I'm sure lots of men look at you that way."

The thought of Morton's viewing her as a woman made her nauseous. "That's not the way he looked at me."

Jake shrugged, neither accepting her denial nor arguing with her. "I'll see if Doris Jordan has anything to say about him when I talk to her tomorrow."

After her protestations that she had no intention of hindering his investigation, Rebecca couldn't ask to go with him no matter how desperately she wanted to.

"What time are you seeing her?" she asked instead.

"I'm meeting her at ten in the morning. Why do you ask? Do you plan to follow me and stand on her front porch, peeking in the window?"

"I expect you to give me an oral report as soon as you get back. I'm in room 102."

His eyes widened slightly. "You're in the room next door?"

She nodded. "This place had plenty of vacancies, and being close seemed logical." Though now she wasn't so sure how logical it was, how well she'd sleep tonight knowing Jake with his bare chest and slate dark eyes was in bed one wall away. Because the room layout was flipped, she'd be sleeping with her head against the same wall as Jake.

She didn't dare look at him for fear that absurd thought would show on her face, that she'd embarrass herself again.

"Well," she said, "I guess I'll see you tomorrow."

"Tomorrow."

***

Jake woke from a tantalizing, erotic dream about Rebecca Patterson.

Damn! She'd kept him awake for a long time just with the thought of her sleeping in the next room, and now he was awake in the middle of the night because of her...awake with his body hard and ready.

A faint ringing sounded, and he realized that must be what woke him. Rebecca's nightstand would be directly behind his, and her phone was ringing.

He turned on a bedside lamp and glanced at the clock. Two fifteen? That was an odd hour to get a phone call.

He lay back and pulled the sheet over him, then kicked it off again.

Why in hell did she have to come here?

Why in hell did it have to bother him that she was here?

He'd thought her attractive when she'd come to his office, but tonight, in jeans and a thin cotton blouse instead of a business suit, she was incredibly provocative. That, combined with the setting, the small motel room, had kept him fighting the urge to take her into his arms and throw her across the bed that was so conveniently near.

She'd felt something too. He'd seen it in those changeable, indecipherable blue-green eyes. But there was so much more going on in those eyes than just desire, and that's what scared him.

Rebecca Patterson needed him. She'd come right out and said it. *I hired you because I need you.* Not *your services* or *your expertise*, but *I need you.*

A Freudian slip, of course. She hadn't meant it to come out that way. But it was true. Not that she needed him specifically. She just needed somebody. She'd lost everybody and she hadn't learned to cope on her own yet.

No matter how much he might want her, he couldn't do that to her, couldn't let her mistake passion for something else, couldn't let her count on him for anything else when passion was all he had to give and all he wanted to take.

"Jake!" A pounding came from the door to his room. "Jake! Please let me in!"

He bolted out of bed, snatched his jeans from the floor and yanked them on then flung open the door.

Rebecca dashed in, closed and locked the door with trembling fingers and leaned against it. Her perfect hair was mussed. She was breathing hard, her high, rounded breasts rising and falling beneath the short, silky white gown that hid nothing.

"Somebody threatened me." Her words and her expression—frightened but trying not to show it—pulled his libido up short.

"What do you mean?"

"I just got a phone call. Somebody told me I'd better go home and forget about finding my mother, that she's dead and if I keep looking, I'll end up that way too."

Chapter 4

"Come sit down." Jake took Rebecca's arm, guiding her toward the chair while trying to ignore the silky softness of her skin and the allure of her nearly nude body.

He switched on the lamp sitting on the desk and pulled out the single chair, offering it to her, resisting the impulse to take her in his arms and comfort her. She was far too appealing in that sexy getup. Only his concern for her obvious distress kept him from making a complete fool of himself.

She made a movement to sit then looked down at herself as if she could read his thoughts...or the lust in his eyes. That was probably pretty easy to do.

"I'll get you...something," he mumbled, his gaze searching all around the room as though he expected a robe to materialize out of nowhere. But at least it gave him something to stare at besides her.

"Do you...is this normal to get threatening phone calls when you're looking for somebody's birth parents?" Her voice sounded so small he half expected to find she'd shrunk to the size of a child.

He yanked one of his denim shirts from a hanger and returned to find she hadn't shrunk at all. She was still tall and elegant, though she now had her arms wrapped self-consciously about herself.

He held the shirt toward her, and she turned, sliding her arms into the sleeves, hiding the sleek curves of her body. But the damage was done. He remembered only too well what she looked like without the shirt.

He stood motionless behind her, paralyzed by her nearness, the faint scents of summer flowers and sleep that wafted from her while she fumbled with the buttons. It would be so easy to wrap his arms around her, pull her to him, murmur soothing, meaningless words in her ear.

And take advantage of her helplessness, her neediness? No, even he had a few rules, like never playing the game with someone who didn't know the score beforehand.

She curled in the chair, looking up at him, her eyes full of pain and fear. "Do you?" she asked, and for a minute he thought she was referring to his self-imposed rules, asking if he really had the strength to ignore his desire for her.

"Do I?" Then he remembered her unanswered question. He cleared his throat. "No. Threatening phone calls are not typical for this sort of case. Do you want something to drink?"

She clutched the shirt tightly and nodded. He headed to the bathroom, the trip really an excuse to take himself away from her physical presence, to get his hormones under control. "Sorry I can't offer you anything but tap water. These rooms don't come equipped with a mini bar."

"Water's fine."

When he returned, she seemed to have regained some of her composure, though her eyes were unusually bright and her skin extremely pale. She accepted the glass as graciously as if it were a crystal snifter of aged brandy. "Thank you."

He sat on the edge of the bed. If these meetings kept up, he was going to have to get another chair in the room. Sitting on the unmade, rumpled bed put too many ideas in his head.

"All right, now tell me exactly what happened, what this caller said."

"I answered the phone." She hesitated, biting her lower lip.

"It's not unusual to have trouble recalling exactly what happened in a stressful situation. Just tell me what you remember."

She shook her head, the movement abrupt and jerky. "I remember every word. *Go away. Go back home and forget about finding your mother. She's dead and if you keep looking, you'll end up that way, too.*"

"Was the caller a man or a woman?"

She shook her head again, more slowly this time, allowing the shadows in her pale hair to shift. "I don't know. The voice was muffled and I was half asleep. It could have been either."

"Any chance it might be our friend, the mayor?"

"It's possible. But why would he do that? Why would anybody do something like that?"

"Most threatening phone calls are bluffs. It's pretty far-fetched to think somebody might want to kill you just because you're trying to find your birth mother."

She studied him silently for a moment. "So you're saying somebody is using empty threats to scare me into leaving before I find her."

He nodded. "That'd be my take on the situation."

"They don't want to kill me. They just want me to go away."

He nodded a second time.

"Why?"

"We haven't found the answer to that yet, but it would seem somebody doesn't want you to find your mother."

"Or my mother doesn't want to be found. If the caller was lying, if she's not really dead, that could have been her on the phone."

She sat with her legs curled under her, his shirt pulled around her knees, her hands clenched in her lap. Without makeup, she lost all traces of a sophisticated veneer. She was young and vulnerable, a sapling bent to the earth by a hurricane, not strong enough to stand on her own.

Rebecca had so much to learn, and before this hunt for her mother was over, he suspected she'd learn a lot more than she expected or wanted to learn.

"You knew going in that your mother didn't want to be found." His words came out more harshly than he'd intended.

"Yes." She straightened abruptly, swinging her feet to the floor, lifting her chin defiantly even as her lower lip quivered ever so slightly. "Yes," she said. "I knew that, but it's still unpleasant to have it confirmed. When you're following somebody's husband or tracking down somebody's parents, doesn't it ever occur to you that what you find might change your client's entire life? Maybe for good, maybe for bad, but it's likely to have a strong effect, one way or the other."

"That's exactly why ninety percent of my business is done for corporate clients. Tracking down a missing heir, finding out who's dipping into the company till, those are the kinds of jobs where no innocent person gets hurt." Jake felt a little uncomfortable, aware he was taking out his irritation with himself on Rebecca, fighting that same need he'd felt the first time he saw her in his office...to go to her, wrap her in his arms, pull her against him, stroke her hair and reassure her that everything was going to be all right.

But that would be the cruel in the long run, for both of them.

He'd had his doubts about this case from the beginning, and that phone call confirmed that she was not going to have a happy reunion with her long-lost mother. She might as well be prepared.

As though suddenly deciding to fight, Rebecca stood, her bare feet wide apart, her entire stance a defiant gesture. His shirt was long. On a smaller woman, it would have been like a robe, loose and concealing. But on Rebecca it was suggestive, reaching only halfway down her thighs, the slits on each side rising up far enough to expose an edge of gauzy white gown and a lot of smooth, ivory thigh. "I'm going with you tomorrow to talk to Mrs. Jordan," she announced.

He rose from the bed and towered over her, aware of the intimidation advantage his height gave him. "The hell you say."

Surprisingly Rebecca, who had seemed so defenseless a few minutes ago, refused to be intimidated. After recovering from her initial fright, she seemed galvanized by the mysterious phone call. "The hell I say. This is what I came for, to act instead of waiting and wondering, to retake control of my life."

While he had to give her credit for guts, he wasn't sure she was ready to hear what Mrs. Jordan might say. That threatening phone call pretty much guaranteed a bad outcome to this whole thing. "Look, the call you got suggests we may be onto something. So why don't you go to the library and check newspapers for the months just before and just after you were born while I talk to Mrs. Jordan?"

"Why should I check the newspapers? You think my mother might have taken out an ad announcing she had a child to give away?"

Jake ignored her sarcasm. "This is a small town. There could be a mention of some teenage girl who left to spend several months with her aunt somewhere up north. Some kids could have run away to get married, then their parents had it annulled. There are a lot of possibilities for stories that might give us a clue."

"You want me to read through five or six months of newspapers?"

Jake nodded. "That's what detective work is about, whether it's with the police force or private investigation. You search through a million grains of sand until you find the one that means something or maybe it only leads you to another one that means something. It's boring and tedious. On the positive side, the newspaper here won't be like the Dallas Morning News. Especially that long ago, it'll be a small paper, probably come out once or twice a week, and all you have to look for is the local news."

She shook her head stubbornly. "I wouldn't know what to look for, and you know I wouldn't. You're just trying to send me off while you question Mrs. Jordan."

He plowed his fingers through his hair. "Didn't we have this discussion earlier tonight? You either hired me to do a job or you're going to do the job yourself. Take your choice."

"That's a totally illogical thing to say. I may not know what questions to ask or what newspaper stories to look for, but I'm a woman. Another woman is much more likely to talk to me than she is to you. Unless you can give me a damned good reason why I shouldn't, I'm going with you."

She was a curious mixture of vulnerability and determination, of fears and courage, of blatant sexuality and dignified sophistication. And she was getting his mind and his body completely messed up.

Telling her she couldn't come with him, making every attempt to avoid her, wasn't the real solution to that problem. Getting his head back on straight was the only real and final solution.

He shrugged, as though the matter were of no consequence. "Fine. I can't stop you from coming with me, but you let me handle the questioning unless I ask for your help."

"Fine. I'll be ready to go at, what? Nine-thirty?"

"Nine-thirty."

She started out the door then stopped. "Oh, your shirt. I—"

"I'll get it tomorrow."

She stared at him for a long moment then her gaze hardened and her jaw firmed. Slowly, deliberately, never taking her eyes from his, she unbuttoned his shirt, slid out of it, handed it to him and strode away. With each step her long legs flashed in the darkness and her rounded rear moved enticingly below her slim waist, the wispy gown accenting more than it hid.

She vanished into her room, but her image remained in Jake's thoughts, imprinted on his eyelids, tingling between his legs.

If she got any more calls tonight, he'd know because he wasn't likely to go back to sleep any time soon.

***

"Good morning."

At the sound of Jake's voice, Rebecca lowered her copy of *The Edgewater Post* and looked up to see him standing there in a denim shirt—the one she'd worn last night?—and faded blue jeans. The jeans were snapped today, thank goodness.

She wasn't surprised to see him there. The motel coffee shop—inappropriately called The Eat Rite Grill—was the only restaurant in the immediate vicinity. However, she was a little surprised to see him still looking so appealing in the light of day. She'd greeted a tired, drawn face in the mirror that morning, but Jake, in spite of—or maybe because of—an indefinable dishevelment, looked more rugged and sexier than ever.

"Good morning," she said politely. "Would you care to join me?"

"Thanks." He slid into the booth across from her, cast a quick glance at her half-empty coffee and picked up the plastic covered menu. "Are you eating or just pumping up on caffeine?"

He almost sounded as if it mattered to him whether or not she ate breakfast. Almost. After his callous treatment of her last night, she knew better than to expect any such thing from Jake Thornton.

When she'd impulsively run to him after the shattering phone call, he'd seemed reassuring and concerned at first. He'd wrapped her in his shirt that smelled of laundry detergent with a faint essence of Jake, and then brought her a glass of tap water. For those few moments he'd seemed human, his dark eyes warm like a summer night. For those few moments she'd leaned on him. Then he retreated from her, brushing aside her fears with a cold reminder that she'd known going in her mother didn't want to be found.

She'd lain awake the rest of the night regretting her impetuous flight to him.

"I've ordered eggs, bacon and biscuits," she said. "I had a rough night, so I figure I need something besides coffee to get me through the day."

A waitress appeared and refilled her cup, then poured coffee for Jake and took his order.

Jake smiled up at the woman, a warm smile Rebecca had never seen from him before. He certainly had never used it on her. "I'll have the same thing this young lady is having."

"Got it." The waitress returned his smile, took his menu and left.

He drank deeply from his coffee before he spoke. "Any more calls?"

"No, none."

"Don't be surprised if you do get another one. If somebody is trying to keep you from finding your mother, they'll probably try again when they figure out the first attempt didn't work."

Jake was being so calm, so rational, so normal that she wanted to fly into his face, grab his broad shoulders and shake him until something sparked in those cold eyes.

She lifted the heavy mug and drank more of the muddy coffee.

The problem was hers, not his. He was doing the job she'd hired him to do. Nothing said he was supposed to get emotional about it.

She, on the other hand, had let her emotions get as much out of control as everything else in her life. The death of her parents had upset her, then finding the note about her birth mother had caused her even more distress. When she met Jake, she'd been in an extremely vulnerable state.

She was attracted to him. There was no point in denying it. He was an attractive man. More importantly, he was the man who was going to help her put herself back together. She'd let that factor confuse her. Being attracted to him and dependent on his skills should not translate into an emotional dependence.

Thank goodness he'd brought her out of that fast enough with his brutal coldness. He'd snapped her back to reality, and she'd taken great delight in defying his objection to her accompanying him to Doris Jordan's house. The righteous anger had felt good, a relief from the emptiness she'd lived with since her parents' deaths...since she'd lost herself.

The anger was, she thought, the healthiest of her rampant emotions.

But she hadn't been able to stop herself from giving him back his shirt and flaunting her nearly-nude body in front of him as she went back to her room. In spite of her distress, she hadn't missed the desire in his eyes when she'd come to his room in the middle of the night. In her anger, the temptation to taunt him had been irresistible.

Though she hadn't looked back, she'd felt his gaze on her, hot and hungry, and she'd loved every second of it. She'd managed to take control of at least that much of her life.

The waitress arrived with heavy plates of eggs, bacon, hash browns and biscuits. Rebecca had lost her appetite when her parents died, but today she resolved to eat every bite. Today she had a feeling she was going to need all the strength she could find.

Chapter 5

Rebecca studied every house, every tree, every lawn of the small town of Edgewater as Jake guided his dark blue, nondescript sedan along the maze of streets toward Doris Jordan's house.

A young boy skated down the sidewalk on roller blades. Two girls sat on a front porch having a tea party with their dolls. A group of kids were shooting baskets in front of somebody's garage. An older couple rocked to and fro in a porch swing.

Had her mother or father grown up in one of those houses, in a world not all that different from her own?

Was her mother or father sitting in one of those houses right now?

Was that teenage boy riding a bicycle her cousin or even her half-brother?

Jake turned down a street with trees so big they formed a canopy overhead. The houses on that street were small and old. He pulled up in front of a yard bursting with a kaleidoscope of disorderly flowers.

"You know," he said, "you don't have to go in." The first words he'd spoken since they'd left the restaurant were brusque but with an underlying note of concern. Or maybe she just wanted to hear that underlying note.

Probably.

She opened the car door and climbed out.

The sidewalk leading up to the porch was cracked, but no grass sprouted between the cracks just as no weeds grew in the profusion of flowers. Morning glory vines twined around a trellis on one side of the porch, and a couple of wrought iron chairs with faded cushions seemed to be waiting for people to visit.

As Rebecca stepped onto the porch, she noticed that the trellis of vines curtained a swing on that side, a place to sit hidden from the world.

The screen door opened, and a regal woman wearing light gray slacks and a matching silvery blouse appeared. "Good morning. You must be Mr. Thornton. I'm Doris Jordan." At first glance, in spite of her perfectly coifed white hair, she looked younger than the seventy-some years Charles Morton had mentioned. But her face was creased with a network of fine lines, and her pale green eyes held depths that could only have been acquired from many years of living.

"I'm Jake Thornton, and this is Rebecca Patterson. I hope you don't mind if she sits in on our discussion."

"Not at all. I'm always glad to have company. Please come in."

Jake had not specified her role in being there, and Doris Jordan was too polite to ask. Rebecca was grateful for that, for the chance to be merely an observer rather than someone with so much at stake.

Jake's hand touched the small of her back as he entered the house behind her. It was a casual gesture, the habit of a man accustomed to walking beside a woman. Nothing in the brief contact justified the surge of heat that shot through her.

Her emotions were running rampant again. She gathered her dignity about her and resolved to keep a tighter rein on her volatile reactions to Jake Thornton, to get in control and stay there.

Though the morning was already warm, Doris Jordan's house with the curtains drawn against the sun still retained the night's cool.

"Would you like some coffee? I've just made a fresh pot."

"Thank you, I'd love a cup." Jake gave the older woman the same charming smile he'd given the waitress.

"And you, Ms. Patterson?"

"Yes, please."

Doris left the room. Jake looked around then sat in a large, overstuffed chair. Rebecca sank onto the far end of a sofa printed with muted or possibly faded flowers and draped with a colorful afghan. The room, like the yard, was filled to overflowing but didn't feel crowded. A roll top desk occupied one corner. A small television housed in an old Victrola cabinet sat in another. The sofa and two chairs were grouped around a marble topped coffee table. Occasional tables holding pictures and lamps dotted the room. Everything was immaculately clean, polished and gleaming warmly in the dim light.

"Here we are." Doris returned with a silver tray holding a matching pot, sugar bowl and creamer, a large mug and two dainty cups and saucers. "My husband, Edgar, and I received this beautiful tea service for a wedding gift. We never drank hot tea, so I've always used it for coffee. I saw no point in letting it go to waste." She set the tray on the table and served them, giving the mug to Jake, then sat down on the other end of the sofa. "Men like the big mugs. I suppose their fingers are simply too large for the smaller handles. My husband and son were both large men like you, Mr. Thornton."

Rebecca accepted the china cup with irises painted in delicate shadings of purple and lavender. "This is beautiful."

"Thank you." Doris held up her own, similar in design but with roses trailing around it. "I began collecting them years ago, back when we thought all our dishes had to match. I saw no reason for that and decided I'd have a flower garden in my china cabinet."

"What a lovely sentiment. A garden inside to match the one outside."

Doris smiled warmly. "Exactly. You obviously noticed my flowers in the front yard have no particular design, either. The random patterns appeal to me with their special brand of unplanned beauty."

Rebecca thought of the kaleidoscopic flowers out front and imagined Doris' china cabinet filled with more of the dainty cups in myriad flowers and designs. "Beauty in chaos."

"I find it wild and soothing at the same time. Would you like more coffee?" She lifted the pot and Jake held out his mug.

"Thank you. It's great," he said.

"Yes, it is," Rebecca agreed. "What we had at the motel coffee shop was less than wonderful."

"Wilbur doesn't supervise his restaurant staff closely enough. I don't believe they clean the pots adequately. It's so important to get rid of the rancid oils."

"You know the motel owner," Jake said, and Rebecca caught the subtle shift in his voice, the hint of business mixed with the conversational tones.

It was enough to pierce the haze of contentment that had settled around her. Doris Jordan's house, her yard, her furniture, her tea service, her manner of speaking had soothed and lulled her. She'd relaxed into Doris' sofa, sipped coffee from her flower-garden cup, luxuriated in the cool dimness of the room and the faint scent of violets or some other old-fashioned flower. Somehow she'd momentarily lost sight of the reason they were there.

"Oh my, yes," Doris said. "I went to school with his mother. I've lived here all my life. I know most of the people."

"I imagine a lot of the women bought dresses from your shop."

"Yes, they did." She set her cup and saucer on the table and folded her hands in her lap. "At one time, having a dress with my label in it was considered special. Not like Neiman Marcus, but special in our little town. Most of the women in Edgewater shopped there as well as many of the women from smaller towns in the area."

Rebecca's heart sank. The chances of this woman's remembering one blue dress were becoming smaller and smaller.

"How'd you come up with the name *Sharise's Shoppe*?" Jake asked, his tone still a careful combination of casual and intense.

Doris smiled, the lines of her face spreading outward in a way that was more wistful than happy. "My son was a twin. His sister, Sharise, died at birth. So when I opened the dress store, it was either *Doris' Dresses* or *Sharise's Shoppe*. Not much of a choice, really."

"It's a beautiful name," Rebecca said. "I don't think I've heard it before." Her own pain of loss reached out and blended with the older woman's. She recalled that Morton had mentioned Doris' son being killed several years ago and her husband dying more recently. He hadn't mentioned the death of an infant too.

For all her pictures and flowers, Doris was alone in the world, as she herself was.

"I'm not sure where I heard the name. Possibly in a book. I read a lot."

A click drew her attention to Jake. His open briefcase sat in his lap, but his intent gaze was focused on her. Immediately he averted his eyes, looked into the briefcase and withdrew the dress. "Any chance you'd remember this?"

"This is the dress you said belonged to your client's mother?"

Jake nodded.

Sally Berneathy

Doris accepted the garment and studied it carefully, her fingers caressing as they slid over the material, as though she would retrieve the era represented by the dress, an era when she had a dress shop and a husband and a son. Finally she looked up, directly at Rebecca. "I sold so many of these."

"The woman would have been short and slim, dark hair, and she wore glasses." Rebecca knew it was useless, but she couldn't give up so easily.

Doris shook her head and handed the dress back to Jake. "I'm sorry. My memory isn't what it used to be."

"It's all right," Jake said smoothly. "I knew it was a long shot. What about somebody who might have come to your shop looking for loose clothes to disguise a pregnancy around 1978 or 1979?"

"I've been thinking about it ever since you phoned me yesterday, but I can't recall anything that might help you. My son, a police officer, was killed on duty in 1979. My husband had his first heart attack when he heard the news, so I'm afraid I didn't notice a lot outside my own family that year."

Doris related the incidents with sadness but without any visible signs of the heart-wrenching grief that still came when Rebecca spoke of her parents' death. Thirty years from now, would she be as accepting of death as Doris Jordan was?

"I'm sorry," Jake said. "I didn't know."

Rebecca impulsively placed her hand over Doris'. "Me too. We didn't mean to revive painful memories."

"It's all right. If we live long enough, we all lose people we love. I've made peace with my losses." She placed her other hand over Rebecca's and gave it a quick squeeze. "Is this your mother you're looking for? Are you Mr. Thornton's client?"

Rebecca looked to Jake as if she thought he had any answers. Of course he didn't.

"Yes," she said. "My parents were killed in an automobile accident recently, and I discovered I was adopted."

Doris took a pair of wire framed glasses from a carved wooden box on the coffee table, put them on and scrutinized her closely, then shook her head. "I've thought since I first saw you standing on the porch that you look vaguely familiar, but I'm afraid I can't quite put my finger on it." She sighed. "I've lived a long time, seen a lot of people and watched a lot of television. You're a lovely young woman. You probably look like someone on my favorite soap opera."

But Rebecca didn't believe that.

She couldn't.

Her mother lived in this town.

The phone call last night and Doris Jordan's comment that she looked vaguely familiar verified that hope.

Jake asked more questions, things Rebecca had to admit she would never have thought of, but elicited no more information.

Finally they rose to leave. Doris walked to the door with them.

"Thank you for talking to us, Mrs. Jordan," Jake said. "You have my number at the motel if you remember anything."

"I'll be sure to call if I do." She turned and lifted slim, dry fingers to Rebecca's cheek. "I hope you find what you're looking for, my dear. But try to keep an open mind. It's more likely to be in the future, not the past."

Rebecca felt a lump rise in her throat and could only nod in response.

She hated to leave this woman's house with its feeling of home and belonging. She and Doris Jordan were two of a kind, alone in the world.

But, Rebecca thought in abrupt self-loathing, Doris had come to terms with her aloneness. She wasn't grasping for any pseudo-family member to fill the void the way Rebecca was.

She walked outside with Jake, into the sweltering mid-day heat. He opened the car door for her, and she slid in, the leather hot through the fabric of her slacks.

"We passed a barbecue place on the way here," he said. "That sound all right for lunch?"

"Sure."

It didn't. It sounded horrible. Hot and greasy, and she wasn't hungry anyway.

Doris Jordan was probably having a salad or cucumber sandwiches with cream cheese and a huge glass of iced tea for lunch.

She thought of the older woman's words.

What you're looking for...it's more likely to be in the future, not the past.

She'd always forged ahead toward the future, optimistic and determined, searching for whatever lay ahead, whatever might be lacking in her life, always certain she would find that something. Now she had no past and couldn't conceive of a future.

The present was a barbecue lunch with Jake Thornton.

A very present, very temporary, very shaky situation.

It was all she had at the moment, and the present moment was the only fragment of time in which she existed.

Chapter 6

September 30, 1979, Edgewater, Texas

Mary stepped back to study the table and see if she'd forgotten anything. The good china Ben's mother had given them, linen napkins, candles....everything had to be perfect.

She spread one hand over her still-flat stomach and smiled. She'd suspected for the last couple of weeks but hadn't wanted to get Ben's hopes up until she was certain. Though she had been certain in her heart, so certain her joy had filled every crevice of her soul and pushed out all but an occasional stab of the pain and horror that had been her constant companion since that day in August.

Blackness tugged at the edges of her mind even now, but she shoved it aside as she heard Ben's car pull into the driveway. Moving quickly, she lit the candles, determinedly focusing on the happy excitement, leaving no room for that darkness to intrude.

A few moments later his key turned in the door she always kept locked now, and he stepped inside, a big bear of a man with a warm smile on his face. "Something sure smells good."

Mary rushed into his arms, lifting her face for his kiss.

"Umm," he murmured. "I don't know whether you or dinner smells the best." He touched his lips to hers again, this kiss more intense, and she felt a response to his passion. He nuzzled her neck. "I know dinner couldn't taste any better than you do. I don't suppose it's one of those meals that could wait a few minutes?" He kissed his way back to her lips. "Better make that a lot of minutes. Maybe an hour or so."

She pulled away from him with a small giggle and took his hand. "No, it can't wait. This is a very special dinner." She tugged him toward the kitchen.

"Uh oh. Is this another new recipe?" he teased. "Are we going to be up half the night with heartburn again? Maybe we better go upstairs first just in case we don't feel like it afterward."

"Oh, you! Stop that! Our steaks are under the broiler and they're going to burn if we don't get in there!"

"Steaks, eh? Hmm." His face took on a mock-pensive expression. "Okay. I guess I can pass up making love with my wife for a big, juicy steak."

Mary danced into the kitchen, Ben's hand clutched firmly in hers.

"Candles and wine, too! Omigosh! It's our anniversary, isn't it? Your birthday? My birthday?"

"Just sit down and pour the wine. Only half a glass for me." Mary gave him an enigmatic smile then bent to turn the steaks.

She went back to the table, sat next to her husband and lifted her half-full glass. She'd planned every moment of this evening for over a year, but now a lump in her throat threatened to interfere with her rehearsed speech, the eloquent toast she'd planned to propose.

"Mar? Are you all right? Are you crying?"

Mary smiled though her eyes were moist. "No. Yes. Oh, Ben! We're having a baby!"

"A baby?" A look of wonder spread over Ben's face. He leaned around and touched Mary's stomach reverently. "Are you sure?"

Mary's heart swelled with love for this man and for the child growing inside her. "Yes, I'm sure. Doctor Wilcox called me with the results today. I had everything planned so carefully, how I'd tell you, what I'd say, but then I forgot everything and just blurted it out! I'm sorry. I wanted to do this right."

"Oh, honey, you can blurt out news like that any day. When? When's she going to...you know...be finished? Be born?"

Mary laughed softly at Ben's flustered questions. "What makes you think it's going to be a girl?"

"Because I'm her father and I know these things."

"What if it's a boy?"

"I guess we can keep him. But I don't think we ought to make him wear that pink dress and booties you've been crocheting."

Mary gasped. "How did you know about that dress?"

"Because I'm her father and I know these...what's that smell?"

71

Mary shot up from her chair. "The steaks! Omigosh!" She jerked them from the oven. "They're ruined!"

"Nah. They're just a little black on one side." He took the broiler pan from her and set it on the stove top then turned her to face him. "For the second time, the first being when you said *I do*, you've made me the happiest man in the world. Right now, your hamburger casserole would even taste like gourmet food. Come on, Mother. Let's enjoy our steaks. You and Sharise need the protein."

Sharise. The name of Ben's twin sister who'd died at birth, the name of his mother's dress shop. It thrilled Mary to know that Ben and his parents wanted to pass such a special name on to her baby, to give the child history and a place in a big, loving family. Her baby would never know the loneliness she'd known since her parents' deaths, the sense of belonging nowhere to no one. This baby would have lots of family to love her and keep her safe...her or him.

"Sharise or—" She broke off, choking on the name Ben had always talked about for a boy. *Charles*.

"Are you all right?" Ben asked, a bite of steak poised in midair halfway to his mouth, his brow wrinkled in concern.

"Of course. I just...I'm sorry about the steaks. I wanted everything to be perfect."

"The important things are perfect. I love you, you love me, and we're both going to love our baby more than anybody's ever loved a baby since the world began. I can't wait to tell Mom and Dad. And Charles. I can just see his face when this kid wraps her tiny little fist around his thumb and calls him *Uncle Charles*. I don't think he had the best of families back in Ohio. This baby is going to be very spoiled with so many people adoring her."

For a fleeting instant an ugly thought reared up amidst all the happiness, but Mary quickly shoved it aside.

It was impossible.

No way could that one nightmare experience, that cruel torture that bore no similarity to making love, result in the miracle of a child, the ultimate gift of love.

"Yes," she agreed, her voice firm, "our baby is going to be spoiled rotten. That's the way it should be."

Chapter 7

Jake held the heavy wooden door open for Rebecca to enter the Smokehouse Barbecue, a roughly hewn wooden building that sat a block off the main street of downtown Edgewater.

They'd had breakfast together, visited Doris Jordan together, and now they were having lunch together. What was wrong with that picture?

Hell, what was right with it?

Nothing that he could see.

He was a loner. Rebecca desperately needed somebody. One hundred eighty degrees out. Opposite ends of the spectrum.

For her sake if not for the sake of doing his job, he had to get rid of her. He couldn't let her start to depend on him, to need him when he had nothing to give.

Nor could he spend any more nights separated from her by nothing but a thin wall. Not after he'd seen what she slept in.

The small restaurant was crowded, but Jake located an empty table and guided Rebecca toward it with a gentle hand at the small of her back.

If you're so damned anxious to get rid of her, why do you keep touching her every chance you get?

Jake ignored the nagging voice in the back of his head since he didn't want to think about the answer to that question.

Smells good in here," she said as they sat down at the square table covered with a red checked vinyl cloth.

Yes, it does. I didn't think I was hungry after that big breakfast, but that smell has changed my mind."

Rebecca frowned. "If you weren't hungry, why did you suggest we come here to eat?"

She was as good with questions as that little voice in his head. He knew the answer but he wasn't about to tell her that he did it because he hadn't known what else to do with her after they left Doris Jordan's house, because she made him uncomfortable and a public restaurant seemed a good place to be with her.

"I thought you might be hungry," he lied.

The waitress came to take their orders—two sandwiches, tea for her and beer for him.

"Doris Jordan's a special lady," Rebecca said when the waitress left.

"Yeah," Jake agreed. "She is. Special and a lady."

"She's lonely."

"Who isn't? She's doing all right."

"I guess." She unrolled her paper napkin and carefully laid out the cheap flatware. "We didn't learn anything from her."

"More than you realize. I told you before, detective work goes one inch at a time. Sometimes it goes by centimeters. It's tedious and time-consuming. That's why you pay me to do the work

Sally Berneathy

75

while you wait at home in air-conditioned comfort for my reports."

"And I told you before, I can't do that."

They sat staring at each other, stalemated.

She was so self-contained today, it was hard to believe this was the same distraught woman who'd run to his room last night.

In the silence that fell between them, the laughter and talking around them punctuated by the clink of silverware on plates seemed to grow louder. The ding of a bell announced another order was up.

Jake didn't like crowds, avoided them as much as possible, and this place was beginning to feel very crowded. When they'd first walked in, the air had felt cool, but that was compared to the noon heat outside. Now it seemed warm and suffocating, the sweet, spicy scent of barbecue overpowering in its tantalizing appeal. If Rebecca weren't with him, he'd get up and leave.

If Rebecca weren't with him, he probably wouldn't feel the need to leave.

The waitress returned with their drinks, and Jake took a long, soothing swallow of his ice-cold beer.

"Okay," Rebecca said, "so I missed whatever it is we learned from Doris Jordan because I'm not a skilled detective. Can I have my report now instead of waiting for you to leave a message on my answering machine in my air-conditioned home which I'm not in right now?"

Jake set his frosty mug back on the table. "Whatever you want. You're paying the bills. Today we learned that your mother very likely came from an affluent family."

"What makes you think that?"

"Because Doris Jordan said that at one time having a dress with her label in it was considered special. She even compared her private label to Neiman Marcus. While she admitted that wasn't a completely valid comparison, any small shop with a private label is going to be in a price range above Wal-Mart. Add this to the visit from His Honor, the Mayor, last night, and I'd say we're looking at a person who's influential in the community."

Rebecca wrapped both hands around her oversized glass of tea and tilted her head briefly in acknowledgment of his deductions. "Very good. I'm impressed."

"Next we consider that your mother came to your parents penniless, gave a phony name on your birth certificate and left with a request that you never try to find her. From this we can assume her parents knew nothing of her pregnancy. The phone call you got last night and our visit from Morton tells me she's still hiding."

"So you really think Morton knows who she is?"

Jake thought about it for a minute, about the assessing way Morton had studied Rebecca, his determined reassurance that they'd find no traces of her parentage in Edgewater. "Yeah," he said. "I think he knows, and I think she's putting the pressure on him to get us out of town."

He realized he'd said the wrong thing as Rebecca's face fell. She was going to have to learn

Secrets Rising

how to keep her every emotion from showing. Such transparency was like an invitation to the sharks of the world to move in for the kill.

He took another drink of his beer, deliberately avoiding her eyes.

"Go on," she said, her voice tentative but firm.

"Nothing else. That's our inch for the morning."

"So what are we doing this afternoon?"

He spread his hands in frustration. "You're going to go back to the motel, get your things and head out for Dallas. You had no business coming with me this morning. You're too involved, too emotional about this whole thing."

She stared at him coldly across the vinyl covered table. At least she no longer looked so damned vulnerable. "Of course I'm emotionally involved. What do you expect? This is my family we're talking about. I assume even you have a family, a mother and father, that you didn't spring fully grown from the seat of that big chair in your office."

"Yeah, I got family. Enough for both of us. I'll tell you what, you take two or three of my step parents, and we'll call off this entire chase. In fact, you can even have my birth parents...if we can figure out which ones they are."

"What are you talking about?"

Jake tossed down the rest of his beer. One part of him didn't want to give her any of him, certainly not his personal life, but another part wanted to warn her, to let her know how foolish she was being.

He gave a mental shrug. What did it matter what he told her? It wasn't like she was going to be a part of his life for more than a few days at most.

"My parents got a divorce when I was a baby. When my dad remarried a couple of years later, I went to live with him so my mother could go back to school. But then my dad divorced his second wife and I went to live with my mother and her new husband. Until they got a divorce. To make a long story short, I never lived with anybody for more than a couple of years, and I have so many step parents, step brothers, step sisters, half-brothers, and half-sisters, we'd have to rent Cowboys Stadium if we ever decided to have a reunion. And you know what? Having all that family hasn't done one damn thing to improve my life. All it's done is create chaos around Christmas. I never know who to buy a present for, who's going to give me a new tie I'll never wear or a bottle of cologne that smells like a service station bathroom. They don't know anything about me, I don't know anything about them, but we're family. Whatever that means."

Her expression had softened as he spoke. "I'm sorry you never had a real family."

He tilted his head back and drew in a deep, frustrated breath. "You're missing the point here. My family was real. Your family was real. Families don't come with rules. I have no complaints about mine. I don't recall ever being unhappy, just a little confused sometimes. But it sounds like you got a good one. So why not leave it at that? Why are you setting yourself up for disappointment? Why are you being greedy and asking for another good one?"

She leaned forward, her voice low and intense. "Greedy? Is it greedy to want to know who I am, what my mother looked like, where my grandparents came from...why my mother gave birth to me and then got away from me as fast as she could run?"

"Howdy!"

Jake's attention jerked toward the sound of the intrusion.

A pulpy-looking, ruddy faced, fortyish man wearing a police uniform smiled down at them. He held his cap politely in his hands, his fingers twisting the brim nervously. "I'm Farley Gates, Chief of Police. Mind if I join you?"

First the mayor, now the chief of police? The city officials must be strapped for entertainment.

"By all means." Jake indicated the chair Farley Gates was already pulling out.

"You folks found the best barbecue in Texas right off the bat," Gates said.

Their waitress appeared so rapidly Jake thought she must have watched Gates come in. "What'll you have, Farley?"

"Just a big, tall glass of iced tea, Phyllis."

"With extra lemon, right?"

Gates grinned and winked up at her. "You got it, honey. Thank you now." He turned back to Jake. "How you folks doing today?"

"Great, Farley, just great," Jake said. "You don't mind if I call you Farley, do you?"

"Of course I don't mind, Jake."

That told Jake what he wanted to know. Farley Gates knew who they were and why they were there. He was not part of an official welcoming committee. Jake would be willing to bet the police chief was going to try to talk them out of searching for Rebecca's mother. She must be one powerful lady in this town to justify so much official interest.

"So what can we do for you today, Farley?" Besides leave town.

"Not a thing. I just wanted to come by and introduce myself to you and Ms. Patterson."

"Rebecca," Jake corrected. "We're all good buddies here, right? All on a first name basis."

Gates looked a little disconcerted, as if the possibility had just occurred to him that perhaps Jake was being sarcastic. But the thought seemed to leave as quickly as it came, and Gates' perpetual smile reappeared. "Charles said you were a good-looking filly. If I'd ever seen your mama, I'd'a remembered her."

"Then perhaps I look like my father," Rebecca said smoothly, though Jake could tell from the tenseness around her lips that Gates' obvious knowledge of her situation had disconcerted her.

Gates nodded. "I reckon that could be, but I can't say as how I know any men you look like, either."

The waitress arrived with his tea and their sandwiches. Gates accepted his drink with another wink. "Thanks, honey."

Jake ignored his sandwich, leaned back in his chair and folded his arms. "And since you've never seen anyone who looks enough like Rebecca to be her mother or father, we might as well pack our bags and head back to Dallas."

Gates' forehead wrinkled as if he was trying very hard to decide how to take Jake's comment. "I don't think there's any call to be rude."

"Was I? My apologies."

Gates grunted and took a long gulp of his tea. "So, are you having any luck?"

Jake shrugged noncommittally. "Some."

Gates looked from him to Rebecca. She gave him a tight smile.

"You know, sometimes it just don't pay to go digging up the past. Some teenage girl gets herself in trouble, goes to the big city to have her baby so nobody will know, comes back, marries a nice guy, has a family, makes a life for herself, then nearly thirty years later that illegitimate baby shows up on her doorstep and ruins that life."

Rebecca went even paler than normal.

"Is that what's happening here?" Jake asked, forcing Gates' attention to him, giving Rebecca a chance to regain her composure. "Does this mean you know who Rebecca's mother is, maybe even who her father is?"

He looked from one to the other, his bonhomie slowly melting into scowling disapproval. "I don't know, and I don't care. This isn't your big city. We take care of each other down here, look out for our own." He focused on Rebecca. "I think by now it oughta be real clear your mama don't want you to find her. Why would you want somebody who doesn't want you?"

Rebecca's eyes rounded in shock, dismay and pain. Jake clenched his fists to keep from punching this jerk in his drooping jaw. Antagonizing the local authorities, even an idiot like Farley Gates, was not a smart thing to do in any investigation.

"Ms. Patterson needs to find her family medical history," he said.

That brought Gates up short. His gaze scanned Rebecca carefully. "She looks pretty healthy to me." Surprisingly, concern edged his voice.

"You're not a doctor."

"What's the matter with her?"

"I can tell you what *isn't* the matter with her. She isn't deaf, and she isn't retarded. You can talk directly to her."

"Oh!" Gates shifted uneasily, his face turning even redder than normal. He cleared his throat. "Are you sick, ma'am?"

Rebecca looked at Jake helplessly. He'd succeeded in two things—diverting her from that hurt despondency at Gates' suggestion that her mother didn't want her and showing her she had no business being in the middle of his investigation.

"You know, Farley, I don't think the three of us are good enough friends that we can discuss something so personal as Rebecca's health."

"Oh, well, yeah, okay." He stood, taking his hat in one hand and rubbing the palm of the other down the side of his uniform. "Well, um, it was nice to meet you folks." He attempted a smile, but it didn't quite work.

He left the restaurant hurriedly, bumping into two tables on his way out.

"There goes one confused police chief," Jake said as soon as the door closed behind Gates.

"Why did you tell him I was sick?" Rebecca demanded.

"I didn't tell him that. He assumed it. You do need to know your family medical history. That's the only legitimate reason I could come up with for you to pursue this. Gates jumped to conclusions all by himself."

Befuddling the enemy gave Jake a smug, satisfied feeling. He took a bite of his sandwich. Gates was right about one thing. It was good barbecue.

From the corner of his eye he saw Rebecca lift the edge of her bread, then put it back down and push the sandwich away. "You think he knows my mother?" she asked in a small voice.

"It's possible. It's also possible he's just following orders from our friend, the mayor." He could leave it there, ought to leave it there. She was starting to have doubts about this whole thing, and that was good. If anything, he should encourage her doubts, encourage her to get her sexy butt back to Dallas and build a life for herself, the way Gates suggested her mother had done.

But some demon in his soul felt compelled to try to erase the sadness from those smoky green eyes. "You thinking he brought you a personal message from your mother, that she doesn't want to see you?"

"I told you before, that doesn't matter to me. I'm not expecting anybody to bring out the fatted calf. I just have to know."

He didn't believe her, but she was working hard at convincing herself.

He shrugged. "You may get your wish. We seem to be stirring up something."

"You mean because of the threatening phone call?"

"That and the mayor's visit to warn us away." He ticked the events off on his fingers. "Then today the mayor sends his number one brown noser to give it another shot. We must be closing in on something real interesting. I gotta admit, I'm starting to get curious."

"This was never about curiosity." The ice in her voice could have cooled the entire restaurant for a week. But at least she didn't look sad and beaten anymore.

"Maybe it ought to be. Your mother must be one important person in this town to justify so much interest from the local big wigs."

"You're a real bastard."

He grinned. "Could be, but I doubt it. My parents were really into marriage. They committed it five or six times each."

She glared at him, pinched white lines etched around her mouth.

He took another bite of his sandwich. She snatched hers up and bit into it viciously.

Good. She was fighting again.

Jake enjoyed the triumphant feeling for at least a minute before realizing he'd only made things worse. What did it matter to him if Rebecca gave up, if she was dejected, if she quit and went home or kept fighting to find her mother? Hadn't he just been trying to talk her into doing that very thing until he'd fallen into the well of despondency in her eyes?

He'd let his competitive personality take over. He didn't like Gates, he didn't like Morton, and he didn't like the idea of their dictating what he and Rebecca should or shouldn't do. That's all it was.

He hadn't done her any favors, though. The evidence was mounting that eventually she would have to give up. If her mother could bring this much pressure to bear, no way would she welcome Rebecca with open arms. More likely she'd call out the troops to escort her long-lost daughter back to Dallas.

Then there wouldn't be a damn thing he could do to remove that crushed, devastated look from her eyes. And in the meantime, she was going to be dogging his every step, not to mention sleeping in the motel room next door to his.

It was his turn to bite viciously into his sandwich.

Chapter 8

Rebecca leaned back and rubbed her neck, rolling her head from side to side. After sitting in the hard wooden chair for most of the day, viewing the Edgewater Public Library's microfiche files of newspapers for the last half of 1979, every muscle in her body ached.

Of course, every muscle in her body was exhausted from two nights of very little sleep. Though last night had not been interrupted by any ominous phone calls, her own mind had kept her either wide awake or in the midst of disturbing dreams in which her mother and father, Charles Morton, Farley Gates, Doris Jordan and Jake, threatened her, cajoled her, served tea to her in flowered cups, chased her, and, in Jake's case, seduced her. She wasn't sure which of the dreams bothered her the most.

Even the dream of Doris, which began happily enough in a flower garden, soon filled with foreboding when a storm came up and Doris climbed into a car with Rebecca's parents. She'd awakened to the familiar empty feeling that had been her constant companion since her parents' deaths, then gone back to sleep to dream of Jake. He'd seduced her but stopped short of making love to her and walked away without a word.

The real Jake, seated at the next viewer, scooted his chair back and looked over at her. "I tried to tell you how exciting detective work can be."

"You never told me how boring a small town could be. Any paper that prints feature articles about Louise Arnold's sugar cookies and Henry Fletcher's home-made bird houses is really scraping the bottom of the news barrel."

To her surprise, Jake smiled, a real smile, not the phony kind they'd been passing back and forth the last couple of days. "Don't let Eunice hear you say that."

To her further surprise, Rebecca heard herself laugh at the memory of the gravely intent librarian with contradictory carrot red hair handing over the requested microfiche to two strangers as if it contained national secrets.

"First time I've heard you laugh," Jake said.

"I haven't done a lot of it the last few weeks."

"Several hours of tedious work will do that, make you slap happy and so bored you forget whatever else was bugging you."

Amazing. Jake sounded like a human being, a real person with a heart beating beneath the muscles of that wide chest. The well-formed muscles, as she recalled from her first night there.

Immediately she tried to erase that image from her mind. Bad enough she'd had those kinds of thoughts about him when they were together in his motel room and he was half naked. Now as they sat in the quiet, musty confines of the old library, surrounded by ceiling-high shelves filled with books, both fully clothed, there was absolutely no reason for her hormones to spill over.

But they were doing just that.

Jake the Smiling Man in the Library was every bit as compelling as Jake the Angry Detective in the Motel Room.

"Well," she said, "guess I better get back to it. I'm only up to the middle of October. I'm sure there'll be big spreads about Jimmy Green's Halloween costume, Thanksgiving dinner at Mrs. Jones' house and Mr. Brown's roof-top display at Christmas."

She slid back to the viewer, reluctant and eager to tear her gaze from Jake's angular, chiseled features that looked so incredibly good wearing a smile.

The day to day minutiae of small town life was even harder to focus on now.

Until the front page headlines of the October 22, 1979, issue.

"Oh, Jake! Here's the story about Doris' son."

She halfway expected Jake to tell her that had nothing to do with their case and to stop wasting time, but instead he gave her a sympathetic glance. "What does it say?"

"*Local policeman slain*," she read. "*Ben Jordan, local police officer, was killed yesterday in a shoot-out at a deserted farmhouse south of town. Jordan and his partner, Charles Morton...*Charles Morton?"

She looked up. "His partner was Charles Morton. Does that mean...?"

"What?" Jake asked when she hesitated.

"I don't know. Nothing, I guess."

"You're thinking if Charles was Ben's partner, that might explain how he knows who your father is, that Ben Jordan might have left a pregnant girlfriend behind." He leaned back and folded his arms, giving her his full attention. "Could be. That might explain why Morton's being so protective of the woman. His former partner's girl. Read the rest of it."

"*Jordan and his partner, Officer Charles Morton, were investigating reports of drug users living in the vacant farmhouse. Morton reports that they knocked on the door and announced themselves as police officers. An unidentified white male shot Jordan from a broken window beside the door. Morton radioed for assistance, but Jordan was pronounced dead upon arrival at Woodward Memorial Hospital.*

"*Police recovered the gun, an unregistered .38 caliber revolver, and assorted drug paraphernalia, but have no clues as to the identity or whereabouts of the assailant. Morton describes the man as medium height and build with long, brown hair and beard, between twenty and thirty years of age and driving an older model Ford automobile, license plates obscured or hidden.*

"*Jordan, an Edgewater native and recipient of the purple heart, is survived by his wife, Mary Baker Jordan, and his parents, Edgar and Doris Jordan.*" She sat back. "Well, so much for the girl friend theory. He had a wife."

"Which doesn't mean he didn't have a girlfriend too, Miss Ivory Tower. In fact, that would be all the

90

more reason to hide her pregnancy. Trade places with me and let me see that article."

Rebecca rose at the same time he did and stepped away, attempting to switch positions without touching Jake, but he moved the same direction. She felt a flush rise to her face as she moved back and he did the same.

Jake put his hands on her shoulders and gazed at her, a faint, suggestive grin tilting the corners of his lips. "This is a tough dance. There's no music and the floor's carpeted, but you just follow my lead, and we'll get this step right."

As Jake turned her, it did seem like a dance, and her blood pulsed faster in rhythm to the primitive beat of some music felt rather than heard. They seemed to be revolving round and round in a waltz of desire though she knew they only moved half a circle.

Then they were still, his hands on her shoulders, his breath warm on her cheek, his nearness setting off some insane electrical storm in her body. His masculine scent along with a faint wisp of the deep blue scent of denim swirled around her, blocking the musty odor of the library just as his deep blue gaze blocked the sight of everything around them.

Without moving his hands or his eyes, he lifted one thumb and traced the line of her jaw. His lips moved, parting ever so slightly. Or maybe it was only a shifting shadow.

His eyelids drooped as though he would close them.

But he didn't. He blinked twice, jerked his hands from her shoulders as if burned and moved away.

Only then did Rebecca realize her own lips were parted, waiting for his to touch them.

Blushing hotly, a little breathless and vaguely disappointed, she fell into the chair where Jake had been sitting, where the warmth of his body lingered.

What was the matter with her? She wasn't even sure she liked Jake Thornton. Certainly she couldn't get along with him. Her hormones, however, completely ignored any problem she had with him. She understood and accepted that she'd lost control of her life, but what had happened to her resolve to at least take charge of her own body chemistry?

"Couple of follow-up articles here. I'm going to see if Eunice will print copies for me." Jake's voice contained faint traces of huskiness. She wasn't the only one dealing with runaway urges. Knowing that made it more exciting but also more difficult. If she knew he had no interest, that she was alone in this absurd attraction, she'd be too embarrassed to even let herself think about him. As it stood now, she not only had to struggle to control her thoughts of him, but she found herself speculating on what he might be thinking.

As if her life wasn't messed up enough, she was fantasizing about a man who embodied exactly what she didn't need right now—someone who held himself aloof from the world, someone who had no need for human involvement.

She focused on the newspaper in the viewer Jake had been scanning. John and Nancy Whittaker's oldest son made the Dean's List at the University of Texas at Austin.

Edgewater was the town of vintage movies. Even now it was like taking a step back into a more innocent time...except for the creepy feeling that had begun with Mayor Morton's visit then been reinforced by the threatening phone call in the middle of the night and Chief of Police Gates' intrusion at lunch. Even sitting in a library, a place she'd always before considered a haven, that eerie sensation of things out of kilter still niggled at the base of her neck.

A hand fell on Rebecca's shoulder. She gasped and whirled, her heart racing.

"Sorry," Jake said. "I had no idea the Edgewater Post could be so absorbing."

"Believe me, it's not. I just didn't hear you come up. Did you get the copies?"

"Yep. Got 'em right here. You didn't find anything else?"

"If I found it, I didn't recognize it."

"Let's knock off for the day. I want to read these stories in detail and see if anything jumps out at me."

Rebecca nodded her agreement. She'd wanted to suggest that herself. After looking at so many articles for so long, she could have seen her own birth announcement and not recognized it. But she wasn't going to admit that to Jake, wasn't going to give him any reason to try to send her home. While that would solve her problem of wrestling with her irrational fascination with the man, she couldn't go back when her life was still in chaos, still unresolved.

"We'll get a couple of cold drinks and go to that park we passed today. If you can stand the heat."

Again she nodded. The afternoon heat in the park wouldn't be anything like the heat if they went back to his motel room.

***

The park was small with half a dozen kids climbing over the playground equipment on one end and a grove of trees on the other. The grass was freshly clipped, and a lanky teenage boy was just pushing a mower into a small wooden shed in the middle.

Jake pulled onto the graveled parking area on the wooded end, and Rebecca spotted a weathered picnic table on the shady side of a huge oak tree.

She sat on one side of the table with Jake on the other.

"It's not so hot here," she observed. "Kind of nice, actually." And surely, separated from Jake by the splintery wooden table, sitting outside in bright daylight with kids shouting and laughing somewhere close by, she could get away from the fluttery sensation of being near him.

Head bent, he shuffled through papers in his briefcase. A breeze stirred the leaves above, and sunlight fluttered patterns across his ebony hair.

"Lots of background stuff here," he said, his voice deep and dark yet filled with streaks of light, sounding just the way his hair looked. "Mayor Morton and Jordan served together in the Army. Morton saved Jordan's life, killed three men who ambushed the two of them and shot Ben in the stomach and him in the shoulder. Both men subsequently received honorable discharges, and Morton came back here with Jordan. Our good old boy with the cowboy hat and down-home drawl is actually from Ohio."

"That's very interesting, but what does it have to do with my mother?"

He looked up. "It may not have anything to do with your mother, or it may have everything. Morton knows something about her, so we need to know more about Morton." He returned his attention to the papers. "They don't seem to have had many leads in Ben Jordan's murder. I don't remember reading anything in the 1980 papers about them catching the guy who did it. Did you see anything?"

"No, nothing. But I could have missed it. I wasn't looking specifically for that."

He studied the photocopies for a few minutes longer then passed them to her. "You might see something I didn't, something that has meaning to you but wouldn't to me."

It was the first time he'd admitted she might actually be a help instead of a hindrance. She took the papers from him and bent over them, reading carefully though she had little hope she'd find anything.

"What the devil?" Jake exclaimed.

She looked up to see him holding a sheet of paper and frowning. "What?"

"Do you know anything about this article on Janelle Griffin?"

"No. Maybe it got mixed in when Eunice was making your copies."

He shook his head. "It wasn't with the copies. It was under the top folder." He turned the paper so she could see it. Across the top in red block letters someone had written: "Go home. Your mother's dead."

The wide-open park seemed to close in around Rebecca. "Janelle. You said since my mother used the name Jane Clark on my birth certificate that Jane might really be her first name."

"This woman died fifteen years ago." His words grated over her like coarse sandpaper, scraping away the skin and drawing blood.

"Let me see it."

Wordlessly he handed it to her.

She stared at the black and red images on the white paper, concentrating all her efforts into forcing them to coherency, something she really didn't want. *Go home. Your mother's dead.* The glaring personal note then the impersonal print of the news story. Janelle Griffin...dead at thirty-one...accidental overdose of prescription sleeping pills...graduate of Edgewater High School...volunteer at Edgewater Memorial Hospital...member of First Pentecostal Church of Edgewater...survived by her parents, the Reverend and Mrs. William Griffin.

In the summer heat, a cold hand gripped her heart and squeezed, shutting out the possibility of warmth ever entering that region again.

Dead.

"Don't go jumping to conclusions. We have no proof this woman is your mother," Jake said.

"Somebody went to a lot of trouble to put this in your briefcase. This article and the note to forget my mother confirms the phone call telling me she's dead." Rebecca was humiliated to feel tears rolling down her cheeks. Angrily she swiped them away with the back of her hand. She wasn't going to cry, especially not in front of Jake.

For a fleeting moment she thought she saw sympathy in his eyes, then the look was gone, replaced by his usual impenetrable expression. She didn't want sympathy from him.

"We've got plenty of time to get to the cemetery before dark," he said.

Her throat tightened. She swallowed twice before she could speak. "Then you do think this is my mother."

"Rebecca, I'm not suggesting we go to the cemetery to mourn this lady. I'm suggesting we go there to check out the stones, her family, dates of birth and death...anything. Research. Investigative work. What you hired me to do."

"Go to a cemetery to check out the stones?" She felt a sob rise and turned it into a semblance of a laugh as it came out. "That's what you call *investigative work?*"

He pushed himself off the bench and rose. "That's right. Unless you're firing me, I plan to continue to do my job. Now are you ready to go back to your air conditioned house in Dallas and check the mailbox and answering machine for my reports?"

97

She swung her legs over the bench and stood also, glaring at him through a film of tears that blurred the harsh angles of his face. "No. I'm going to that cemetery. If that is my mother, I want to see her grave."

"Suit yourself." He closed his briefcase and picked it up then walked away. She followed close behind.

***

The cemetery was small, but even so it took them almost two hours to find Janelle Griffin's grave. The area was well-tended, the grass newly mown.

Jake walked around, studying the inscriptions and making notes.

Rebecca stood beside the stone that marked the passing of Janelle Griffin.

Her mother?

She studied every word, every carving on the gray marble, trying to ferret out the secrets of the woman's life. *Beloved daughter*, it read. Not wife or mother. The two words told their own story of loneliness. The sensation surrounded Rebecca, and she couldn't tell if it came from the grave, from the inscription on the stone or from her own heart.

"Her father died five years after her," Jake said. "Apparently her mother's still alive. Paternal grandparents and great-grandparents are here. All Reverends. Three infants." She looked up, and he hastily added, "Born in 1895, 1904 and 1906. Infant mortality was high in those days. Here's another single woman, Janelle's great-aunt, judging from the year of birth, dead in her fifties. Looks like Janelle's family has lived in Edgewater for generations."

Rebecca walked around the area, reading the story carved in stone. "A prominent family, like you said, a long line of ministers, the kind of people who would have been scandalized if their unmarried daughter had turned up pregnant. The kind of family who just might have enough influence to get the police department to declare an overdose of sleeping pills accidental. Her mother's still alive, and the mayor and the chief of police are still protecting her. Janelle would have been sixteen or seventeen when I was born. A teenage girl, again like you said."

He moved over to stand close beside her. "There's nothing here to prove this is your mother, Rebecca."

"There's nothing to prove she isn't."

"Stop it. You're jumping to conclusions."

"Am I? How much more evidence do we need? Do you want to have the body exhumed so we can do DNA testing?" She looked away, toward the last sliver of sun resting on the horizon. "This whole thing has been pointless. I never had a mother to search for. I've been chasing a ghost, a will-o'-the-wisp."

The enervating loneliness wrapped its tendrils around her, stealing the energy from her body, from her soul. She started to sink to the ground, to rest for a moment or a lifetime on the cool grass, but Jake's strong arm stopped her.

"Rebecca, don't do this."

Anger surged through her, mingling with the grief and filling the empty spaces. She whirled on him. "Leave me alone!"

To her complete humiliation, she burst into tears. Jake pulled her against him in spite of her efforts to push away.

Painful sobs she could no longer suppress heaved themselves up from somewhere deep inside, pouring onto Jake's broad chest, drenching his denim shirt, while he held her firmly with one hand on her back and stroked her hair with the other. She willed herself to stop, but her body was no longer under her control. Even as one corner of her mind berated her for her weakness, she leaned against Jake, crying in huge gulps.

Gradually when enough of the inner tension had been thrust outside of her, she was able to catch her breath and again tried to push away.

He loosened the circle of his arms enough to allow her to pull a handful of tissues from her purse and blow her nose. Gently he coaxed her back to him and continued to stroke her hair. In spite of herself, she relaxed, unballing her fists and pressing her hands against him instead.

"Just because your parents loved every stray that crossed their paths doesn't mean they put you in that category." His words whispered past her, so soft she wondered for a moment if they existed only in her mind.

"I never said that," she murmured against him, refusing to look up and meet his gaze.

"Not in so many words. But you thought it, didn't you?"

She took in a long breath, wondering if she could answer that question, if the answer would be a betrayal of the two people she'd loved most in the world. Probably.

Jake didn't press her, and suddenly the words began pouring out as uncontrollably as her earlier sobs.

"One day when I was ten years old, I was playing at my girlfriend's house, and I said to her that I wished my mom and dad loved me special the way hers loved her. Her mother overheard me, and she called me in for a talk. She told me how proud I should be of my parents, how wonderful it was that they were so kind and loving to anyone in need. She made me feel very selfish because I resented something everybody else admired."

Waiting for the expected censure, Rebecca stood with every muscle in her body tense.

"I don't think that sounds selfish. It sounds like every little kid in the world."

"I thought I should be special to them because I was their little girl, their only little girl. When I grew up, I was more adult about it. I knew they loved me. I knew they were terrific people with big hearts and plenty of room for everybody. But then they died, and I couldn't be adult about it anymore. I understood then why I'd never been special to them. I was just another homeless person they took care of. It was like I'd been an orphan all my life, like I'd never had a home or a family."

"And you thought if you found your birth mother, you'd have a real family, a real life."

She leaned back in his arms and looked up at him. The sun had almost vanished from the sky and his face was shadowed, unreadable. "Pretty dumb, huh?"

He chuckled quietly without humor. "Been there, done that. Trust me, it is possible to survive."

She recalled Jake's farcical recitation of his own family life. Had he once been a small boy looking for someone who'd love him in a special way?

She searched his face for the softness, the vulnerability that must have been there once. He moved his head slightly, and a final glimmer from the sunset reflected in his eyes, bringing to life bright flames of raw desire, igniting an answering flame deep inside her.

For a long moment he stared at her, his gaze flicking across her face and back again. She tried to turn away so he couldn't see the way he affected her, but she remained immobile, as if her body had somehow linked itself with his. His head dipped toward her, and she could only lift her lips to his as all rational thought disintegrated into pure sensation. His mouth on hers, warm and soft, firm and demanding, carried her away from the empty world she'd been trapped in, created a whole universe of twinkling stars and swirling galaxies, of moons and planets and suns waiting to be explored.

Her arms wrapped around him, her hands splaying across his back, her fingers searching the corded muscles beneath his denim shirt. Her heart pounded in rhythm with his ragged breathing as though the two of them comprised a single entity. He pulled her more tightly against him, one hand sliding down her hip while the other tangled in her hair.

With every breath she drank in more of him. The scents of denim and masculinity she'd noticed in the library mingled with the green scent of the freshly-mown grass, and all seemed to belong to Jake. He surrounded her, his lips devouring hers, his arms wrapping her body, his essence invading her soul. She could feel his hardness against her and she wanted him, wanted all of him, needed to be a part of him, as if by a physical union he could fill the black hole she'd become.

Somewhere in the back of her mind, an alarm bell clanged. She wanted to ignore it, to immerse herself in the wild sensations Jake's kiss created in her, to grasp for the elusive quality of completion, but the alarm kept screaming discordantly.

She'd just lost her family, maybe twice. This frantic need for Jake wasn't going to change that. He wasn't going to fill the void.

Reluctantly she pushed away, and this time he let her.

The summer evening turned cold when his lips and his body left hers.

"It's getting late," she said breathlessly. "We should go back."

His eyes searched hers for a long moment, then he nodded. "You're right," he said, and she wasn't sure if he was responding to what she'd said or what he'd seen in her eyes. Or both.

They crossed the cemetery side by side but not together, and the setting sun cast long shadows before them.

When they were seated in the car, Jake sat for a moment with his hand on the key. "I shouldn't have done that," he said, not looking at her.

That made a horrible situation even worse, made her eager participation one-sided, desperate. "It's all right," she mumbled, studying her hands in her lap.

"It wasn't professional."

"It's all right," she repeated, unable to come up with anything more original to say.

He started the engine, and they drove into the gathering darkness.

If Rebecca had felt alone before, the sensation was multiplied exponentially now. For a few brief moments she'd known a joining to someone else, a belonging. With the withdrawal of that connection, the barren wasteland inside her seemed even more stark.

"As soon as we get to the motel, I'm going to pack up and drive back to Dallas," she said. "Tonight."

"Good idea. I'll keep you up-to-date on anything I find."

"I don't think you'll find anything else. I think Janelle Griffin was my mother." The last of her hope had gone with Jake's withdrawal. The bleakness in her soul was complete. "I think my mother's dead. I've got to accept that and do as you said, get on with my life. Go back to work, reclaim my friends, carve out a place for myself."

"Good idea," he repeated.

So it was sealed. She'd leave and never see Jake again, never again experience the heady sensation of his touch, his kiss. The night stole into the car, seeping inside her pores, running through her veins where hot blood had flowed only a few minutes before.

Two blocks away from the motel, red lights flashed behind them and a siren sounded.

"What the hell?" Jake pulled over.

"Were you speeding?"

"In this town? Considering our relationship with the local police chief, I wouldn't dare change lanes without giving a signal. Assuming we could find a street here with an extra lane to change to."

Farley Gates lumbered up to their car door.

"What's the problem, Gates?"

"Need to see your driver's license."

Jake reached into his back pocket, took out his wallet, removed the license and handed it to the police chief.

Gates copied information onto a ticket.

"What are you doing?" Jake demanded. "I wasn't speeding and you don't have any red lights for me to run."

"Got five, but that's not the problem. You got a busted out head light."

"The hell you say! Look!" He flung his arm toward the windshield. "You can see both beams from here."

Gates walked to the front of the car, took out his club and swung it downward. Rebecca gasped in shock as the sound of breaking glass filled the quiet summer night. He walked back to the window and handed Jake a ticket. "Like I said, you got a busted head light."

Gates returned to his car and drove away.

"What's going on?" Rebecca asked. "Why did he do that?"

Jake shook his head and continued to stare out the windshield until the tail lights disappeared.

Finally he turned to Rebecca. "I've got a real strong hunch Janelle Griffin is not your mother. Otherwise, he wouldn't still be trying to get rid of us."

Comprehension finally penetrated Rebecca's shock, followed by righteous anger and a new determination. "I'm not going back to Dallas."

"I had another hunch you'd say that."

He didn't sound upset, but he didn't sound glad either.

It didn't matter. No more than it mattered that her mother didn't want to be found. At the cemetery she'd given up her mother, had accepted that she would never be special to anyone, that she had no identity. Dealing with the pain only to find it was a false alarm had hardened something inside her. She would find her mother. Even though the woman might slam the door in her face, she'd find her and meet her and see the color of her eyes, the shape of her chin, the slant of her nose, then turn and walk away from her.

And then she'd be in control of her life. Then she'd be able to take her hard-won identity and go forward to that future Doris Jordan had urged on her.

Chapter 9

October 20, 1979, Edgewater, Texas

Mary sat curled on the sofa with a book open in her lap. She'd just read the same page three times and still had no idea what it said.

It was five minutes after eleven. Ben should be home soon. This month he was on the evening shift, 3:00 to 11:00, and she hated the long hours of darkness until he returned.

She hadn't always felt like this. She'd lived in Edgewater all her life. Nobody locked their doors. Nobody worried.

Except now she did. She compulsively locked her doors and windows and jumped at every noise, especially every time the phone rang.

Of course, some of that concern wasn't new. Every policeman's wife lived with the fear of the phone call telling her that her husband had been injured...or worse.

Not that such things happened in Edgewater where calls to the police department were usually teenagers having a loud party or Horace Drake drunk in public again.

Still her fears ran rampant, especially after the sun went down.

Pregnancy. That's all it was. Hormones. The changes her body was going through making her more emotional, bringing back all the old fears she'd thought were behind her, fears of losing those she loved the way she'd lost her parents. And now, added to that old fear was apprehension for the fragile new life growing inside her that she already loved more powerfully than she could ever have imagined.

Resolutely she turned away from the other explanation for her fears, from the black place in her memory. Like the black holes in outer space, it would suck her in, steal the sunshine from her life, whirl her someplace far away where only pain existed.

She wouldn't look at it. It was in the past and she and Ben and their baby had a whole world of future before them.

The past was dead. It couldn't hurt her.

As long as she kept the doors and windows of her house and of her mind locked.

The phone shrieked and Mary gave an echoing gasp. Her book slipped from her fingers and fell to the floor. Who would be calling at that hour? Not Ben. He encouraged her to go to bed, to be asleep when he got home, especially now that she was pregnant.

The menacing black plastic instrument screamed at her again, demanding her attention.

The always ominous phone call in the middle of the night became even more ominous when Ben was on duty.

It rang a third time before she could find the courage to answer it.

She reached toward it, the movement slow and difficult, as movements in a nightmare when some evil creature pursued the dreamer.

"Hello?" The sound that issued from her mouth was more a croak than a word.

"I hear congratulations are in order."

Charles.

She should be relieved that Ben was safe, that no one was calling to say, *I'm sorry, Mrs. Morton. There's been an accident*. But she wasn't relieved. The gargoyle creature of fear still sat on her shoulder and taunted her.

"My partner tells me he's going to be a daddy," he continued when she didn't respond. "At least, he thinks he's going to be a daddy. You and I know different, don't we?"

Her heart crawled into her throat, pounding so hard she couldn't talk, couldn't deny the unspeakable thing he'd just suggested.

"Let me tell you what else I know. I'm not having any damn kid messing up my life again just because you women are too stupid to use birth control. You wanted what happened as much as I did. You teased me and flirted with me and now you think you're going to have some squalling brat and prove it's mine and ruin everything for me. Well, you're dead wrong, bitch. I've got somebody who'll take care of things. You meet me tomorrow at—"

"No!" The word erupted as a volcano, propelled by the horror in Charles' diatribe.

For a moment Charles said nothing, just long enough for Mary to think perhaps she was having a nightmare, this wasn't really happening. It couldn't be happening.

"No?" His voice, deceptively soft, sent a chill down her spine. "I don't think you mean that. I don't think you want Ben to know what we did, how you seduced me into betraying my partner." He paused for a long moment then continued in a slower, deeper tone. "I don't think you want to worry about whether your husband won't make it home some night."

Oh, God! It wasn't a dream. It was all real...the attack, the insinuations Charles was making about her baby, what he wanted to do to her baby.

"This isn't your baby!" she protested, finding her voice at last. "It's Ben's! Ben's and mine!" She slammed the phone down, refusing to listen to any more of his insanity.

Blood rushed past her ears in a loud roar, and cold invaded her chest. She wrapped her arms about herself to warm and protect her baby.

Charles was insane.

There was no doubt about that.

But he wasn't the father of her child.

Tears streaked down her face, icy tears as though she'd frozen solid inside.

He couldn't be the father of her child.

The phone rang again.

Clasping her hands to her ears, she ran upstairs and crawled under the covers, hiding her head beneath the pillow.

Ben's baby! Not Charles'!

She curled into a ball, pulling her knees to her chest, shielding the tiny child inside her. Tears welled up from a bottomless pit, uncontrollable sobs shaking her body so hard she feared for her baby's safety.

A minute or an hour later a hand grasped her shoulder.

"Noooo!" she wailed, jerking away and rolling to the other side of the bed. Had she left the door unlocked? Had he come in?

Two arms grabbed her, hauling her upright, into the cold darkness of the room. She kicked and hit and screamed and flailed against her assailant.

"Mary! Mary! Wake up! It's me, Ben! Wake up!"

Slowly the voice, the familiar scent of her husband, penetrated the black veil of her fears.

She flung her arms around him, holding on tightly and sobbing against his neck.

He patted her back comfortingly. "It's okay, sweetheart. You were having a bad dream, that's all."

For a split second she tried to believe him, wanted to believe that she'd dreamed the phone call, the threats, the attack.

"I wasn't asleep," she said between sobs. "He wants to kill our baby!"

Ben sat on the bed, pulling her across his lap and rocking her."Shhh. It was a dream. Just a dream."

She shook her head. "No." She gripped the front of his shirt with both hands and looked up at him, steadying herself against Charles' voice that still reverberated inside her head. "It wasn't a dream. I tried to pretend to myself it was, but it wasn't. Charles raped me."

"Charles? Mary, listen to what you're saying. You've had a bad dream. Charles would never hurt you."

"Please, you've got to believe me!" She turned loose of his shirt and dropped her face into her hands. Of course he didn't believe her. She was acting hysterical. She was hysterical.

Taking a deep, ragged breath, she lifted her head and tried to sound rational. "I haven't been asleep. I haven't been dreaming. You know I never go to sleep until you get home." She pushed forcibly away from him and struggled to her feet then reached down and switched on the bedside lamp. "Look at me. I'm still dressed."

Ben's forehead furrowed with confusion. His eyes shadowed with concern, he rose slowly and put one big arm about her shoulders. "Let's go downstairs and I'll make you a cup of cocoa."

Mary nodded, the movement a jerking of strained, uncontrollable muscles. Hysteria still screamed through her mind, but she had to be calm and rational. She had to convince Ben of the danger.

As she walked on trembling legs down the stairs beside her husband, for the first time his presence failed to reassure her. She wasn't safe. He wasn't safe.

Nobody was safe.

She'd prayed and begged, and still her father had died. Still her mother had left her to go into her own private world of insanity and grief. Again she'd prayed and cajoled and hoped, but her mother had never emerged except to drift quietly into death.

Mary had done what Charles had told her to do, had kept his secret, yet now he was threatening Ben and her baby.

Once again her safe, happy world had changed to one of chaos and uncertainty.

Ben guided her to a chair at the kitchen table then set about heating milk in the microwave, not looking at her or speaking to her. He didn't want to believe her, didn't want to believe the man who'd once saved his life could do something so contemptible.

Was Charles right? Would Ben choose his friend over his wife?

Of course he wouldn't. Ben loved her. He loved their baby.

Nevertheless, her heart felt as though it had turned to lead...cold and heavy and sinking to the pit of her stomach. She wrapped her arms about herself, and her fingers were icy.

"Why did you tell him about the baby?" she asked and was amazed that the words came out sounding so calm. Coming from inside her, they should be cold and frozen too. "I asked you not to tell anybody."

Ben took the cup of hot milk from the microwave. "I told Charles because he's my best friend," he said in a monotone, not looking at her. "Because I want him to be our baby's godfather."

He didn't believe her. He was ignoring everything she'd said.

He added cocoa powder to the cup of hot milk, stirred and set it on the table in front of her. She

114

wrapped her hands around the cup, trying to find some warmth.

Ben sat down beside her, and she saw that he wasn't unaffected. His pupils had contracted to pinpoints. He lifted one hand and pushed the damp tendrils of hair back from her face. His fingers on her skin were as cold as her own.

"Mary, you fell asleep in your clothes and had a bad dream, didn't you? A horrible nightmare." His voice, his eyes, the set of his mouth all begged her to say *yes*.

"No," she whispered. "I didn't fall asleep. It wasn't a dream. Charles attacked me."

"He hit you?"

"He raped me."

Ben's eyes darted from side to side as if seeking some way around her pronouncement, the deed that would forever separate him from the man who'd saved his life, the man who now shared that life as his partner.

"He raped me," she repeated dully. "Last summer. You were late coming home. He said you had to do paperwork. He came to the door. I let him in. He tore my clothes and forced me down on the floor."

Dark red suffused Ben's face as grim acceptance finally surfaced in his eyes. For a moment he sat paralyzed, then he slammed his fist onto the tabletop. "I'll kill the bastard!" He pulled her into his arms. "Oh, my God, my God, my God!"

Tears sprang from her eyes again, but now they were tears of hope, cleansing tears, washing out all the anguish she'd held clenched inside for so long. "I was afraid to tell you. He said if I did, you wouldn't come home from work one day. I can't lose you. You're my world. I love you so much."

"You're not going to lose me. Not ever."

He slid his chair back and stood, plowed a hand through his hair then began to pace.

"How could this happen? How could he smile at me and work with me and eat dinner in my home and pretend to be my best friend? I shared your chocolate chip cookies with him just today! I asked him to be our child's godfather!"

He strode to the far wall of the kitchen and punched one big fist through the sheetrock. Mary flinched. She'd known Ben Jordan since grade school, and she'd never seen him lose his temper before.

He whirled on her, his expression fierce, his shaggy brows almost meeting over his nose, his lips a thin line. A vein stood out on his forehead, throbbing perceptibly. "How did you know I told him about the baby?"

"He called. Tonight. He—" Mary swallowed hard. She'd thought the worst was over, but it wasn't. She still had to tell him what Charles had said. "He thinks the baby's his. He wants me to...to get rid of it. He said he knows somebody." She looked down at her lap, picking imaginary lint off her skirt, waiting for Ben to condemn her baby.

Ben came back to the table, yanked out his chair and sat down again. "What did he say? Tell me as exactly as you can remember."

116

"I remember every word. I'll never forget." She swallowed again and forced herself to maintain a calm veneer in spite of the chaos roiling inside. "He said, *I'm not having any damn kid messing up my life again*—" She grabbed Ben's sleeve. "He said *again*! That means this must have happened before! I used to wonder why he came home with you instead of going back to Ohio!"

"He said his family was wealthy and wanted him to go into their business, but he wanted to be a cop, same as I'd told him I wanted to be." Ben shook his head, anguish mingling with the rage in his eyes. "I never really believed that story. He used to scream in his sleep, begging his dad and sometimes his mother to stop, not to do it again, stuff like that. I figured his parents beat him or something. I wanted to show him that not everybody was like that. I wanted to help him. And look what he did to repay me."

He shot to his feet and kicked his chair across the room. "I'll kill him with my bare hands." He spread those hands in front of him, the fingers curled upward.

Icy tendrils of fear wrapped around Mary again. "If you kill him, they'll put you in prison. He'll still win. I'll lose you. You can't kill him. He—he saved your life."

Ben's lips tilted upward in a macabre imitation of a smile. "Yeah, I've told you the story, how the two of us were ambushed by three men, both of us shot, me in the gut and him in the shoulder. I went down, but he fought like he didn't even know he was

117

hit, not even when they shot him two more times. He killed all of them."

She nodded numbly. "I know."

"But you don't know the whole story. Charles shot those men until he ran out of bullets, then he stabbed them until their bodies were unrecognizable. When it was all over, he looked around and saw me, but I don't think he really knew who I was. He passed out, and that's how they found us. He did save my life and I've always been grateful, but I'm not real sure he even remembered doing it. I think his goal was to kill those men, not to save me. That was kind of incidental to his rage."

He returned to her in two long strides and pulled her up to stand facing him. Tears brimmed from his eyes and slid silently down his cheeks. "Mary, I'm so sorry! I brought him into our lives. I thought I could help him and look what's happened. This is all my fault."

"Don't say that! It's Charles' fault. He's the one to blame. He's the one we've got to stop before he can hurt you or our baby or some other woman."

"You're right. He's got to be stopped. First thing tomorrow I'll call the police department in his hometown and see what I can find out, see what he meant about somebody messing up his life again. Then I'll take it to the chief." He pulled her close. "It's going to be okay," he whispered, his lips against her ear. "Everything's going to be okay."

She clutched him tightly, almost believing him, wanting to believe him. Ben could do anything. He could make it okay. He could keep her and their baby safe.

"The baby," he said quietly. "Is it his?"

Her newborn flower of hope wilted into the murky pit of despair.

"No! It's our baby!" She ducked her head. "I don't know," she whispered.

For an eternity of agony, he held her wordlessly, then he leaned away from her, forcing her to look into his eyes. "That's right," he said fiercely. "This baby is ours. I don't care whose eyes or hair she has. I don't care who started the process, who planted the seed. It's our baby, yours and mine."

She wanted to assure him that the baby was his, would be born with his green eyes, his dark hair, his incredible capacity for love, but she couldn't speak for the sobs of relief welling up in her throat.

It wasn't necessary anyway. Ben understood. He understood and accepted everything. Her Ben. Her wonderful husband.

She leaned against him and he held her close.

Ben would take care of everything. Somehow he'd get rid of Charles, and she and Ben and the baby would be safe and happy together for the rest of their lives.

Chapter 10

Jake knocked on the wall that separated his room from Rebecca's. "Pizza's here!"

He knew he was out of his mind inviting her to share a pizza with him, but she'd just received another devastating blow and didn't need to be alone.

Which was precisely why he didn't need to be with her. He couldn't pick up the pieces, couldn't put her back together.

But he'd been as powerless to stop the invitation from coming out of his mouth as he'd been to stop himself from kissing her at the cemetery. There was something about Rebecca Patterson that made him wish he still believed in Santa Claus, that he was Santa Claus and could bring her all those fantasy gifts she wanted so damned bad...someone to love her special and forever, someone to fill in the empty spaces in her life, a family as defined by television in the fifties.

Of course he didn't, and he wasn't, and nobody could. He'd be doing her a favor if he could teach her to savor the present, forget the past and the future...leave the former for dead and accept that the latter came with no guarantees.

A tapping sounded at his door.

"Come on in. It's open."

She came in wearing a white cotton shirt and khaki shorts, her long legs bare, her pale hair pulled into a pony tail with wispy tendrils curling about her face.

"I took a shower and changed clothes," she said, and he realized he was staring.

"I know. I heard the water running." And he'd seen in his mind's eye exactly how she looked with that water sluicing down her naked skin, cascading over her rounded breasts—

"Have a seat." He interrupted his own thoughts before they got completely out of hand.

"I brought my own." Only then did he take his eyes off her body sufficiently to notice that she was dragging a chair behind her.

"Good idea." Keep him off that bed. Maybe keep his mind off that bed.

She pulled her chair over to the desk where he'd set the pizza box and soft drinks.

He sat across from her.

Much better. He could still see the bed behind her, a background, but at least he wasn't sitting on it, and the covers weren't rumpled. The maid had straightened the worn spread, tucking it around the pillows and sheets, leaving it pristine.

He picked up a piece of pizza and bit off a big chunk. Rebecca did the same, and for a few minutes they ate in silence.

"Pretty good," she said, reaching for a second slice.

"Yeah. Good barbecue, good pizza. This town has a couple of things to recommend it in spite of Mayor Morton and Chief Gates."

She grimaced. "It's going to take more than barbecue and pizza to compensate for those two. So what's our next step?"

Our next step, she'd said, not *your*. What the hell, he was getting used to that. She wasn't going home any time soon. There was nothing he could do about it. She was surprisingly stubborn for someone he'd originally thought weak. She was determined to plunge headfirst into a lake of quicksand that could very well suck her down so far she'd never be able to get back to the surface.

He couldn't stop her, and what did it matter to him anyway?

"The library. I'm going back there to see if good old Eunice has any idea who might have put that clipping in my briefcase. I have a feeling she doesn't miss much that goes on in her library."

"Do you think she'll tell us?"

"Well, that's a whole other story. Only one way to find out. After that we need to run a check on Janelle Griffin."

Rebecca laid down her last bite of pizza and frowned, the aura of fragility returning to hover about her. "I thought you said you didn't think she was my mother."

"I said I have a hunch she isn't. If she is, our Chief Gates is into overkill. Nevertheless, we can't discount the possibility that she's somehow involved. Otherwise why, of all the dead women in the Edgewater cemetery, did our mysterious visitor leave us an article about her death?"

"I see. What about Doris Jordan? Do you think she's telling us everything she knows?"

"My gut feeling is that she is. Which is too bad. It would have been nice if she'd remembered exactly who bought that dress thirty years ago."

"That's terrible about her son's murder." She shuddered. "Reading about it in the newspaper made it..."

"Real?" he finished for her.

"Yes. When she told us, it was sad, but it was something that happened a long time ago. I guess because the newspaper story was written the day after the shooting, now it's like it only happened yesterday."

"Well, it didn't," he said brusquely, needing to vanquish her fears about Janelle Griffin and her sentimental feelings for Doris Jordan's losses as well as his own out-of-character tendency to be sucked into those feelings, into Rebecca's losses.

"I know. But don't you think it's interesting that Charles Morton was involved in that situation too?"

"Not really. It's a small town. The cast of characters is small. You're bound to see some repeats. Especially a high-profile guy like our friend, the mayor."

She nodded as she drew one slim finger slowly through the condensation on the outside of the paper cup holding her soft drink. It was an unconscious gesture, the kind people make when their minds are far away, but Jake could almost feel that finger drawing patterns on his skin instead of on the cup, wiping away a path of sweat rather than condensation, sweat from the exertion and excitement of making love—

"Jake?"

"Huh? What?"

"I said, am I being paranoid, or do you think there's some kind of conspiracy going on here?"

"You know what they say, just because you're paranoid doesn't mean somebody's not out to get you." He picked up his own paper cup and downed a large gulp of the flat and watery but icy cold liquid. He ought to pour it into his lap.

"I kind of expected that people might be reluctant to talk to you," she said, "but I would never have expected somebody to slip us a false lead or break out the headlight of your car."

"Yeah, they're definitely trying to get rid of us. But all they're doing is pissing me off. I wouldn't quit now if you told me to."

A slow smile spread across her face. "Good."

"How about you? Are you okay with all this? I mean, it's pretty obvious your parents aren't cleaning the guest room and chilling the champagne in preparation for your arrival."

There it was again, that far-reaching emptiness in her smoky eyes as if she were the only person in a dark, starless galaxy that stretched ahead of her into forever. But when she spoke, her voice was firm. "I told you from the beginning, that doesn't matter. I just need to know."

I didn't believe you then, and I don't believe you now, he wanted to say. But he didn't. He had to give her credit for one thing. She had guts. Anybody could be brave when they had no fear. Rebecca had plenty of fear yet she kept pushing forward in spite of it.

"Glad to hear it," he said instead, pretending he believed her. "Because this whole thing is starting to stink. I have no idea what our friendly mayor's next move will be, but I can almost guarantee he'll make one."

"I keep wondering if he might be my father." She tore the remaining piece of crust into little bits as she talked, her gaze focused on that activity.

He knew she wanted him to deny the possibility, but he couldn't. If she was so determined to find the truth, she'd better be ready to face whatever she found.

"You don't look anything like him except for the mandatory one nose, two eyes and two lips." That brought her attention to him and even tilted the two lips mentioned upward in a slight smile. "He does have snow white hair which could mean he was a blonde when he was younger. He has blue eyes, and yours are blue mixed with green. But there are only a few eye and hair colors to go around, so that doesn't mean much."

"Wouldn't I know? Wouldn't I feel some sort of connection to him if he was my father?"

"Nope," he said, squashing down the desire to agree with her, to respond to the plea in her eyes. "Now that's something I do know about since I come equipped with family members of every size, shape and degree." He leaned back in the rigid motel room chair and grinned. "When they put me in kindergarten, I called my teacher *mother*. I thought all grown women were *mother* and all grown men were *dad*. The other kids were my brothers and sisters. Hell, I had to be careful when I started dating to be sure I wasn't dating one of my half-sisters."

She smiled. "How many sets of parents could you have had by the time you were in kindergarten?"

"Let me see. I think Dad was on his third wife and Mom was on her second husband, but each one of the step parents had kids who had other parents. I swear I remember living with my father's second wife's first husband and his third wife for a couple of months."

She arched a dubious eyebrow.

He burst into laughter...at her, at the absurdity of his life, her life, the whole world. She joined him, her laughter clear and mellow, like a well-tuned violin.

"It's funny," he said. "But it's true."

She sobered. "It is?"

"Yep. I told you I have enough family for both of us. I was a teenager before I was certain which two people were my original parents. And they weren't my favorites, by any means.'"

She studied him intently, her forehead wrinkling. "Don't you feel detached, at loose ends?"

"Doesn't everybody? Isn't everybody? We come into this world alone and go out the same way."

She shifted her gaze from him to the curtain over the single window in the small room, as if she would see through it, find some answers in the darkened parking lot outside. Her profile was classic and elegant, her skin fine-pored and translucent with no makeup, her nose straight, lips full and faintly pink, chin curving down to the creamy sweep of her throat.

A ringing sounded from far away.

She turned to him, her eyes still hazy with distant images and thoughts.

The ringing came again, and she blinked away the fog. "Is that my phone?"

"Yeah, it sounds like it. Are you expecting any calls?"

She shook her head, and they both charged out the door. If this was another threat, he wanted to be there to hear the voice, to speak to the caller.

Rebecca fumbled with her key, got her door unlocked and ran to snatch up the phone.

"Hello?"

Jake followed her, leaning his head against hers so he could hear the conversation.

"Rebecca, this is Doris Jordan."

"Hello, Mrs. Jordan. How nice to hear from you."

Jake could tell from the sound of Rebecca's voice that she was genuinely pleased to get a call from the older woman. A connection, he thought. Something she desperately needed. A surrogate grandmother.

In spite of everything that had happened and everything he'd told her, Rebecca still wanted to believe in fairy tales and happy ever after.

At the rate things were progressing, that hope couldn't survive much longer.

"Would it be possible for you to bring that blue dress over and let me look at it again? I've been thinking about it ever since you left. It was so long ago, but I think that dress might have been in a 1978 shipment. I can't promise that it'll do any good, but I'd really like to look at the garment again, if you wouldn't mind."

"Of course. When would you like me to bring it by?"

"I'd love to have you and Mr. Thornton join me for lunch tomorrow."

Without giving him a chance to agree or disagree, she accepted. "We'd love it."

"Shall we say about 1:00? Is that too late for you all?"

"No, that's perfect. See you then."

She replaced the receiver and turned to him, her face glowing. "She wants to see the dress again. She's starting to remember."

"Maybe. Or maybe she just wants the company. She said she was always glad to have company."

Rebecca's expression didn't change with his pronouncement, and he realized Doris' motivation didn't matter. Rebecca's enthusiasm was inspired almost as much by the luncheon invitation as by the possibility of Doris' having pertinent memories of the blue dress.

"Okay," he said. "At least we won't have to go back to the barbecue place for lunch tomorrow and risk meeting Chief Gates again."

Rebecca smiled at him, at his small attempt at tact, and Jake was suddenly very aware of being close to her, of the way she smelled...like soap and an open meadow in full summer bloom.

He stepped away, moving toward the door before he did something really dumb like kissing her again, like throwing her across that bed and making love to her until they both forgot how pointless such an action would be, how ill-equipped she was to deal with the consequences of such an action.

"Well, it's been a long day. Guess I'll go get some sleep. Let me know if you have any more strange phone calls."

"I will."

***

Rebecca closed the door behind Jake, glad and sorry he was gone.

She was exhausted, bone tired. It had indeed been a long day after a short night. Two short nights.

She wanted nothing more than to crawl into bed and sleep deep and hard. Nothing more, that is, than to crawl into that bed with Jake and make love deep and hard.

She yanked the band off her pony tail and shook her hair loose then sat on the bed to brush it. Her chair was still in Jake's room, right where she wished she was.

She'd had a couple of relationships with men, relationships that began with mutual respect and friendship then segued into mutually enjoyable sex. Pleasant relationships that provided her with an escort to company functions and someone to eat dinner with when she didn't want to be alone. Looking back, she couldn't remember why she'd stopped seeing either of them. The partings had been as insignificant as the relationships.

Nobody special.

Nobody who'd ever disrupted her life.

Nobody she'd ever wanted the way she wanted Jake.

She and Jake weren't friends, and she was pretty sure enjoyable would not be a term that would apply to their lovemaking. Hot, out-of-control, wild, life-changing...but *enjoyable* was far too tame a word.

She didn't understand the pull, and she certainly didn't trust it. Her whole world was chaos. She had to somehow get it stabilized, not get involved with someone who would make it even crazier. Not someone like Jake Thornton, someone who, she felt certain, could make her want him in a special way, take her self-control away again, then leave without a backward glance. His entire family had left no lasting impressions on him. Certainly she wasn't likely to.

She jumped at the sound of a knock on her door. "Rebecca?"

Jake.

He'd come back, and she wasn't sure she had the strength to send him away.

"Yes?" If she didn't open the door, didn't look at him, didn't feel the electrical charges that sprang from him to her and tingled along her skin, maybe she could resist.

"Are you dressed?"

As if that made any difference.

"Yes."

"Then would you let me in?"

A hint of anxiety in his voice reached her, and she rose to open the door.

A cloud of heat, heavy and sultry, rushed in, pushing aside the air conditioning and surrounding them as he stood with one hand on the door frame. The world beyond him was dark and distant, and the heat seemed to come from inside the two of them rather than from that outside world.

His eyes narrowed with recognition of the feeling, but then he stood straight, scowled and compressed his lips.

"Did you take the dress?" he asked.

"What dress?"

"The blue dress. Your mother's dress."

"No, you did. You put it in your briefcase at Doris Jordan's house yesterday."

"After that, I mean. I took it out of my briefcase and put it in one of the drawers in my room last night."

"Then why are you asking me if I took it?"

"Because it isn't in that drawer anymore."

Rebecca shook her head uncomprehendingly. "When would I have taken it? Where is it? What are you saying?"

"It's gone. The blue dress is gone."

Chapter 11

Their only clue was gone.

Rebecca had anticipated another restless night of fluctuating between bad dreams and insomnia. Instead her fatigue had finally caught up with her, and she'd slept soundly, awakening refreshed and in a surprisingly good frame of mind. Her emotional overload had acted in the same way as her physical.

She resolved to enjoy the respite, however brief it might be, and began by dressing in a peach colored scooped neck cotton blouse and matching gathered skirt with a wide white belt and white sandals, the happiest, most capricious outfit she'd brought with her.

She'd just finished dressing when Jake called. "Are you ready to go?" he asked without preliminaries.

"Yes. I'll meet you outside."

She stepped from her motel room into a glorious morning, the sky a wide, cloudless blue, the breeze pleasantly warm and scented with the fragrance of unseen honeysuckle. Taking advantage of the moment, she drew in a deep breath, savoring the clean, innocent essence of the day, knowing soon the temperatures would be scorching and she and Jake would be embroiled in the nasty little secrets of the town.

Jake's door opened and he came out wearing another pair of faded blue jeans with a white knit shirt that hugged the muscles of his chest and allowed a few dark hairs to escape from the open V-neck.

"Good morning," she said, but his gaze slid over her to focus on something behind her.

She turned to see what held his attention. The motel maid was rounding the corner with her cart.

"Come on," he said curtly.

Rebecca followed him down the sidewalk, almost running to keep up.

The woman, short and plump with streaks of gray in her shiny black hair smiled as they approached.

"Hi, I'm Jake Thornton in room 103."

Though the woman's expression didn't change, Rebecca thought her smile became stiff. Or perhaps she imagined it, was becoming paranoid.

"Did you clean my room yesterday?"

She hadn't imagined it. The woman's dark eyes widened in fright. She shook her head, the motion jerky. "No hablo inglès."

Jake folded his arms and rocked back on his heels."¿Limpia usted el cuarto de numero cien y tres ayer?" The woman's gaze darted from side to side as if seeking an avenue of escape."¿Ve usted un vestido azul?" Jake continued.

The woman shook her head vehemently and darted away.

"I don't know what you asked her, but she's not being honest," Rebecca said, watching the woman disappear into a room and close the door behind her.

"I asked her if she cleaned my room and if she saw a blue dress. And I agree. She's lying. She knows something about it."

"Why would she take the dress? It's out of style. It's old and faded. It wouldn't even fit her."

The question was rhetorical, but Jake answered it anyway. "Get rid of the evidence. My guess would be that she either owes a favor to good old boy Charles, or he has something on her."

The morning had lost its glory. The air hung languid about them, sticky with grease fumes from the restaurant next door.

"You ready to go to the library and see if we can get rebuffed there too?" Jake asked.

She nodded, her eyes meeting his, searching for reassurance that they weren't really going to be rebuffed, that this situation wasn't as hopeless as it was beginning to look.

Of course he gave none.

She turned and headed for his car anyway.

***

Jake parked in the small lot behind the Edgewater Public Library. Rebecca stepped out immediately, not giving him the chance to come around and open her door, to remind her of his overwhelmingly male presence.

He joined her, squinting into the sun as they walked to the front of the big old stone building. "July in Texas. Every day's a carbon copy of the day before. It'll be a hundred degrees by noon."

"Shortly after noon we'll be inside Doris Jordan's cool, comfortable house," she pointed out.

She was very much looking forward to that lunch, to being with the older woman who had so much chaos in her life and so much peace in her soul.

"Without the dress she asked to see again," he reminded her.

"Maybe she'll be able to remember something without actually having to see it this time."

He shrugged. "Maybe. At least the fact that somebody stole the dress tells us there's something there to be remembered."

"Did you ever doubt it?"

"Nothing's certain until you have proof, and then sometimes you're still wrong."

She wasn't sure if he was trying to reassure her about the terrible possibility that Charles Morton might be her father or prepare her for the possibility of never finding her heritage.

They turned the corner of the big old building where yesterday they'd found the story of Ben Jordan's death, and she let Jake's comment pass without a reply. He probably didn't expect one anyway. He seemed to think it was part of his job to dispense pessimistic advice.

The front of the library was impressive with wide steps leading up to large double doors of dark, shiny wood. Stone lions on each side guarded the town's collection of reading material. On the surface, Edgewater was an idyllic town, a remnant of a bygone era when life was slower and simpler.

But ugliness seethed just beneath the picturesque surface.

And her search was causing the town's ugly little secrets to rise to the surface. She was bringing up the skeletons of her birth for everybody—herself included—to see.

Jake held the door for her to enter the library.

Wooden card catalogues—no computers for Edgewater—and reading tables spread to the left with an Oxford English Dictionary on a stand in the middle. On the right was the desk where they'd obtained the microfiche the day before, but Eunice wasn't presiding that day. Instead, a short woman with pale hair—blond or silver or a mixture—in a medium length nondescript style stood talking to a tall, slender man. From their postures and expressions, the quiet conversation appeared to be intensely personal.

"Excuse me," Jake said, and both people turned to look at him. The man had a pleasant, disinterested expression as anyone, interrupted by strangers, might have. However, Rebecca thought she saw a flicker of something else in the woman's blue eyes...a momentary dilation of the pupils, a flash of sharp darkness...but a curtain of ambiguity descended immediately.

"Can I help you?" the woman asked, looking directly at Jake and ignoring Rebecca. A hollow essence in her low-pitched voice, a translucent overlay on her pale face and in her veiled eyes gave her a quality Rebecca could only define as haunted.

"I'd like to speak to Eunice," Jake said.

"Eunice isn't here today. I'm her assistant."

"I see." Jake tunneled his fingers through his hair, obviously frustrated by this latest hindrance to their investigation. "We were here yesterday, and someone left something in my briefcase. I need to find out who it might have been so I can return the item."

"If you'd care to leave the item with me, I'll try to locate the owner."

"I really need to talk to the person who left it."

"But you don't know who that person is."

"No, I don't."

"Then I don't see how I can help you." The woman gazed up at him, waiting, volunteering nothing. Her small chin jutted forward, the muscle in her jaw knotted.

The tall man beside her regarded them with a confused expression. During the woman's verbal exchange with Jake, he'd shifted his attention from one to the other as if surprised at his companion's reactions to the two strangers.

Jake shifted his weight from one leg to the other. Even he appeared a little disconcerted with the assistant's total lack of cooperation. "I thought you might have a list of everybody who checked out a book or brought back a book yesterday."

"I'm sorry but that information's confidential."

Jake gave her the same smile he'd given Doris Jordan. Rebecca could have told him he was wasting the wattage on this woman.

"I understand," he said. "Were you working here yesterday?"

"Yes."

137

"Then maybe you could just give me some idea of who might have been downstairs around two or three."

"I'm sorry but that information's confidential," she repeated, more emphatically this time.

Rebecca moved closer to Jake, trying to insert herself into the woman's line of vision. Maybe she'd have more luck than he was having.

And if she did, maybe she could even convince him she needed to be there. She certainly couldn't do any worse than he was doing in this instance.

"Please," she said, "this is very important." The woman didn't look at her, didn't admit by so much as the blink of an eye that she heard. "I'm Rebecca Patterson." Rebecca held out her hand, forcing some kind of acknowledgment.

Slowly, as if with great effort, the assistant turned her veiled gaze toward Rebecca but ignored the outstretched hand.

Haunted.

The woman was being incredibly rude, but somehow Rebecca couldn't get upset with her. She could almost reach inside the stranger and feel the inconceivable anguish that quivered behind her stony gaze.

"The item was a note," Rebecca explained, "and it's very important that I find out who wrote it."

The woman—Rebecca realized she hadn't even told them her name—shook her head, the movement a series of short, staccato jerks. "I can't help you." She spaced each word out in a staccato rhythm that matched her movements. "Please excuse me. I have

138

work to do." She turned away, heading toward an open office door behind her.

"Please, I'm trying to locate my mother." Rebecca could only assume the entire town knew already, so she might as well use the information if she could.

The woman kept going, disappearing into the office and closing the door as if she hadn't heard...or didn't care.

The man gave them an apologetic smile, shrugged then started after the woman. He was attractive in a quiet, artistic way, tall and thin with curly salt and pepper hair. The woman's husband? Lover? Had he seen a new side to her today?

He pushed the door open and stuck his head inside. "Mary?"

A soft murmur came from the room, and the man entered, closing the door behind him.

"Well," Jake said. "I'd say we need to come back tomorrow and talk to Eunice."

"Apparently." Rebecca stared at the closed door. "He called her Mary. Do you suppose that's Mary Jordan, Ben Jordan's widow?"

"Could be. Like I said, it's a small town. If we stay here long enough, we're bound to run into everybody. On the other hand, Mary's a common name."

"I guess so." Rebecca couldn't seem to tear her gaze away from the door which hid Mary and her friend. "I think it's her, though. She seems so..." She hesitated, reluctant to use such an intangible term as *haunted* in the presence of Jake's pragmatism.

"Rude?" he suggested.

She shook her head and faced him squarely. "Your job may be detective work, but my job is working with people. And that woman has had tragedy in her life."

Jake shrugged. "Whatever. She wasn't much help to us. To you."

Of course he couldn't let the *us* stand. For Jake Thornton, there was no *us* even in the two of them working together.

"Do you think that guy was her husband?" she asked.

"Could be. She was wearing a wedding ring. He wasn't, but that doesn't necessarily mean anything. Well, there's no point in hanging around here. I doubt if that lady will even give us the trays of microfiche to go through. We'll come tomorrow when Eunice is here. Let's go back to the motel room. I need to make a couple of phone calls."

Reluctantly Rebecca left the library with Jake.

Or, at least, in the company of Jake. She doubted that anyone was ever *with* him.

At the big doors, she turned one more time to see if Mary and her friend had come out of the office.

They hadn't. She could see nothing but the closed, silent door.

Chapter 12

October 21, 1979, Edgewater, Texas

A knock sounded on the front door.

The candy dish Mary had been dusting slipped from her fingers and crashed to the floor.

She chided herself for being silly. Ben had assured her that he'd take care of everything.

Like your mother said your father would come back from the hospital. Like she promised at his funeral that she'd never leave.

Like anybody had any control over the dangers of living.

Heart pounding furiously, she dashed to the door, praying to see a neighbor, a girl scout selling cookies, even an insurance salesman.

Charles and another officer, Clyde Hartman, his and Ben's sergeant, stood on the front porch, hats in their hands. Clyde's broad, freckled face was distorted, his eyes sad, his lips compressed as if holding in words he didn't want to speak. Charles frowned solemnly but his eyes glittered with anger and something else. Triumph?

Mary's hand went to her throat as the world spun dizzily around her. "Ben—" The word came out a croak, a desperate plea.

"I'm sorry, Mary," Clyde said. "There was a shooting."

She shook her head. "No!"

"I tried to save him," Charles said smoothly. "But I couldn't. He died instantly."

Blackness surged up to envelop her, to wrap around her and keep out the awful lie Charles had just told.

Strong arms grabbed her, holding her just above the night. Ben had caught her. Ben would always catch her. He'd promised to keep her and their baby safe.

A scent of too-sweet cologne assailed her nostrils, a scent imposed over but not hiding the dark, musty odor of death.

It wasn't Ben who'd caught her.

"She's fainted!" The concerned voice came from far away. She wondered briefly who was talking and who'd fainted, but the comforting darkness beckoned.

"She'll be all right. I'll take her by the doctor to be sure. Get her a sedative. Ben would want me to take care of her."

The doctor. Ben had been hurt, but they were going to the doctor. Ben was going to be all right.

She let herself drift into the safe shroud of darkness.

***

Pain.

Stabbing, hurting, pulling her out of the darkness. Someone was groaning.

Ben!

She tried to sit up, to see if it was Ben who was groaning, ask the doctor if he'd be all right, but someone held her down. Someone who smelled of too-sweet cologne and death.

Charles.

A woman swore. "This'll hurt a lot less if you'll lay still."

"Who are you? Where's my husband?" She was lying on her back on a table. A bare bulb dangled from the ceiling, the harsh light blinding her. She squirmed, trying to rise, to see where she was, who the invisible woman was...to get away from Charles. The movement increased the pain between her legs. Panic burst through her. "What's going on? I want to get up!"

"I can't do this if you don't hold her still."

"Give her something." Charles.

The other person snorted. "You want drugs, you go down to the hospital and ask them to do your abortion for you."

Abortion?

This couldn't be happening! She was having another horrible nightmare.

The room spun dizzily, the light above swirling like a drunken sun. Mary felt herself sinking back into that black oblivion where Ben was still alive and—

No! She couldn't go there. She had to stay awake, remain in the terrifying nightmare. She had to fight for her baby's life.

"Please don't do this!" she begged the woman. "My husband—"

"Ben's dead." The brutal pronouncement came from Charles' lips on a gust of fetid breath.

Tears sprang to her eyes, and a sob rose in her throat.

"I warned you what would happen if you started mouthing off," he said. "Now you'll lie still if you know what's good for you. Let us get this over with."

Charles had killed Ben because Ben knew. She'd told Ben and because of her, he was dead.

The horror engulfed her, invading her soul, sinking its tendrils into every part of her body, bleak and painful and forever.

She thought of the child growing inside her. Ben's child. Or—

For a second she considered doing as he said, lying still, letting them take this baby who might not have been conceived in love.

But only for a second. As Ben had said, it didn't matter who started the process, this was her child. Hers and Ben's. And she loved her baby with all her heart.

And hated Charles with a like intensity.

That hatred gave her strength to do whatever it took to save her child. She swallowed hard and sucked in a deep breath. "You're right." The calm, cold voice seemed to come from a stranger, couldn't possibly be hers. "I don't want any child that might grow up to be like you. I'll lie still but only if you go in the other room. I don't want you to see me...to see my body."

He laughed. "It's not like I haven't already seen everything you've got. It's a little late for modesty."

She pulled her knees together with every ounce of strength she possessed, ignoring the stabbing pain the action brought.

"Go on in the other room," the female voice instructed. "A woman's got a right to a little privacy at a time like this."

Charles was silent for several heartbeats. "You know what happens if you don't do this right."

"I know." The voice was hollow and dull, devoid of hope.

"All right then. Whatever it takes to get on with things."

She heard and felt every footstep as he left the room, closing the door behind him and taking the stench of death with him.

"I need to sit up a minute," she begged. "I think I'm going to be sick."

The woman sighed. "Okay. Hang on just a minute. Let me get this speculum out."

The pain eased, and Mary sat upright on the table. For the first time, she was able to see the woman, a very ordinary, somewhat mousy person who looked to be in her forties but could be younger. The hard edge to her plain face made it difficult to be certain.

"Why are you doing this?" Mary asked, her voice low to keep Charles from hearing and because every word, every movement, was an effort.

The hard edge deepened. "I owe Charles, and Charles always collects on his debts."

"You owe him enough to take the child of someone you don't even know?"

145

The woman reached for a package of cigarettes on a nearby lamp table, extracted one, lit it and blew out a stream of smoke. "Yeah," she said, "I owe him enough."

"Look, what if you just tell him you did it. Tell him the baby's gone."

She took a long draw on the cigarette then shook her head slowly. "Can't do that."

"Why not?"

"You think he's not gonna notice when you swell up like a house?"

"It'll be too late then!" She leaned forward in her fervor, her hands held out beseechingly.

The woman took several short, nervous puffs on her cigarette then crushed it out in an overflowing ashtray, her eyes on her action, refusing to meet Mary's gaze. "Not too late for him to ruin my life. I'm a nurse. I got a kid, a boy ten years old. I'll lose all that if Charles throws me in jail for doing abortions. That man is pure evil. He uses his job to collect evidence on people, then he owns that person. Like he owns me."

"I'll go away! Leave town! He'll never know. I promise!"

The woman's brown eyes lifted to hers and softened, but her mouth remained hard. "Come on, honey, why would you want to have the kid of a man like that?"

"It's not his baby!" *This baby is ours*, Ben had said. *I don't care whose eyes or hair she has. I don't care who started the process, who planted the seed. It's our baby.*

"He says it's his."

"He's lying! This baby belongs to my husband and me."

"Your husband's dead."

Mary shut out the hateful words. She couldn't think about that now. Later she'd have to face it, accept it, figure out how she could possibly live with it, but not now. Now she needed every resource she could muster to fight for the life of her child.

"This baby's all I have left. You're a mother. Surely you can understand."

The woman pushed her short brown hair away from her face and sighed again. "Yeah, I can understand. I don't know what I'd have done without my kid when my husband took a walk." She shook her head. "I gotta take care of that kid, and I can't do it from the inside of a jail cell."

"I swear Charles will never know. I have a friend who'll help me. She lives—"

The woman lifted a hand. "No. Don't tell me. Lord, I can't believe I'm even thinking about this. Okay, listen. You go in that bathroom over there and close the door then turn on the water. And get your ass out the window as fast as you can. You got five minutes. That's all before I go in and tell Charles that you tricked me. And, so help me God, if you ever show up in this town again, I'll do worse than an abortion."

Tears sprang to Mary's eyes as she slid off the table. "Thank you! You won't be sorry. Thank you!"

"Five minutes."

Chapter 13

When they returned from the library, Jake went to his room and Rebecca to hers. Trapped there for the morning, she paced restlessly for miles, turned the television on and off dozens of times, tried in vain to understand the bursts of muffled, one-sided conversations from Jake's room and grew more distraught with every slowly passing minute. This was the way she'd felt before she left Dallas to come down here...wandering in aimless circles, going nowhere with no goal in sight.

Since she'd arrived in Edgewater, she and Jake had been busy every minute. She'd felt as though they were accomplishing something, as if she was once again taking control of her life. No matter that they hadn't ended up with a lot to show for their efforts. It had felt good to try, to push forward.

But now Jake was in his room making phone calls, and she hadn't dared to demand to go in with him. Being in the confining, bed-filled space of Jake's room tended to dull her brain processes and intensify her hormonal processes.

If she had any sense, she'd take his advice and go back to Dallas, let him finish the job and send her those reports he kept talking about.

She picked up the phone and dialed her home number, intending to see if she had any messages. But before the second ring, she hung up. Nothing that could conceivably be on that machine would have any relevance for her. She couldn't go back because she had nothing to go back to. She was disconnected from that part of her life and not yet connected to another.

And Jake Thornton was her only link to that nebulous, unknown world.

How ironic that, to find herself, she had to risk losing the small bits of herself she had left, had to relinquish whatever remnant of control she still retained. Even though she was doing all she could, in the long run she had to trust Jake to help her, to do his job.

It would be far too easy to lean on him for more, the way she'd done in the cemetery.

She felt like a vacuum, needing to suck in the touch of another human being, to bond with that human being, to take from him the missing parts necessary to make her complete.

As a child, she'd done that with her parents, needing more than they could give. Was it possible she'd always remembered, somewhere on a subconscious level, the rejection by her birth mother? She'd heard that hypnosis had been known to bring up memories from time spent still in the womb.

As an adult, she'd thought herself past all that, but now she was right back in that trap. Except she knew only too well the futility of looking to anyone, especially someone like Jake. She had to find herself, get herself back together...and then she wouldn't need Jake or anyone else.

Or would need only what Jake needed from her...physical satisfaction. Nothing more. Nothing he couldn't deliver. She suspected he could deliver the physical satisfaction quite competently.

The ringing of her phone pulled her from her thoughts.

Heart pounding, she stared at it through two more rings before she mustered the courage to lift the receiver. Even then she couldn't speak, couldn't bring herself to invite another mystery caller to give her another message of discouragement about her mother...about her own future.

"Rebecca?"

"Jake!" She let out a long breath.

"You okay? You sound funny."

"I'm fine."

"You ready to go to Doris Jordan's?"

"I'll be right out."

When she left her room that time, the heat from the sidewalk slapped her in the face. At least it wasn't as misleading as the beautiful, hopeful morning she'd come out to earlier.

"Who did you call?" she asked as soon as they pulled away from the motel. "Unless they were personal calls," she added, the possibility suddenly rearing in her mind. "In which case, of course it's none of my business."

The possibility that he'd been making personal calls, that he had someone to call, hadn't occurred to her until then, until she heard the demanding tone in her voice...until a sick sensation rolled over her at the idea that he could have been talking to a woman.

That immediately produced another sick sensation at the thought that it would bother her if Jake had someone to call, if he was involved with someone, if he felt close to someone and shared his feelings with that unknown woman.

Of course she had no reason to get upset at those images. Jake was her investigator. She neither wanted nor expected anything more. He couldn't and wouldn't fill the void in her soul.

So she'd kissed him. So they had a man/woman attraction. They'd get over that as soon as this case was finished and each of them returned to his own world.

As soon as she had a world to return to.

Jake's lips quirked upward in an expression that more nearly resembled a smirk than a smile. He cast her a quick, knowing glance that sent the blood rushing to her face.

"All business, ma'am," he said. "I'm on the clock." He drove in silence for long enough that she wondered if he was going to refuse to discuss his mysterious calls. "I talked to a couple of guys on the police force in Dallas who owe me favors," he finally said when he'd apparently decided he'd tortured her sufficiently. "I asked them to check out Charles Morton's past in Williford, Ohio."

"Why?"

"Standard procedure. A hunch. Whatever. He seems to be involved in this cover up. We probably won't learn anything, but you have to follow a lot of blind alleys until you find the right one."

The thought of Charles Morton being in any way involved in her life sent a shudder of revulsion along Rebecca's spine.

"Cold? Want me to turn down the air?"

"No. I'm comfortable." Or at least her discomfort couldn't be solved by something so simple as turning down the air conditioning.

As they drove to Doris Jordan's house, the veneer of the small town seemed to have slipped, and Rebecca noticed things she'd missed the day before...peeling paint on some of the houses, weeds that dotted occasional yards, two kids fighting over a bicycle, another with a skateboard who'd fallen and skinned his knee. Like her hopes, the town had acquired a big dose of reality overnight.

Doris' house, however, still held its haphazard charm. She greeted them at the door with a welcoming smile.

"Come in. I'm so delighted to see both of you again."

"It was kind of you to invite us, Mrs. Jordan." Jake held the door for Rebecca to enter and placed his hand at the small of her back, just the way he'd done the first time they'd visited Doris. And she had the same reaction as the first time, as every time he touched her...an electrical surge, a desire for the touching to continue, to accelerate.

Deliberately she moved away from him, past Doris and into the house.

"Jake—may I call you Jake?" Jake nodded and returned Doris' smile. "And Rebecca. You must call me Doris. Mrs. Jordan sounds so formal, and I've never been a formal person." She led them through the living room.

Rebecca felt as though she had left her problems on the porch. They would still be there when she went out again, ready to leap onto her back and drag her down, but for the moment she could share the tranquility of Doris' world.

"I hope neither of you is a vegetarian. I've made chicken salad sandwiches. My own recipes for both the chicken salad and the bread. Edgar always called this my ladies'-club-lunch, though I never belonged to a ladies' club, and he seemed to like it well enough."

The dining room table was set with more of her flower garden dishes, a platter of thick sandwiches, a large bowl of potato salad, a plate of brownies and tall glasses of iced tea with an extra pitcher on the sideboard.

"It looks delicious." Rebecca took the chair indicated, across from Jake. It would be so easy...and so reckless...to let him become a part of this escape from reality, to relax for the course of this meal and lapse into the feeling that the two of them shared more than a job, that he was her luncheon partner.

But then the meal would be over.

And reality had a way of cutting into the soul with a sharp, jagged edge when it hit those who foolishly lived in a fantasy world.

As they ate, Doris led the conversation along avenues as light and palatable as her homemade bread, avoiding the issues of the dress and Rebecca's parentage. Doris was a true Texas lady. Meals were not the place for business topics or anything stressful.

Jake was doubtless right about her wanting their company, but Rebecca didn't care. She needed Doris' nonthreatening company too. She needed this time out from the unfamiliar world she'd been thrust into with her parents' deaths.

"What do you think of our little town?" Doris asked as she passed the plate of brownies to Jake who'd inhaled two sandwiches and one brownie already. "Quite a change from Dallas, I imagine."

Jake took two more brownies. "Thanks. Yeah, Edgewater is definitely different."

"Are you both from Dallas originally?"

"The Metroplex area," Jake replied. "I lived pretty much all over, from Mesquite to Ft. Worth to Red Oak to Lewisville and all points in between."

"So your family moved around a lot?"

"You could say that." He gave Rebecca a conspiratorial glance, acknowledging shared information to which the two were privy, information which almost gave them a link. Almost, but not quite.

"Rebecca's from Plano," he continued. "I think her family stayed put a little better than mine." He neatly diverted the conversation from himself.

Rebecca experienced a small, illogical thrill that Jake had shared his family history with her but not with someone else, though she knew he was probably only protecting Doris' genteel sensibilities.

"My parents had a restaurant in Plano and a house a few blocks away. We spent more time at the restaurant than at home."

"Then you never had to do dishes."

Rebecca laughed. "Actually, I did. My mother thought it was important that we lead as normal a life as possible so every chance she got, we ate at home even if she and Dad had to run back to the restaurant immediately. Which left me to clean up."

"Your mother sounds like a wise woman. You must have loved her a lot. It shows when you talk about her."

"Yes," Rebecca said. "I loved them both a lot." It was true. Whatever might have been lacking in their relationships, she had loved her parents. A fact which only made their betrayal harder to accept.

"And now you're feeling very confused."

"A little." That was an understatement.

"Perfectly normal. It takes a while to adjust to death, and you've suffered a double loss. Not only did your parents die, but you've discovered they weren't what they seemed."

Rebecca nodded. The crushing events, spoken in Doris' calm voice, became, if not less devastating, at least shoved into a category that might one day be dealt with.

"More tea?" Doris lifted the pitcher, her hand trembling slightly with the weight. A strong woman who had survived more than her share of tragedy.

Rebecca extended her glass, and Doris poured the translucent amber liquid. "On the other hand," she continued, "your parents were exactly what they seemed." She refilled Jake's glass and her own, set the pitcher down and returned her gaze to Rebecca. "They were people who loved you. I don't know

155

what I would have done after Ben's death then Edgar's heart attack and subsequent death a few years ago if it hadn't been for my daughter-in-law, Mary. She's the light in my life. I couldn't love her any more if she was my natural daughter."

Rebecca swallowed around the sudden lump in her throat. "I understand what you're saying. Nothing will change my love for my parents. I just need to know the truth—where I came from, what my mother looks like, why she didn't want me."

Doris' eyes were suddenly sad. "I wish I could change your mind, convince you to take what you have and be happy with it."

"What I had," Rebecca corrected. "I was happy with what I had, blissful in my ignorance, but with some little piece always missing. Anyway, now it's gone, all in the past."

Doris rose, laying her napkin on the table. "Our past is a part of us. It's never gone. Shall we move into the living room? Please feel free to take your tea with you. I'll bring the brownies."

The time out was over. Back to the big game.

"We have bad news," Jake said as they went into the comfortable living room. Again he took a seat in the large chair while she and Doris sat on the sofa. "We've lost the blue dress that belonged to Rebecca's birth mother."

Doris frowned. "Lost it? How did you lose it?"

"Actually, I'm pretty sure somebody took it from my motel room."

"I don't understand. Why would anyone do that?"

156

"We were hoping you might help us figure it out. I questioned the maid who cleaned my room, and she suddenly lost the ability to speak English."

"Lucinda?"

"I don't know her name."

"A short woman, early fifties, a bit overweight, silver streaks in her black hair?"

Jake nodded.

Doris frowned. "That has to be Lucinda. She's worked at the motel for years. Of course she speaks English. She was born right here in Edgewater." She looked from Jake to Rebecca, confusion deepening on her soft features. "Lucinda's always been a completely honest person. She used to clean house for me when I had the dress shop. She went to school with my daughter-in-law."

"Mary Jordan?"

"Yes. Have you met Mary?" Doris and her daughter-in-law apparently had a good relationship which probably meant the Mary they'd met at the library wasn't Mary Jordan. That Mary was not a content, loved person.

"Does she work at the library?" Jake asked.

"Yes, she does. She's been there for years." So much for Rebecca's perspicacity. But she had been right about one thing. The woman in the library had tragedy in her life. "She ought to be the head librarian," Doris continued, "but Eunice Waters won't retire. She acts as though all the words will fall out of all the books if she isn't there every day to keep them in line."

157

"Mary was talking to a man," Rebecca said, "a tall, thin man. Did she remarry after your son's death?"

"That would be David. He teaches at the high school. He'd like to marry her, but she's never gotten over Ben. I've encouraged her to get on with her life, but..." She shook her head sadly. "Mary's never been the same. Ben's death changed her completely. She almost had a nervous breakdown when he died. She wasn't even able to attend his funeral. I understand how she felt. He was my son, and a part of me died with him, but we have to go on. For all she's done for me and as close as we are, she can't seem to help herself or even let me help her. She reminds me a lot of you. Much too stubborn for her own good."

Against her will, Rebecca thought of Jake's suggestion that Ben Jordan had been having an affair and left the woman—her mother—pregnant when he died so suddenly. Knowing her husband had been unfaithful would explain Mary's change after her husband's death. It would even explain her animosity to Rebecca, assuming she somehow knew Rebecca's identity. Everybody else in town seemed to.

"Your son must have been quite a guy," Jake said, encouraging Doris to talk about Ben Jordan, his mind apparently running along the same channels as Rebecca's.

"Yes, he was," Doris agreed. "Edgar and I were always so proud of him. Edgar owned a hardware store, and we'd hoped Ben would take over. But from the time he was a little boy, he had his heart set on becoming a police officer." The lines in Doris' face seemed to soften as she gazed into the past. "We worried about his choice of career, of course, but then he went off to the army and nearly died. We thought if he survived that, surely he could survive being a policeman in a quiet place like Edgewater." She blinked away the hint of moisture that appeared in her faded eyes.

"Did they ever find the man who killed him?"

"No," Doris replied. "They never did. I always thought..."

"What?" Jake prompted, leaning forward when she stopped in midsentence.

Doris smiled and picked up the plate of brownies from the coffee table. "Would you like another?"

Rebecca exchanged glances with Jake. Was Doris simply trying to change the subject, or was there something about her son's murder she didn't want to discuss with strangers?

"You always thought what?" Jake prompted heartlessly.

"Nothing, really. It's hard to be objective when you're personally involved. As a mother, of course I felt they didn't try hard enough to find Ben's killer, though I'm sure they did. He probably headed straight for Mexico. We didn't have computers and instant communication in those days. He could have gotten away fairly easily."

"Charles Morton must have been devastated."

Rebecca looked up sharply at the overly-casual, pointed tone in Jake's voice.

"He seemed to be." Doris' words had a strained quality.

"You sound skeptical," Rebecca said, reaching for confirmation of her own aversion to Mayor Morton.

"Edgar and I accepted Charles into our lives because he saved Ben's life, but…" She shook her head slowly as she studied the depths of her glass of tea.

"Please," Rebecca encouraged. "I need to know."

"We need to know anything you can tell us," Jake interpreted smoothly, putting her request on more of an impersonal level. As it should be. However, left to her own devices, Rebecca would have told Doris how she felt about Charles.

Doris sipped from her glass of tea then set it on a coaster on the coffee table and folded her hands in her lap. "My son was a rescuer, always bringing home stray cats and dogs. When he started school, he was already a head taller than most of the children his age. He was a self-appointed guardian for the underdog. I can't tell you how many times he got into fights because a larger child was picking on a little one. That's why he was so determined to become a policeman, to protect the defenseless, to help people."

She hesitated, looking from Rebecca to Jake, down to her hands then up again. "I always thought Charles was one of Ben's rescues. He settled in here as though he had no past. He never went home and never talked about any of his family. Ben gave such a glowing account of how Charles saved his life, but I was never sure it was quite so clear-cut. Of course, Charles has made a place for himself here in

Edgewater. He advanced to sergeant on the police force then lieutenant then chief, and now he's the mayor. I suppose that says something about him."

"I don't like him, either," Rebecca said, defying Jake's attempt to keep the subject impersonal.

"You've met Charles?"

Jake shot her a warning glance. "He came by to offer his help."

"And to discourage me from trying to find my mother," Rebecca added stubbornly. She trusted Doris, and they could certainly use a friend in this town where someone made threatening phone calls and slipped them a misleading newspaper clipping, where the chief of police broke out headlights and the motel maid forgot how to speak English. "Can you think of any reason he might do that? Anybody he might be protecting?"

Doris looked troubled but not as startled as Rebecca might have expected before the woman had admitted her own reservations about Charles. "No, I have no idea why he would do that. But Charles and I haven't been close since Ben's death."

"Is Charles married?" Jake asked.

"No, he's never been married. As you might imagine, he's considered a very eligible bachelor. He escorts most of the single women from time to time, but never anybody in particular."

"Don't people find that a little strange?"

"Oh, yes. People talk. But never to his face. Charles is a formidable person in this town."

"What do people say about him?"

Doris shrugged. "The usual things. That he doesn't like women, though there's no evidence he likes men either. He travels a lot, and people speculate that he has a married girlfriend in Dallas or Ft. Worth."

"What do you think?"

"Charles is...different. He's very focused. If he has someone in another city, I'd guess that it's—excuse my frankness—a paid escort."

"So he's never been linked with a woman?"

"Well, there was one time a lot of years ago. Nothing ever came of it, though. I always thought it was just wishful thinking on the part of the woman."

"Who was she? What happened?" From the corner of her eye, Rebecca could see Jake lean forward as he spoke, waiting for Doris' answer.

"She was a really nice young woman. She'd always been shy and didn't mix well with the other young people. Her father was a minister of the Pentecostal church. He was very strict with her, and even though she must have been in her thirties, I don't believe she ever dated. I'm not sure anybody saw Charles and her in public together, but for a while, the rumor went around that they were to be married. Then abruptly she became a complete recluse, and that rumor died. She refused to come out of the house for several months and finally died from an overdose of sleeping pills. They said it was accidental, but I have always felt the poor tortured soul took her own life."

Rebecca sucked in her breath, trying to get enough oxygen to her brain so she wouldn't pass out. It couldn't be.

"What was her name?"

"Griffin. Janelle Griffin."

Chapter 14

It was late afternoon when they left Doris Jordan's house. Doris had given them the address and phone number for Lorraine Griffin, Janelle's mother. Jake had expected Rebecca to leap up and insist they go question the woman immediately, but she didn't. Probably because she didn't want to consider the possibility that Charles could be her father. He couldn't blame her for that.

Or maybe her lack of reaction was because Doris seemed to weave a spell about Rebecca, pulling her into a sense of security Rebecca no longer had...if she'd ever had it. Her parents' deaths and her subsequent discovery of her adoption had thrown her for a loop, but he suspected she'd always looked for too much from others. She still hadn't accepted that the only person she could count on, the only person who could give her security, was herself.

"Let's go to dinner tomorrow," Rebecca suggested to Doris as they walked out on the porch into the stifling heat. Any sign of a breeze had died. The leaves overhead were still, drooping as if their energy had been sapped.

"That would be lovely," Doris said without hesitation. He had to hand it to her. She was an up-front lady, open and without coyness in her need for and extension of friendship. She seemed to have achieved a rare balance...the ability to take from and give to other people while still relying on herself.

"Let's go to the best restaurant in town, my treat," Rebecca continued. "And I hope it's better than the one at the motel."

"We have a couple of very nice places here."

"Good. We'll pick you up about seven."

We'll, she'd said, and he hated the pleasure that rippled through him at her use of the word that included him.

They reached the end of the walk, and he opened the car door for her. "Nice of you to include me in your dinner party plans," he said, and even he wasn't sure if he was being sarcastic or genuine.

She looked puzzled then startled and finally shrugged. "You needn't come along if you don't want to."

"I might as well. I'd like to eat somewhere decent for a change."

They drove down the street, and Rebecca leaned out the window to wave to Doris.

They turned the corner, and she slumped back in her seat, as if she'd left her vitality behind with Doris Jordan, as if their descent from Doris' cool house into the unrestrained heat had wilted her.

He flicked on the air conditioning. The temperature was going up instead of down. Or maybe the surge of heat rose from the thought that he was heading back to the motel with Rebecca, from the memory of her in his room in that gauzy white gown combined with the memory of the way she'd kissed him in the cemetery.

"I don't want to go back to that horrible motel," she said as if reading his mind.

"Then go back to Dallas. That's your only other option."

"No."

The argument had lost its strength. He knew she wasn't going back, and she knew that he knew and there was no point in wasting energy arguing. Not when he really didn't want her to go back. At least, his body didn't want her to. His mind knew better, but his body wanted her right there, close to him, tantalizing, teasing, tempting him to do something foolish.

"In that case we're stuck with the motel. I figured you'd want me to get right on the Janelle Griffin thing and to do that, we need a telephone."

She offered no response, continuing to stare straight ahead through the windshield at the darkening sky. It must be later than he'd thought. Surely the days weren't already becoming short in July.

"You do realize, don't you, that if Janelle Griffin is your mother, not only is she dead, but that means all your search will turn up is a not very desirable father, Charles Morton?" He made himself say the words, be deliberately cruel, force her to face reality.

"I understand the implications of Janelle's connection with Morton." Her voice was tense, and the same tension emanated from her, filling the close confines of the vehicle, combining with the oppressive heat that even the blasting air conditioner couldn't seem to dissipate.

166

"As long as you're ready to deal with that possibility." He had to push her, force her to confront the circumstances that could break her.

She gazed out the window in silence for several moments. "Storm's coming," she finally said.

Yes, he thought, that's what he was pushing her toward. A storm. A release of that tension that had been growing since the first day she walked into his office...the tension inside her and the tension between the two of them.

Thunder rumbled in the distance, and he realized she was speaking literally. That's why the sky was getting dark, why the atmosphere pushed against him with so much force it was difficult to breathe. It was the approaching storm that filled the air around and inside him with minute charges of electricity, making him want to crawl out of his skin...or into Rebecca's.

Only the storm.

"Stop," she said. "Up there."

A block away he saw the park where they'd gone the day before to study the newspaper clippings from the library. "Under all those trees? Are you crazy or you just like to tempt lightning?"

"For a few minutes. Please. I've always loved storms. We had a screened in porch that faced the west, and we'd sit out there and watch them roll in. I want to see it from here instead of from that awful motel."

The lost quality in her voice touched a long-forgotten chord, sending the haunting note echoing through Jake. It was silly and even dangerous, but he pulled into the graveled area near the trees.

She got out of the car, and he followed her to stand gazing westward toward the ever-darkening sky. Though no breath of air stirred, currents seemed to roil about them.

She turned her gaze to him, her body amplifying and sending back the unfocused electricity that crackled silently all around them. Her eyes mirrored the dark, turbulent sky.

"Doesn't it feel like the whole world will explode if something doesn't give?" The timbre of her voice was pitched lower than normal, and her words sizzled along his skin, setting his nerve endings on fire, bringing hot blood rushing to his loins.

"Yeah, it does," he agreed.

"I don't mean just the storm. I mean all of it." She spun around, her back to him, facing the clouds that had begun to churn and tumble along the horizon. Her blond hair fanned across her back, lying softly on the fabric of her peach colored dress. "All of it," she repeated. "Charles Morton, Janelle Griffin, the disappearing dress, the threatening phone call, Farley Gates knocking out your head light. It feels like everything's going to explode any minute now, just like that storm is going to."

She ran one hand under her hair, lifting it off her neck, exposing the smooth, ivory skin above the scooped neck of her dress. The gesture was, he supposed, meant to cool her, but it had the opposite effect on him. That explosion she was talking about was getting closer and closer.

Without thinking—surely he would have stopped himself if he'd thought about it—he raised his hands to the back of her neck, touching the silky skin, stroking each separate vertebra.

She tilted her head forward and moaned softly as if she found the pleasure as exquisite as he did.

God, he wanted her! He ought to move away from her, stop touching her. All he wanted was a release from the terrible tension in his body while she wanted a release from the tension in her heart, something he couldn't give her.

Instead of moving away, he bent closer to her and pressed his lips to her neck, tasting the warm saltiness of her.

That wasn't what he'd intended to do at all.

He wasn't sure what he had intended to do. The blood pounding in his ears and the world spinning around him and inside him muddled his thinking. All he seemed capable of doing was feeling.

She moved back against him...or he moved toward her. He couldn't be sure which and didn't really care. All he knew for certain was that her bottom pressing against him was almost enough to send him over the edge.

"The storm's about to break," she said, her voice husky with desire and with a dual meaning to her words.

His gaze followed the direction she pointed, to where the leaves in the tops of the trees were beginning to swirl. He knew she wasn't referring to that storm only. The storm between the two of them was moving in just as fast.

He felt the cool breeze on his face, though it wasn't refreshing. Instead, the contrast only made his body hotter.

He slid his arms around her from behind, holding her more tightly to him and nuzzling the side of her neck.

Stop, Jake!

The words screamed inside his head. If Rebecca would only say them, he could find the strength to stop, to take a cold shower, to regain his common sense.

But she didn't tell him to stop. Instead, she swayed against him, the pulse in her neck thudding rapidly against his lips. Didn't she know he couldn't give her the emotional connection she needed, couldn't offer anything but a momentary release from the storm raging outside and inside their bodies?

He pulled her blouse from the waistband of her skirt and laid his bare hands on her bare stomach.

The wind picked up, blowing her hair across his face, soft silk that flooded his senses with the intense fragrance of a field of brilliant flowers in the broiling heat of mid-summer.

"Rebecca," he whispered, his lips against her ear, and then he didn't know what else to say.

Lightning streaked across the sky. Thunder boomed nearby.

"Yes," she said breathlessly. The word could have been a response to his unfinished comment or to the unspoken question between them or approval of what they were doing...or all three.

"God help us both, I want you, Rebecca. Right here in the middle of this public park, with Farley Gates liable to come along any minute and throw us in jail for obscene public behavior. Protect yourself from me. Tell me to stop. Tell me and I will. I swear I will."

She turned slowly in his arms and pressed her lips to his, the hunger in her kiss destroying any control he had left. Lightning struck so close it made the hair on his arms stand on end, but he barely heard the thunder over the thunder of his own heart.

The first big, heavy drop of rain splatted on his cheek, and, reluctantly, he withdrew his mouth from hers.

Her eyes, greenish blue like the tumultuous sky, blazed with their own storm. "Stop telling me things for my own good. Stop warning me about how badly my search could turn out. Stop telling me to go home. Stop telling me to make you stop touching me. My whole life has gone crazy, and all you can do is tell me what not to do. That's not good enough. I have to do something. I have to find something that makes sense."

"You think making love would make sense?" The rain came faster now, streaking down both their faces, but she didn't seem to notice and he didn't care.

"I don't know. Do you think wanting to make love and not doing it makes sense? Do you think standing in the rain arguing about it makes sense?"

"No. It doesn't. Come on. Let's go back to the motel." He urged her toward the car, knowing the ride would give them time for their passion to cool, for her to decide if this was really what she wanted to do.

Rebecca shook her head, refusing to let Jake steer her to his car. Once they got inside the familiar vehicle, they'd both have time to think about what they were doing, and at that moment she didn't want to think. At that moment she wanted to touch another person and make a connection, no matter how temporary. She wanted to touch Jake, to find that tentative connection with him that she'd found so briefly yesterday in the cemetery.

She pointed to the small shack where they'd seen the boy take his lawnmower the day before.

"You're crazy!" he shouted as the storm grew in fury around them.

She turned, ran across the wet grass to the shed, flung open the door and darted inside, breathing a short prayer of gratitude that small towns didn't feel the compulsive need to lock every door as they did in big cities.

For an instant she thought Jake wasn't going to follow her, that he didn't want her as badly as she wanted him.

Then he charged inside, almost tripping over the lawnmower, and closed the door behind him. His action plunged the room into semi-darkness with only one small window letting in the dim light and intermittent flashes from outside. Other gardening tools leaned in one corner, and a wooden table held plastic jars and bottles.

Jake pulled her into his arms and kissed her, his lips wet and warm and demanding, and she surged against him. When they'd kissed yesterday, she'd been bereft after the fleeting encounter ended. Today she accepted that fleeting encounters would be all they'd have, and she was going to savor every second of pleasure, store it up against whatever new pain awaited her in this futile search she'd undertaken for her family, for somewhere to belong. For the next few minutes, she belonged with Jake in the tool shed of the park. Maybe that was the extent to which any person could belong to another, could touch another.

She opened herself to him, tasting the rain on his lips, inhaling the scent of wet denim and musky desire, letting the tumult inside merge and escalate with the booming thunder, the sizzling lightning and pounding rain outside.

With one movement, he pulled her dress over her head and tossed it aside. His hands cupped her breasts, and his mouth fastened on a nipple, the suction creating an unbearably delicious streak of internal lightning that spread along every nerve in her body, centering between her legs, fueling the urgency that already tormented her.

She tangled one hand in his hair and clutched his shoulder with the other, needing to touch him, to feel the solidity of his body, to confirm that he was real and substantial and with her, not separated by a veil the way she'd felt separated from everybody recently.

His tongue teased the other nipple as he lifted one side of her skirt and slid his hand inside her panties, urging her legs apart. He was completely in

173

control, detached and uninvolved even in the most intimate act two people could perform, making love to her while staying fully clothed himself.

She clasped her hand around his, stopping him. He straightened and looked at her, his eyes half-closed and smoky. "You want me to stop?" His voice was as smoky as his eyes, and his breathing came ragged and harsh. "You want me to stop now?"

She groped for the buttons of his shirt. "No, I just want to be together with you. I need to touch all of you. I need to do the same things to you that you're doing to me so we're at the same place together."

He yanked his shirt over his head, and Rebecca heard several buttons ping on the wooden floor. Before she could reach for the hairs on his chest that she'd longed to explore since that first night he'd answered his door without a shirt, he unzipped his jeans and pulled them off. His skimpy black briefs barely contained his bulging erection.

She unbuckled her own belt and let it drop to the floor, then reached behind her to unfasten her skirt, but this time he stopped her.

Kneeling, he lifted the skirt and slid her bikini panties down her legs, tracing their path with kisses, then raised each foot in turn and slipped the underwear off. Finally he plunged his hand beneath her skirt and slid one finger inside her while his mouth again sought her nipple. Frenzied, tortured pleasure swept over her, pulsing in an elemental rhythm that matched the rain pelting the roof and the window.

With trembling hands, she reached for him, wrapping her fingers around the bulge in his shorts, needing to take him to the same place he was taking her.

He groaned and pulled away from her and for a moment she tensed. This couldn't be one-sided. They had to be together. He couldn't be detached.

"I'm ready to explode, and I don't want it to be in your hand." He slid off his briefs, freeing his erection to rise against his taut stomach. "Pull off your skirt," he growled. "I want to see the body I've been dreaming about every night that leaves me with an erection every morning."

The knowledge that he had been dreaming of her, wanting her as she wanted him, further inflamed her, made her feel special, that he wanted *her*, not just sex but sex with her. She unfastened her skirt and let it pool on the floor at the same moment as a bright flash of lightning lit the room. His naked, aroused body was magnificent, and she ached to have him inside her, a part of her.

He ran his fingers gently over her breasts, the hollow of her waist, along her hips. "You're beautiful," he said, "just like in every dream I've had about you."

He cupped her bottom and pulled her against him, his hardness against her stomach, her breasts against his chest. His lips claimed hers, his tongue darting inside her mouth to tangle with hers, pushing in then out, a rehearsal of the ultimate penetration. She clutched him to her, her hands on the bare skin of his back, her body arching against his, her desire a shrieking hurricane.

When she thought she could bear it no longer, he stooped to retrieve his shirt from the floor and threw it over the edge of the table. "I don't want you getting splinters in that gorgeous bottom." He bent again to take a foil square from the pocket of his jeans.

He was a gentleman, considerate of her needs. For this one moment, this one act, she was important to him, special. However many women Jake might have had in the past or would have in the future, right now she was the one he wanted.

She leaned back, and he sheathed himself inside her with one deep lunge, filling her, making her aware of every inch of her that he touched.

"I'm sorry," he gasped. "I meant to go slow, but I can't. You've got me completely out of control."

"Don't apologize. Don't stop!" Her muscles clenched around him involuntarily, urging him to continue.

His hands cupped her bottom again, cushioning her against the table and pulling her closer as he thrust in and out, each stroke bringing her higher and higher, whirling in a tornado of increasing sensations. The storm outside had reached a peak, the lightning flashing almost continuously, creating a strobe-like effect that made his movements appear jerky, an illusion that contrasted sharply with and heightened the smooth silkiness of Jake moving inside her.

She clutched his arms and met his thrusts until the world exploded in a white-hot burst of flame and roaring thunder, and she wasn't sure if the storm outside had risen along with their fury or if it all came from inside.

As Jake held her, his head drooped on her shoulder, his rapid breath on her neck gradually slowing, Rebecca became aware of her uncomfortable position against the table.

"I need to move," she whispered, straining against him.

Jake stepped back and pulled her upright. "I'm sorry."

She tensed as he said the same thing he'd said after their first kiss, the words that had negated the entire act. Logically she knew he wasn't apologizing for their lovemaking, just for her discomfort.

She knew that logically, but his repetition of the apology brought her down from the high she'd been on, back to the small, dim shack with the rain pelting outside and Jake stooping to pick up his clothes.

Lightning from a distance brightened the room briefly and weakly. The storm had spent its fury leaving only the rain behind.

Jake straightened, holding a pile of their mingled clothing. "They're a mess from the rain and the dirty floor. I guess the good news is, we'll get washed off when we run back to the car in this downpour."

His voice was impersonal, as though talking about laundry rather than clothing discarded in the haste of lovemaking. The connection between them—tenuous at best—now seemed weaker than before.

Suddenly aware of her state of nakedness in front of this lover who'd reverted to being a stranger,

Rebecca disentangled her underwear from the pile and began to dress, keeping her gaze lowered.

Making love with Jake had been the most incredible experience of her life, but now that it was over, now that her body was satisfied and her adrenaline ebbing, embarrassment and emptiness crept over her. Had she really behaved so wantonly with him, let herself go so completely...lost every shred of control?

For those extraordinary moments, she'd felt connected. Now that it was over, he seemed more remote than ever which shouldn't bother her, but it did. She'd told herself she only wanted that temporary physical connection, would be satisfied with that much.

Apparently she'd lied to herself.

Post coitum omne animal triste.

After sex, every animal is sad.

Was that all it was, the normal backlash after reaching such a peak?

Or was it that she was faced once more with her aloneness, the knowledge that even the ultimate act of joining with another still left her alone?

They finished dressing, and Jake opened the door then turned to her. He lifted one hand and cupped her cheek. His eyes, dark like the storm clouds outside, flicked over her face as if searching for answers in her chin, her lips, her forehead, avoiding her eyes. He turned away from her. "You deserve better than this." He waved a hand toward the dim interior. "Sex in a gardening shed. I should have been able to restrain myself until we could at least get back to the motel and have a bed."

Sex. He couldn't even refer to it as making love.

She shrugged and refrained from reminding him that she had been the one who'd insisted they go into the shack. "This place beats that crummy motel room, hands down," she said flippantly.

He smiled and finally met her gaze. "You could be right. Are you ready to head back to that crummy motel room?"

She nodded, and they dashed through the rain to the car. She was glad he hadn't suggested waiting until it let up. The shack had become confining and claustrophobic. She had to get away as quickly as possible, even if it meant going back to the dreary motel.

She had to get away from the memory of that brief, glorious touching that only resulted in more distance.

Jake drove in silence back to the motel.

He'd completely lost his mind, making love to Rebecca in that hovel. She deserved a five hundred dollar a night room with a king size bed and a Jacuzzi. She deserved a man who had something to give instead of one who could only take.

She deserved someone who, having taken once, at least had enough control, enough decency to be satisfied and not to be aching to hold her again, love her again, to wrap her in his arms and his body and keep her until everything was finally finished, however long or short that might be.

And therein lay the problem. Rebecca hadn't yet accepted that *forever* had no real meaning in human relationships, that everything had an end, that a moment of touching another was the best anybody could hope for. She was bound to learn it sooner or later. But he didn't want to be the one to teach her.

He stole a glance at her as she sat beside him in the car. She stared straight ahead, her wet hair clinging to her cheeks and shoulders without altering in the slightest her look of pride and vulnerability.

Making love to her had been a major mistake. Instead of quenching the fire, it had only fanned the flames. Now he knew what her lips felt like beneath his. He knew the firmness and satiny texture of her breasts so temptingly outlined by her wet dress. And he knew the silky heat between her thighs, knew how it could steal his common sense and take him to heights he'd never before imagined.

Rebecca wasn't going back to Dallas, and he wasn't sure how he was going to keep his hands off her. Especially now.

He parked in front of the motel.

"I'll go in and call Mrs. Griffin. See what I can find out," he said and waited tensely for her response, for the possibility that she'd insist on coming to his room to hear the conversation.

He wanted her with him, alone in his room, in his bed, wanted her more than he'd known it was possible to want a woman. And wanted just as badly for her to stay out of his room, to remove the temptation he had no will power to resist, the void in her soul that he couldn't fill. That nobody could in the long run.

She nodded without looking at him, opened her car door and got out into the rain that had slowed to a drizzle.

He slid out and followed her up to her door. "I'll call you after I talk to her."

She nodded again. "I'd appreciate that." She opened her door and went inside.

When Jake entered his room, he noticed the red message light on his phone blinking. He hesitated, torn between wanting to get out of his wet clothes and take a shower or find out who might have called, what he and Rebecca might have flushed out with their investigations.

Curiosity won. He peeled off his shirt, picked up the phone and dialed the office.

A woman answered.

"Jake Thornton. Do I have a message?"

"Oh, Mr. Thornton. Yeah, Wilbur wants to talk to you. Hang on a minute."

The line was silent for a moment, then the voice of an elderly man came on. "Wilbur Caswell. We got a problem here, Mr. Thornton. We got people coming in tomorrow that have your room and Ms. Patterson's reserved."

"You do? Okay, we'll move to other rooms."

Wilbur cleared his throat nervously. "Well, that's the problem, you see. All the other rooms are booked, too."

"All the other rooms? You're not even half full." The man was obviously lying.

"We will be tomorrow. Every room. Not a single one open."

"When I made my reservations for an indefinite time, your clerk said there wouldn't be a problem."

"She was wrong. You have to leave tomorrow morning."

"I see. Okay, tomorrow's Friday, and you're booked for the weekend. How about Monday?"

A long silence followed as if Wilbur hadn't been prepared for that question. "No," he finally said, "I'm all booked up for the next month."

Jake hung up the phone and stared at it. He'd flushed out something all right. Flushed Rebecca and him right out of their rooms. At least she wouldn't have to be concerned with this ratty place anymore. They might be sleeping in the streets, but they wouldn't be coming back here.

A rapid knocking sounded at the door.

What now?

He opened the door to see Rebecca huddled there, her eyes wide with fear and sadness though she was making an obvious effort not to let him see it.

She pushed her damp hair off her face and he saw that her hand was trembling.

Only by clenching his fists was he able to stop himself from reaching for her, from pulling her into his arms and trying to right whatever was wrong.

"Did you talk to the front desk, too?" he asked.

"Front desk?" She shook her head. "No." She swallowed hard. "I was going to take a shower but there's a snake in my tub."

He did reach for her then, but she pulled back, turned and headed toward her room.

He followed.

The snake, a nonpoisonous garden variety, writhed in her tub, trying unsuccessfully to scale the slick porcelain sides.

She stood outside the bathroom, hugging herself and watching him with that defenseless expression. "Jake, what's going on?"

"Be damned if I know, but you haven't heard the latest. I just talked to the office, and we've lost our rooms."

"What?"

"They claim they're all booked up for a month starting tomorrow. Somebody wants us out of town real bad." He looked back to the snake, black and menacing against the white porcelain, but essentially harmless. "We're getting into overkill here. With the manager kicking us out, we don't have any choice except to leave. So why the snake? What purpose does it serve if we're already on our way out the door?"

"To frighten me. To make us stop looking for my mother. To make us leave town for good, not just find another motel and commute."

"Maybe. But it almost seems like we're battling more than one person."

"What do you mean?"

"I'm not sure. It just seems to me that we're dealing with two different approaches here. One is powerful and intimidating, sending the mayor to talk to us, the chief of police to break my headlight, influencing the motel owner to kick us out. The other is quieter, makes a late night phone call, writes a note, steals a dress and leaves a harmless snake. They're both trying to run us out of town, but the methods are worlds apart."

Rebecca gave a short, brave bark of a laugh and rubbed her arms. "So what are you saying? You think my mother and my father are working separately to get rid of me? How can they hate me so much when they don't even know me?"

He could feel the sadness emanating from her, and he wanted to reassure her. But he'd be lying. He'd tried to warn her from the beginning that things could turn out this way. Eventually she'd have to face reality. She could postpone it but not avoid it. Her mother, her father, the family of one of her parents...those were the only logical people who could be doing these things.

Still he couldn't bring himself to tell her she was very possibly right on target.

"We have insufficient evidence to form any conclusions." Straight out of Criminology 101.

"Then let's get busy finding that evidence. Did you call Mrs. Griffin yet?"

She was tough. He had to give her that. A spine of tempered steel that kept her going in spite of the broken spirit that showed in her eyes.

Chapter 15

November 5, 1979, Cottonwood Bend, Texas

Mary dried the last skillet from breakfast and put it in the cupboard.

"It's a perfect morning," Sharon said, looking out the window as the dish water gurgled down the drain. "What do you say we grab a second cup of coffee and go sit on the porch awhile?"

"Sounds good to me." Mary shook out the dish towel and hung it on the rack to dry then reached down to Sharon's eight-month old baby playing contentedly on the vinyl floor. "If you get the coffee, I'll get the little trouble maker here." The infant cooed and clapped her tiny hands as Mary lifted her. "Oh, you love your Aunt Mary, don't you, sweet thing?"

"That she does." Sharon poured two cups of coffee, added cream and sugar, and led the way through her house to the front porch.

The green metal of the lawn chair was a little cold as Mary sat down, but it felt good after the stuffy warmth of the kitchen. She pulled her hair back and clipped it on top of her head, away from tiny grasping hands, then settled in beside her friend and arranged the baby, Pam, in her lap.

It was, indeed, a perfect morning. A cloudless blue sky rode high overhead with a bright yellow sun that gave off warmth but lacked the scorching heat of summer. Several trees were vibrant with the red and gold leaves of fall while others, like the live oaks and magnolias, would wear their shiny green all winter.

A dirt road led away from the house and down to the main road five miles away. The place was secluded. Safe. So why couldn't she stop worrying?

"This is my favorite time of the year," Sharon said, handing Mary a cup of coffee. "The garden's in, the canning's done, all those jars lined up in the cellar to keep us fed this winter, but it's still warm enough to get outside."

"It's beautiful," Mary agreed.

"In a few years, Nick and I will have a small herd of cattle out here that will, we hope, grow into a big herd. That's what he's always wanted to do. Have a big herd of cattle and a small herd of kids."

Mary gave the obligatory laugh though her heart ached at her friend's words. Just so confidently had she and Ben once planned their future. Now Ben had no future, and hers looked bleak except for one bright spot, the child growing quietly beneath her heart, giving her the courage to go on.

"Thank goodness Nick didn't want it the other way around," Mary said. "I think you've already got your hands full with this one." Pam squirmed to get down, and Mary reluctantly let her slide to the porch where she held onto one finger with both hands and balanced on chubby legs. "You're soon going to be walking and then your mommy won't be able to stop you from getting into absolutely everything!"

Pam gurgled happily in response, showing two teeth on top and two on the bottom.

"You're spoiling her rotten," Sharon said.

"That's okay. Isn't it, sweetie pie? That's what aunties are for." She ruffled the baby's soft blond curls, eliciting more gurgling, a couple of foot stomps and some jabbering.

"You also fret over her. A lot. More than I do. It's like you're scared to let her out of your sight."

Mary tensed and looked at Sharon to see if she was being censured, but her friend's face held only concern.

"She's precious," Mary said.

"But durable." Sharon set her half-full cup of coffee on the wooden porch and leaned forward intently. "What's wrong, Mary? Besides losing Ben, I mean. Oh, I know that's enough. But there's something you're not telling me. We've been friends since we were Pam's age, and this is the first time you've kept secrets from me. What are you scared of?"

Mary shook her head, looking away from Sharon's probing gaze and biting her lip. Tears, always close to the surface, threatened to spill over if she tried to talk. Not that she would talk anyway. The last person she'd confided in was dead. Ben had been murdered because she'd talked.

She ought to be safe on the farm twenty miles outside the small town of Cottonwood which was another twenty miles away from Edgewater...away from Charles.

But she'd thought she was safe with Ben looking out for her and the baby. Nobody was ever really safe, and she wasn't going to endanger her friend or her friend's baby any more than she already had by coming to them for shelter.

"I've tried not to ask questions," Sharon continued. "But I can tell something's wrong, and I'm worried about you."

"Everything's fine." It was the first lie she'd ever told her best friend.

"Yeah, right. Two weeks ago you call us to come get you at a bar outside of Edgewater. We do, no questions asked. You have nothing with you but the clothes on your back, not even your purse, you beg us not to tell anybody you're here, and now you say everything's fine. I don't think so."

Mary's head jerked up. "You haven't told anyone, have you?"

"Of course we haven't. And we won't. You know you can trust me completely and you know you're welcome to stay with Nick and me for as long as you want. Forever. No questions asked. But it's breaking my heart to see you this way. You jump at every noise, every time the phone rings, every time Nick drives up in the evening. You worry about Pam constantly. You look scared, like you're being pursued by the devil himself. And you never cry even though I know your heart's broken. I want so much to help you, but I don't know what to do."

Mary nodded, drawing one finger around the rim of her cup, avoiding Sharon's gaze. "I know. I'm sorry."

Her friend waited as if expecting her to continue, but Mary had nothing else she dared say. Finally Sharon sighed resignedly. "I know how much you loved Ben and how upset you are over his death. But I don't understand why his being killed by some druggie who's long gone would make you so afraid. You're not worried the man who did it is going to come after you, are you?"

Mary didn't answer. She turned away, studying the trees in the yard, the rosebushes now bereft of blooms, the faint tire tracks left by Nick's pickup earlier that morning. Down the road the wind stirred up a cloud of dust.

Or a car was coming.

"Why would he do that?" Sharon continued. "He's a stranger. He shot Ben because he didn't want to go to jail. You're no threat to him."

But Ben's murderer thought she was. Charles thought her baby was a threat to him, and she knew she could never convince him otherwise. She squinted against the morning sun, telling herself the dust was only that, not a car, not Charles. He could never find her here.

"You're pregnant, aren't you?"

Mary gasped and turned back to Sharon.

"I know the signs. I've been there." She rose from her chair and knelt in front of Mary with Pam between them. The baby turned to her mother and lifted her arms to be held. Sharon wrapped one arm around her daughter and took Mary's hand with the other. "That's another thing I don't understand. You should be thrilled. I know you've always wanted babies. You adore Pam. And this means you still have a little bit of Ben, his child."

Tears pooled in Mary's eyes. She and Sharon had always been closer than sisters. They'd shared every part of growing up from their favorite dolls through their first bras and crushes on boys. Sharon cared about her and wanted to help, and Mary wanted to tell her everything, share this latest secret and depend on Sharon's friendship to help her get through it.

A sound intruded on the still morning, the distant sound of an engine.

She looked up. The cloud was moving closer, and she could discern the shape of a car.

Nick wouldn't be home for hours. The road ended at Sharon's house. No one else would be coming down that road.

Her heartbeat accelerated. The tears dried or turned to stone.

She couldn't tell Sharon anything. By her very presence, she'd put her friend in danger. Somehow she had to protect Sharon and Pam as well as her own baby.

She yanked her hand away from Sharon's grasp. "Take Pam and go in the house." The voice that came from her mouth sounded strange and harsh to her own ears.

"What?"

"Please! Take Pam, go in the house and lock the door."

Sharon rose, holding her baby close as if frightened that Mary had suddenly gone insane. Maybe she had.

A police car pulled up to the house.

"That's strange," Sharon said. "What's an Edgewater policeman doing here?"

Charles got out of the car, and Mary rose even though a few minutes ago she'd have sworn she wouldn't be able to, that her legs would never support her, that she'd faint from the sheer terror and hopelessness of it all.

Charles came to the edge of the porch, and she went to meet him. "How you ladies doing this beautiful morning?"

"Sharon," she said stiffly, knowing what she had to do to protect her friend, "this is Charles Morton, Ben's partner. He moved to Edgewater after you left. I'll be going back with him." She had to lure him away from Sharon and Pam. After that, she'd figure out how to save her own baby. Somehow.

"Pleased to meet you, Charles. Didn't you serve with Ben in the Army?"

Charles pulled off his cap and smiled. "Yes, ma'am. I did indeed."

"Oh, you're the one who saved Ben's life. Well, it really is a pleasure to meet you! Come on in and I'll make a fresh pot of coffee."

Thank God she hadn't told Sharon anything about Charles. Her friend's words held the unmistakable ring of truth. Charles must know he had nothing to fear from Sharon. If only she could get away before Sharon mentioned that she knew about the pregnancy.

"Charles doesn't have time to come in. We have to leave now, don't we?"

"I appreciate your kind invitation, ma'am, but we'll have to make it another time. Mary and I do have some important business that can't wait."

"You take care of her, then. She's been awfully upset since Ben's death." Balancing Pam on one hip, Sharon turned to Mary and hugged her. "Call me, okay? And you come back here any time you want to. There'll always be a place here for you and yours."

Gratitude, love, fear, helplessness...a thousand emotions tried to sweep over Mary, but she pushed them back. She had to think, not feel. Think and plan and calculate. She couldn't allow any emotion to interfere, or both she and her child would surely die.

"I've really enjoyed our visit. I'll call you as soon as I get everything settled." She walked off the porch toward Charles' car, her back ramrod straight as though a steel beam had been welded to her spine.

She got into the passenger side and closed the door. Charles slid in beside her. "What did she mean, *you and yours?*"

She faced him, letting him see her eyes so he'd believe her. He didn't know she'd turned to stone inside and would never betray herself by so much as a flicker of emotion. "I didn't tell her. She doesn't know anything. It's just a Texas expression."

He nodded, apparently satisfied she was telling the truth. "So do I take it you've decided to be smart and get this little problem taken care of so we can both get on with our lives?"

"Yes. I've decided I don't want anything to do with a child that belongs to you." It was amazing how easily she'd become a proficient liar. Not that her statement had been a complete lie. Her child didn't belong to him.

"I don't believe you any more than I believed you when we were at Margaret's, but I'm glad you see the futility of resisting." He started the car. They pulled away, and Mary's mind shifted into high gear, observing everything—how far away Charles sat, how fast they were going, where the door handle was—making notes of everything so she'd be ready when the opportunity came. The opportunity would come. She couldn't accept any other possibility. Somewhere, somehow, her chance to escape would come.

"Are we going back to that woman's house? Margaret, is it?" she asked, gathering information, storing data.

"I had to arrest poor Margaret. Caught her doing illegal abortions. Can you believe it?"

Guilt swarmed over Mary. Charles had punished the woman because of her, because Mary had begged for the woman's help, and she'd given it.

But she couldn't dwell on it, had to shove it away. She couldn't do anything to help Margaret and couldn't afford to indulge in useless emotions. Her only focus was saving her baby.

"What's going to happen to her?"

His face hardened, and Mary allowed herself a brief surge of relief. His expression could only mean Margaret had somehow thwarted him. "The bitch jumped bail and skipped town. But I'll find her. She won't get away with that. She's a whore, no better than you. No better than any of you. I know what to do with whores."

Ignore the threat! she ordered herself. Just because he says it doesn't mean he can do it. She wouldn't let him do it.

"What about your mother?" she asked. Even Charles must have a mother, must have once been somebody's little boy, somebody's baby. Perhaps she could reach him through that avenue.

"What about her?"

"She raised you. She loves you. She's not a whore."

"*She raised you. She loves you. She's not a whore*," he mimicked in a falsetto voice. "Of course she is."

That line of questioning seemed to make Charles more agitated. Mary dropped it and was silent until they reached the highway, her mind racing in all directions at once, searching for that opportunity she knew must come.

"How did you find me?" she finally asked.

"I have friends everywhere."

"Friends? Or people who owe you?"

He laughed. "Isn't that what friends are? You tell each other your dirty little secrets and then you each hold it over the other's head, and you smile and do each other favors so neither one of you will betray the other, and that makes you friends."

She looked outside the car, focusing on the rutted road ahead, the trees along the sides, anything to avoid letting herself be intimidated by Charles' insanity. She would get away from this madman. Somewhere, somehow.

"Ben was your friend," she said. "He never held anything over your head."

Charles snorted. "No? How about the Army thing?"

"He let everybody think you were a hero."

"Sure he did. As long as I played his games. But he never let me forget that he could take away everything he gave with just one word to the right people."

She turned to stare at him in amazement. "That's not true! Ben wasn't like that at all!"

"Grow up. Everybody's like that. Your precious Ben even took your word, the word of a whore, over my word. He went nosing around in things that were none of his business. He was getting ready to ruin my life. He asked me to come to that stinking little town in the first place. He got me on the police force. He gave it all to me and he thought he could take it all away whenever he wanted. Well, he was wrong."

The coldness in Charles' voice told her she was dealing with a man who was completely insane. He wasn't even angry. He merely hated—Ben, her, his mother, everyone, probably even himself. Charles was the most dangerous person she could ever have imagined. If he'd been angry, she could have hoped that anger would eventually dissipate, that he'd be distracted by something else or that logic would prevail.

But black, unreasoning, unemotional hatred was something she had no defense against.

So she'd have to go around it.

Somewhere, somehow.

"Where are we headed if Margaret is no longer available?"

"Don't worry. I have another friend who's willing to help us. A doctor. You might even get drugs this time."

"I'd appreciate that." Drugs! She wouldn't be able to think or talk or run. She'd be helpless. She had to get away before they reached their destination.

They were approaching the outskirts of Edgewater already. Ahead she could see a gas station and a Dairy Queen on either side of the highway.

"Could you stop at that station for just a minute? I think I'm going to be sick."

"And let you go to the bathroom again like you did at Margaret's house?" He laughed without humor. "How stupid do you think I am?"

"No," she said quickly. "Not the bathroom. I just want to get some crackers for my nausea. I've always gotten car sick, and now that I'm pregnant, it's much worse. I threw up in Nick and Sharon's truck, and I'm about to throw up in your patrol car." So many lies, and Mary had a horrible feeling they were only beginning.

"Aren't you lucky you're not going to have this problem much longer?" Charles asked, but he slowed and pulled into the service station.

This was it. Somehow she'd have to get away now. It wouldn't be easy. She couldn't count on anyone to help her. The attendant was more likely to believe a police officer than a woman without any identification. She reached for the door handle, but Charles grabbed her arm and pulled her back to him.

He slapped handcuffs around one wrist, through the steering wheel and around the other.

"I'll be right back with those crackers."

He got out of the car and closed the door behind him. Blind, unreasoning panic threatened to overwhelm her. She yanked futilely on the cuffs, knowing she had no chance to escape.

Stop it! she ordered herself. Be calm and think!

Her baby's life was at stake. She had no room for the self-indulgence of panic.

She took a deep breath and forced herself to relax, to stop focusing on the problem and look for the solution.

Somehow she had to figure out a way to bring a third party into the picture.

Think!

If only the car would refuse to start when he came out. Then he'd have to call a tow truck. That would get them out of the patrol car and into the truck with the driver. That would give her a chance.

But she couldn't count on a miracle to save her. She had to make her own miracles. She had to disable the car.

How could she do that? The only thing she could reach was the steering wheel, and she'd already tried unsuccessfully to break that.

No, that wasn't all. She could reach the pedals with her feet. She could reach the turn indicator, the gear shift, the ignition. For a split second, hope surged that she could steal the key. But he'd taken it with him. A cop. He knew all the tricks.

If he couldn't put the key back in the ignition...

As a teenager, she'd lost the key to her diary and tried to pick the lock with a bobby pin. The plastic tip had come off inside and even when she'd found the key, she'd been unable to open it, had resorted to cutting the tab.

She lowered her head to the steering wheel so she could reach her hair then pulled out the plastic clip. If only Charles didn't come back too soon!

She shoved one angled plastic tip into the ignition as far as it would go then broke it off and shoved it farther inside with a second plastic tip.

Charles came out of the door of the station.

She yanked the second piece out and lowered her head so fast it hit the steering wheel. If there was pain, she had no time to acknowledge it as she frantically pulled her hair back up and secured it with the broken clip.

Looking up, she erased all expression from her face. Her heart was pounding so hard she feared it would leap from her chest. She couldn't seem to make it slow, but she could keep Charles from knowing.

He slid into the car, unlocked her cuffs and handed her a box of saltine crackers. "Don't get crumbs in my car."

Forcing herself to look away from him as he tried to shove the key into the ignition, she opened the box, took out a cracker and nibbled though her mouth was so dry she knew she'd never be able to swallow it.

Several seconds went by and the engine did not roar to life. She dared to hope.

Charles cursed, and her hopes rose.

"You God damn bitch, what did you do?"

She lifted her head and looked at him. "You left me handcuffed. What could I do?"

He glared at her, then jiggled the gear shift and tried the key again.

After several minutes, he was perspiring. "I know you did something, but it's not going to help you. You've slowed things down. That's all. Put off the inevitable. All I have to do is radio in and have them send out a tow truck. We'll ride back in the cab, you in handcuffs as my prisoner. Then we'll get the tow truck operator to drop us off at Sam Wilcox's office."

"Dr. Wilcox?" she blurted in shock. "He's my doctor! He delivered me. He did my pregnancy test! Why would he…?" She shook her head, unable to complete the horrible thought.

"The good doctor got greedy. He saw a chance to make a little extra money what with everybody wanting drugs and him having access to them. Fortunately for him, I was the one who caught him, and I'm a reasonable man. I did him a favor, now he does favors for me. You could say we're *friends*."

If Charles had a man like Sam Wilcox under his thumb, how far did his power reach? How far would she have to go to get away from him?

She wouldn't despair, Mary told herself resolutely. For the sake of her baby, she couldn't.

But it was getting harder and harder to hope.

***

Twenty long minutes later a city-owned tow truck pulled up. Charles cuffed her with her hands in her lap and got out to talk to the driver.

Another patrol car arrived and parked behind the tow truck. The door opened, and Clyde Hartman stepped out.

Thank God! Clyde knew her! He'd save her!

She opened her mouth to call to him then closed it. If Charles had control of Dr. Wilcox, he could have Clyde too. Hadn't Clyde released her to him so he could take her to that woman for an abortion?

The three men talked, and she heard Charles explaining the problem with the ignition. Clyde separated from the trio and started toward her. Charles grabbed his arm, and he stopped.

"Trust me," Charles said with a laugh. "I tried everything."

"I trust you, Charles. I just want to take a quick look. I used to work on cars a lot before I joined the force. Souping them up, making hot rods out of Chevys."

Clyde shook off Charles' arm and continued toward the car. He opened the door and started to slide in, then stopped. "Mary!" His broad face broke into a smile, and it was the most beautiful sight Mary had ever seen.

"Hello, Clyde."

His expression sobering, Clyde slid in beside her. "How are you doing? We've all been worried about you. Charles told us you were too upset to come to Ben's funeral and were going to stay with some of your folks for a while. Are you doing better now?"

She smiled reassuringly. "I'm fine now."

"Has anybody told you about Edgar?" he asked tentatively, as if he feared to upset her all over again.

"Edgar? My father-in-law? No! What about him? Is he all right?" Please God, don't take him too.

"He's going to be fine." Mary dared to breathe again. "It was touch and go there for a while. He had a heart attack from the shock of Ben's death. But the doctor says he can still have a long life if he takes it easy and avoids worrying." Clyde reached to take her hand then stopped when he saw the cuffs. "What's this?"

Charles leaned in the window on her side. "For her own protection. The people she was staying with brought her back up here so she could get some help. She's having some really bad emotional problems. Even tried to hurt herself. I'm taking her to the doctor."

Clyde's eyes widened in shock. He grasped both her hands in his. "Oh, Mary! Ben wouldn't want you to do that!"

"I didn't," she said firmly. For a moment she considered telling Clyde the truth, taking the chance that he'd believe enough of what she said to at least check things out. But her story might only add credence to Charles' assertion of her mental instability.

Even if Clyde did listen, would he end up like Ben when he started checking?

"It was all a mistake," she improvised. "I woke in the middle of the night with a terrible headache and went to get some aspirin. But being half asleep and in pain and in a strange house, I got the wrong bottle and took three of my...my aunt's sleeping pills. She's elderly and when she had trouble waking me up, she jumped to the wrong conclusion." This business of lying was getting easier and easier.

Clyde studied her carefully for a few seconds then looked at Charles. "Is that what happened?"

"No. She took the entire bottle."

"No, I didn't. Aunt Gertrude's nearly ninety. She gets confused easily."

"I think you can take off these cuffs," Clyde said quietly.

Mary turned and lifted her hands to Charles. As he unlocked the cuffs, she'd have liked to give him a triumphant look, but she didn't dare taunt him...and she hadn't emerged triumphant yet. This was only the first step. She kept her expression neutral. Charles did the same.

"Now, Mary," Clyde said, "you've had quite a shock. I do think you ought to see a doctor."

Mary rubbed her wrists. "I will, Clyde. I'll call and make an appointment with Dr. Wilcox. But right now I just want to get home again. I've had two weeks to deal with Ben's death, and now I've got to start getting on with my life."

"Good girl." Clyde smiled and patted her hand.

"Will you take me home?"

"Mary," Charles interrupted, "I said I'd take you home."

"No, you said you were taking me to a doctor. I'm quite capable of taking myself to a doctor. Besides, you've got to go back in that tow truck. Clyde can run me by the house a lot more easily."

"I'd be pleased to do that, Mary," Clyde said. "When I heard Charles' radio message about having car trouble, I came out to see if I could help since things are pretty slow right now. I don't have anything to do that's nearly as important as taking you home."

"Thank you, Clyde. I'd really appreciate that." She pushed open the door and got out. As she walked away from Charles, she could feel his hatred following her, surrounding her like a black, roaring tornado. She wouldn't have much time when she got home. Grab a few things, get in the car and go.

She was on her own. She couldn't even look to Doris and Edgar for help. That would not only put them in jeopardy from Charles but also from Edgar's heart. She had no one to rely on but herself.

She needed money, needed to close out Ben's and her bank account. Maybe she could get Clyde to stop by the bank so she wouldn't have to worry about Charles' intercepting her there.

She could call later and arrange to have the utilities turned off then decide what to do about the house. She'd probably never go back there, never see Doris and Edgar again. Tears formed somewhere deep inside at this latest reminder of the loss of everything she and Ben had planned.

But she had no time to shed those tears. Ben was gone. All their hopes and dreams were gone. All except one, and her entire focus, her entire life, had to be directed toward saving that one, her child.

How far would she have to go to be safe from Charles?

A big city. Los Angeles? New York? The only knowledge she had of those cities was from geography classes and what she'd seen on television. They seemed like foreign countries, and the thought of going there was frightening. But not as frightening as Charles, not as frightening as losing her baby before that baby took a breath, before she even got to hold that baby in her arms.

She climbed into the passenger seat of Clyde's patrol car, leaned back and pressed a hand to her gently rounded stomach as if she could touch and soothe the child within.

It's going to be all right, precious one. Your mother loves you more than anything in this world. I know love wasn't enough to keep Ben safe or my mother or my father, but somehow, whatever it takes, I will keep you safe. You just concentrate on growing, and your mother will take care of everything else. I promise I won't let anything happen to you. I swear I'll keep you safe.

Chapter 16

The morning was cool after the rain the day before, but the sun blazed as relentlessly as ever. The cool wouldn't last long.

Rebecca stashed her suitcase in the trunk of her car and looked back at the rundown motel where she'd spent the last few nights. Less than a week, certainly not enough time that it should bother her to leave it when she'd hated the dreary place from the first night there.

Was she so bereft that she could become attached to any place or anyone?

"Okay," Jake said, opening the door of his car. "We're due at Lorraine Griffin's in twenty minutes. The directions sound pretty simple so we should be there in plenty of time." He hesitated, one foot inside his car. "You're sure you want to go with me? You could wait here. Checkout's not until eleven."

She smiled ruefully. "If I'm still here at 10:59, they'll probably send somebody over to dynamite the door and toss in a herd of tarantulas."

Jake rubbed his hand over the back of his neck. "You could be right. Well, you shouldn't have any trouble following me. Not much traffic to get in the way." He climbed inside his car and started the engine.

Rebecca did the same and drove behind him across town.

Going to the same place in two different cars. That was appropriate.

Last night after he'd disposed of the snake, an uncomfortable tension had developed between them. She knew from the look in Jake's eyes that he'd like to spend the night with her. Or at least, part of the night. Doubtless he couldn't commit to an entire night. But he wanted to make love again. And so did she. Yet equally as strong as her desire for him was her fear of the letdown that would follow, the hollow despair she'd felt when it was over in the gardening shed and would feel again when he left her in the middle of the night.

They'd parted and gone to their rooms, and she'd made a decision to return to Dallas and wait for Jake to send her reports, just as he kept suggesting. Perhaps she had nothing to go back to there, but all the occurrences in Edgewater only served to increase her emptiness.

Contrary to her original feeling, that she needed to be there to take control of her life, she seemed to be losing a little bit more of that control every day. It was becoming increasingly obvious that her parents didn't want to be found, didn't want her. Jake wanted her, but only for a limited time, an achingly beautiful time that made the minutes and hours that followed more barren by comparison.

Being kicked out of the motel had come at an opportune time. Tomorrow was Saturday, and Jake would probably go back to Dallas for the weekend. She wasn't sure if private investigators worked on weekends or not. In any event, he'd find somewhere else to stay, and she'd return to her condo in Dallas.

After dinner with Doris.

Doris Jordan was the one bright spot in this trip, the one person who made her feel comfortable and wanted, as though somebody cared. She wouldn't leave without telling Doris good-bye.

She followed Jake across town to an older home with a well-kept lawn and carefully trimmed shrubs. Though larger, the house was similar in age and appearance to Doris Jordan's, but no riot of flowers greeted them. Nothing about this house greeted. It was simply a house sitting in the middle of a yard.

She parked behind Jake's car and got out.

Side by side but not together, she and Jake walked up to the house.

Lorraine Griffin came to the storm door as they stepped up onto the porch. She didn't open the door, however, just stood looking out at them.

Like Doris Jordan, this woman had lost a child and a husband. She was tall like Doris and about the same age, but there the resemblance ended. They were no more similar than their houses.

Janelle Griffin's mother was a large woman, big-boned so she would never be slim even if she weren't carrying an extra fifty pounds. She wore her graying hair pulled back into a tight bun, and her face drooped, its melancholy attitude at odds with her robust appearance. The brown dress she wore suited her.

"Mrs. Griffin?"

She nodded curtly.

"I'm Jake Thornton and this is Rebecca Patterson. I called you a few minutes ago."

She looked Rebecca up and down, and Rebecca suddenly felt that her white sundress, sedate as it had seemed when she'd put it on that morning, was inappropriate, too revealing.

She found herself fervently hoping this sour woman was not her grandmother.

"You're the woman who wants to find her parents?"

"My biological parents, yes."

"So why do you want to talk to me? Are you trying to accuse my Janelle of having relations with a man? My daughter was a good girl. Went to church every Sunday, not like some I could name."

"We're not accusing your daughter of anything," Jake soothed. "And any information you can give me about those others you could name will, of course, be kept strictly confidential."

"I'm not one to gossip."

"I understand. We don't want to cause anybody any problems. My client is simply trying to locate her natural mother for health reasons."

Lorraine lifted the glasses that hung from a chain around her neck and put them on then peered at Rebecca. "She doesn't look too good. What's the matter with her?"

Not deafness! Rebecca wanted to shout. "Nothing fatal," she said instead.

"Could we come in?" Jake requested.

"Is she contagious?"

"No. She's not contagious."

This woman was the widow of a minister? Rebecca could only hope her husband had had more compassion than she did.

Lorraine Griffin held the door open for them to enter.

Again Rebecca couldn't help but make a comparison to Doris. The house and furniture were of a similar age and style, but this place was another world. An arrangement of gold plastic flowers that matched the gold shag carpet sat precisely in the middle of the coffee table which was centered in front of the brown Naugahyde sofa. End tables which matched the coffee table and held matching lamps with the plastic covers still on the shades sat on each side of the sofa. Everything was precise and tidy and perfectly squared. Lorraine Griffin's cupboard would hold no flower garden of riotously mismatched dishes.

"Have a seat. Can I get you something to drink?"

It was the obligatory Texas courtesy, but it lacked the Texas warmth.

"No, thank you," Rebecca replied.

"None for me either. We had a big breakfast."

She and Jake perched on the cold brown sofa while Lorraine sat in the matching chair, her legs crossed primly at her swollen ankles. Though an air conditioner purred continuously in one window keeping the temperature cool, the room seemed stifling with a faintly chemical odor as of pesticide. Surely no bug would dare to intrude on Lorraine Griffin's domain.

"How long did your daughter date Charles Morton?"

Lorraine scowled. "My daughter never had anything to do with that son of Satan. Who told you she did?"

Rebecca's heart went out to Janelle Griffin. Having this woman for a mother couldn't have been easy.

"You know how people gossip," Jake replied.

"I know how people lie."

"Of course," Jake said smoothly. "I realize that, but I have to check out every lead. And I can see how a slick, successful man like Charles Morton could have insinuated himself into the graces of an innocent, unworldly girl like your daughter."

Lorraine sighed, and Rebecca caught a glimpse of sadness that blended with the bitterness. "She was innocent. Sheltered. Her father was a minister of the gospel, you know, and she thought the whole world was like our church. She didn't know about all the wickedness out there."

"That was a hard way for her to find out." Jake's voice was soft, and Rebecca held her breath, wondering if Lorraine would take the bait.

Lorraine compressed her thin lips. "Charles Morton is evil. Of course he wanted to corrupt my daughter. Darkness hates the light and wants to stamp it out so darkness can rule. If somebody doesn't stop him, he's going to spread that dark evil of his over this entire country just like he did—like he tried to do to my Janelle."

Jake nodded and leaned slightly forward, silently encouraging Lorraine. He was good, Rebecca thought. Definitely good at manipulating people—a skill doubtless made easier since he had no personal involvement in any of it.

"He met her at a bake sale," Lorraine continued, "and you could tell right away he was up to no good. Came to our church a few times. I'm surprised God didn't strike him dead when he walked in that holy building. He went to some of the socials we had for our young folks, but Janelle didn't want anything to do with him."

"You sound like you were very proud of your daughter."

"Of course I was."

"I'd love to see a picture of her, if you have one."

Lorraine looked suspiciously from Jake to Rebecca then left the room.

"My mother was tiny," Rebecca whispered. "If Janelle looks like her mother, that lets her out."

Jake nodded. "I know. We'll find out how tall she was."

Lorraine returned with a framed picture and handed it to Jake. Rebecca leaned closer to peer at the family portrait, to search for familiar features.

"That's my husband." Lorraine pointed to a dumpy man a couple of inches shorter than her. Except for having darker hair in the picture, Lorraine hadn't changed much over the years. "And that's Janelle."

The woman standing beside Lorraine was short and slim with dark hair pulled back from her face in a style identical to her mother's. Janelle's features were unremarkable and would have been attractive with a different hair style and a little makeup...and with a smile.

Was it possible this sad, colorless woman had given her life? Even in the picture, which was far from being a close-up, Janelle exuded sadness, loneliness, uncertainty. She would have been easy prey for a man like Charles.

"Some say there was talk of them getting married," Jake said.

Lorraine took back her picture and resumed her seat, her thin lips becoming thinner with tight white lines at the corners. "Times were different then. If a single man came sniffing around a single woman, people assumed he had honorable intentions. Not like now with women crawling into bed with every man they meet."

The older woman's narrowed gaze indicated she suspected Jake and Rebecca of doing exactly that. Rebecca had to suppress an urge to shock the woman, to assure her they hadn't crawled into any bed but had done the deed half-on and half-off an old table in the shed in the park.

She bit her lip and allowed Jake to continue to conduct this part of the investigation.

Jake took a small notebook and pencil out of his pocket. "Who?" he asked.

"Who?" Lorraine repeated.

"Yeah. Who was crawling into bed with who back around 1979? I'd say it's a pretty safe bet Rebecca's parents weren't joined in holy matrimony or they wouldn't have given her up for adoption. If we know who was fooling around with who, that would give us a place to start."

Lorraine Griffin set her family picture on the coffee table and folded her hands primly. "I'm not one to gossip."

"This isn't gossip, Mrs. Griffin. This is a very serious investigation."

It was all the encouragement she needed. "Well, Kay Langley and Murray Johnson were awful thick, holding hands and kissing in public. And Bob Horton and the Wilson girl. Let me see...what was her name?"

Jake dutifully took notes as Lorraine ran through a list that surely included the entire town and a longer time period than 1979.

Finally she concluded. "My memory's not what it used to be. That's all I can come up with right now."

"You've been very helpful. If no one on this list checks out, we'll get back to you and see if you've remembered more."

Lorraine nodded. "I'm sure I will."

Jake stood, and Rebecca followed his lead. She couldn't wait to get out of the stifling, chemical-scented house.

"Thank you very much for all your help, Mrs. Griffin," he said. "And allow me to express my condolences on the death of your daughter. I know it was a long time ago, but wounds like that don't heal."

Lorraine Griffin rose too. "No, they don't. A mother shouldn't outlive her child."

"How did she die?"

Lorraine's eyes narrowed suspiciously. "It was an accident." She waited as if she expected him to contradict her.

"I assumed it must be. She was so young. A car wreck?"

Lorraine's mouth twisted. "No. She was having a hard time sleeping, and that fool doctor, Sam Wilcox, gave her a prescription for drugs. I didn't know about it or I'd have taken it away from her and flushed it down the toilet stool."

She drew herself up and Rebecca felt a moment of sympathy for her. Even this insensitive woman had loved her daughter. Perhaps the loss had hardened her. Perhaps she hadn't always been like that.

"She didn't know how strong those drugs were. She took too many. The doctor said sometimes people woke up in the middle of the night and didn't remember how many they'd already taken and took some more. Janelle must have done that. She went to bed one night and didn't get up the next morning."

She looked at Rebecca, bestowing her full attention for the first time. "Any mother that would give up her child isn't worth looking for. I don't believe you're sick except at heart and finding somebody who'd do that kind of thing isn't going to help you."

"I'll keep that in mind." Even the woman's good advice had a cruel edge to it.

Jake thanked Lorraine Griffin again, and they left.

At the end of the sidewalk, Jake stopped and turned to her. "You want to go pick up some chicken or something and go to the park to eat it? I don't know about you, but after that house, I'm not anxious to be inside anywhere for a while."

"Sure. Sounds good to me." He'd mentioned the park as casually as if yesterday had never happened, as if they'd never made love in the park.

Or even had sex.

***

The day was still comfortable when they reached the park a little after noon, though Jake suspected it would soon be hot and muggy with the humidity from the rain the day before.

He set the sack of fried chicken on the picnic table closest to the shed where he and Rebecca had made love yesterday. Not because he wanted to be as close as possible to the reminder of their encounter but because he needed to desensitize himself to the memory. He needed to associate it with mundane things such as eating fried chicken, talking about the case, watching squirrels play in the trees, anything but that mind-bending episode that replayed itself in vivid detail every time he was near Rebecca or even thought about her.

Pretty much continuously.

She sat across from him in a white sundress that gave the fair skin of her neck and shoulders a creamy glow by contrast. Her slim fingers moved gracefully as she peeled the paper off a straw and stuck it through the plastic lid of her soft drink.

Damn! He'd be hard pressed to find something more mundane than that action yet she seemed to be moving to music...erotic music. Even over the strong smell of fried chicken, he caught her scent—summer flowers along with the essence of the rain-washed grass and trees, all imbedded in his brain as a part of making love with Rebecca.

He jabbed a straw into his own drink, ripped open the sack of food, pulled a drumstick out of one of the boxes and bit into the crispy meat.

Rebecca took out a wing and separated the sections then stared down at it. "That was a waste of time, wasn't it? Talking to Lorraine Griffin. We didn't learn anything new."

Jake shrugged. "We learned that if Janelle Griffin got pregnant, she wouldn't dare keep the baby."

She looked up at him skeptically. "You think that, even after what Lorraine said about women who give up their babies?"

"Maybe that's why she said it. To mislead us."

"I hope not. If that woman is my grandmother, then she's right. I don't want to find her."

"Yeah, that's certainly something to think about."

They ate in silence except for the lyrical chirping of birds and the occasional raucous call of a blue jay. Jake noticed Rebecca was doing more picking at her food than eating it. She munched on a fry, holding it between thumb and index finger while slowly sucking it between her lips and into her mouth. Her gaze was unfocused and he knew she was probably thinking about Lorraine Griffin, but her actions with the fry struck him as intensely sensual. Of course, most things she did struck him as intensely sensual.

They were going to have to find a different motel in a different town tonight, and he was either going to have to see that they got rooms on opposite sides of the place...or one room with a big bed. Avoid it entirely or dive in completely.

"My adoptive grandparents were wonderful people," she said, and Jake made an effort to wrench his thoughts away from his lust. "They're all dead now, but I adored them when I was a little girl. My dad's parents were the more stereotypical, I guess. They lived north of Plano in McKinney, and when I'd go to see them, Grams would do the cookie thing and Gramps would take me fishing. Mom's parents were more like her, always busy, involved with the community, doing volunteer work. They'd take me to Six Flags Amusement Park and the zoo but also to visit people in hospitals and nursing homes."

With her straw, she stirred the crushed ice left from her drink. "And all that time, everybody knew about me, that I wasn't really a part of the family."

"Doesn't sound like it made any difference that you weren't born into it."

"How can I ever know how they'd have treated me if I'd been their real daughter and granddaughter?"

Jake gave an unamused bark of laughter. "Let's hope it wouldn't have been the way somebody— maybe your real parents—are treating you now...a threatening phone call, a snake in the bathtub. I think I'd prefer the homemade cookies, trips to Six Flags and even visits to nursing homes."

She leaned forward, her arms on the rough wood of the tabletop, her hands clasped tightly together. "How did your grandparents treat you?"

This time his burst of laughter was from genuine amusement. "Which ones? The real ones or one of the sets of steps?"

She didn't laugh. "All of them," she replied.

Jake shifted on the bench that had suddenly become hard and uncomfortable. He forced himself to smile. "It's tough to keep them separated, remember which was which. My family tree, especially with the grafted on sections and the sawed off branches, is too complicated."

"Like the way my family tree is turning out." She waited, watching him intently, her chameleon eyes a mixture of the sharp green hues of the leaves overhead and the blue of the sky.

He'd always felt there was little point in recalling the past. It was over and dead and had no bearing on the present. But now it did. Rebecca needed a comparison, and he had all varieties of relationships to give her. He sighed and folded his arms.

"Okay, let me think. Grandparents. One set—I'm pretty sure this was my mom's parents—used to send me really inappropriate gifts. Like one year when I was five or six, I asked for a guitar and they sent an electric one with so many attachments, I didn't have a clue what to do with it. Or when I wanted a set of weights, something small that I could take along when I moved from one place to another, they had a full size home gym delivered."

"They had money," Rebecca guessed.

"Several of the branches had money. Some handled it better than others. I remember one set of grandparents that didn't bring me a lot of gifts but the ones they did bring were neat. Like a baseball and bat. They lived in the country, and I thought it was great fun to go out and pick tomatoes that we'd eat for dinner. They even let me have a go at milking a cow. I got one little stream of milk, and you'd have thought it was pure gold the way I carried on. The way they carried on, for that matter. But they belonged to my dad's second wife, and when he married his third or maybe it was his fourth...anyway, she went ballistic when she found out her husband's son was hanging out with the ex-wife's parents. So we got a divorce and they got custody of the cow." He chuckled at his own humor.

She frowned, a vertical crease marring the smooth skin between her eyebrows. "Why did you laugh? That's not funny."

"You don't see the humor in that? I guess you had to be there."

She still didn't laugh or even smile. In fact, her eyes had gone a soft blue as if with compassion...something he neither needed nor wanted.

220

He leaned forward, covering one of her hands with both of his, turning the compassion back to her where it belonged. "You know how when you exercise really hard, to the point of exhaustion, of physical pain even, you gradually build up muscles. Pretty soon you're much stronger, and the same exercise that used to wear you out and make you ache all over is a breeze. Well, that's the way it is with life. You had a good life. You didn't have to exercise your emotional muscles. Until now. One day you'll wake up and realize that you're stronger, and even somebody like Lorraine Griffin won't be able to cause you so much as a moment's discomfort."

Her gaze flickered over his face then down to their joined hands. Gently she pulled her hand from beneath his and laid it on top. "I'm not sure I believe that or even want to believe it."

Her hand was soft, the fingers long and slim, the skin silky. Like all of her. "When the time comes," he said quietly, "you will. When you wake up with those muscles fully developed, you'll know it, and you'll be glad."

She took her hand away and lifted her soft drink, taking the straw between her lips and sipping the melting ice, then setting it down. "Why did you become a private detective?"

"I didn't like being a cop."

"Oh. Well, why did you become a cop?"

He closed his box of chicken bones and set it on the torn bag. "Control, I guess. It didn't seem like I had much when I was a kid, being shuttled from one place to another at somebody else's whim with a new set of rules every time. When you become a cop, you have one set of rules that you and everybody else have to live by. If they don't, then you can force them to."

"So what didn't you like about it?"

"It didn't work. Nobody wanted to play by the rules. The victims, the perps, they all have problems, and they expect you to solve them. You haul in a kid for doing drugs, and his mother hits the ceiling, the same mother who called you last week to report a prostitute working her neighborhood. Somebody gets killed and you bring in the killer. So the victim's family wants his head while his family screams that he's innocent and they want him released. Nobody's happy. Now I find information for people. They may not like the information I get for them, but I've done what I said I would. The rules are clear-cut. Nobody has any right to be upset. It's just a job, no emotional confusion, nobody expecting things I can't give."

She nodded slowly, the dappled sunlight and shadows gliding over her hair and her face. "I see. But you've warned me from the beginning that I might not like what you find for me. Is that part of your job? The warning?"

"Sometimes."

She studied him in silence for several moments.

A woodpecker beat his rat-a-tat-tat rhythm in a nearby tree, the sound hollow and lonely.

"I'm going back to Dallas tonight," she said abruptly. "Right after we have dinner with Doris."

He blinked twice, scratched an eyebrow that didn't itch and gave himself a few seconds to assimilate her announcement. "You mean for the weekend."

"No, for good. I'm going to get out of your way and let you do the job I hired you to do." She gave a half-hearted, crooked grin. "To quote somebody we all know."

"When did you make that decision?"

"Last night. I decided, as long as we have to move out of the motel, I might as well go back to my condo. You seem to have things under control down here. And talking to Lorraine Griffin confirmed that I don't need to be here. If that woman should turn out to be my grandmother, I'm not sure I want to be around when we make that discovery."

"Well." He picked up a limp fry that had escaped his cleaning efforts and laid it on the torn paper bag. What was the matter with him? This was what he wanted, wasn't it? For her to go away, remove temptation, protect herself from the harsh realities they were bound to uncover...from the harsh reality of getting involved with him.

"Good," he said. "That's a wise choice. I'll call you every night. To keep you updated on the progress."

You'll call her every night to hear her voice.

He wanted to groan aloud at the startling revelation. He'd been so damned careful to protect Rebecca that he'd forgotten to watch out for himself. He'd let her get under his skin, let himself become accustomed to being around her. She'd become a habit of sorts. A damned attractive habit, one that sent his libido into overdrive.

But habits could be broken.

Thank goodness she was leaving. A couple of days and he wouldn't even remember what she looked like. It always happened that way. All those muscles acquired through the years automatically came into play.

He stood, gathering up their trash. "You ready to go?" He wasn't at all sure where they were going. He'd planned to spend the afternoon locating another motel. He supposed he could do that, but Rebecca would be left alone to fend for herself until time for dinner with Doris.

Not that taking care of her was his responsibility.

"If this is going to be our last day together—" He stopped in midsentence. Somehow that hadn't come out the way he'd intended. "If this is going to be the last day you're down here, I'd like to try to talk to Charles again with you along and see how he reacts to your presence. Yank his chain a little. Check out a hunch I've got."

Disgust and fear shadowed her delicate features. He realized her fear came from the possibility that they might discover Charles was her father rather than from physical fear. Accordingly, he recognized and admired the courage it took for her to lift her chin and agree.

"All right," she said. "I'll admit I'd as soon visit the city sewer as see him, but if it's what we need to do, let's go."

"There's no point in taking both cars, and this is probably as good a place as any to leave one of them." A totally logical thing to do so why did he feel guilty and a little excited to be riding in the same car as her?

"Let's take mine," she suggested, "since yours has that broken headlight. You're probably driving on borrowed time as it is. If you run into Farley Gates again, I have no doubt he'll be thrilled to give you another ticket, maybe take you to jail."

"Good idea." Reminding himself that he wasn't some drooling teenager with lustful thoughts of what could happen in a car after dark, he turned and strode toward the automobiles parked a short distance away. "I need to get that headlight fixed, but since I've put it off this long, I might as well wait until I get back to Dallas and get a friend of mine to help me." He should have done it the day after it happened. Surely they had an auto parts store in Edgewater. Even without the proper tools, he could have probably done the job in a couple of hours. But he'd been busy.

And he hadn't wanted to leave Rebecca alone after that threatening phone call.

Or was it just that he hadn't wanted to leave Rebecca?

He reached his car and realized he'd carried their trash with him. Damn! He never got distracted like that. When Rebecca was long gone and out of his hair, he'd be able to focus better.

She was already getting into her car. "Be right back," he told her.

He loped over to the refuse container near the table where they'd eaten and shoved the sack and paper cups inside.

Rebecca started her car and backed out of the parking space, and for a moment he thought she was leaving him. The brief spurt of disappointment that knifed though him was, he assured himself, merely the overreaction of his hormones. Anyway, she wasn't leaving, just moving the car into position.

He jogged back to where she waited, opened the door and slid in then looked out to the dark spot in the area where she'd been parked. "Do you have an oil leak?"

"Not that I know of. This car's only two years old, and I have it checked regularly."

"Probably condensation from your air conditioner." He fastened his seat belt and turned to her. "Are you ready to beard the mayor in his den?"

She didn't look any more ready for that experience than he was ready for her to leave, but they'd both do whatever was necessary.

Chapter 17

Rebecca leafed through the six-month old issue of Newsweek for the third time. Even if the reading material in the reception area of Charles Morton's office had been timely and interesting, she'd have found it difficult to concentrate, especially after they'd been waiting for almost an hour.

Jake, sitting in the molded plastic chair next to her, seemed fascinated with the old magazines, going through each one page by page. He'd warned her before they came in that they might be turned away without seeing Morton or might have to wait a long time before being admitted. The waiting didn't seem to bother him at all.

She supposed that was normal, though. This was only a job to him. It was her life, her future.

And the longer she waited, the more inclined she was to take Jake's advice and walk away, take him off the case, tell him to forget this whole nightmare.

Could it possibly be any worse never to know who her parents were than to have Lorraine Griffin for a grandmother and Charles Morton for a father, people who put a snake in her bathtub and had her evicted from her motel room?

"Bingo!" Jake muttered. He handed her the magazine he was reading, a regional publication.

"Mr. Thornton, Ms. Patterson, His Honor the Mayor will see you now," the receptionist announced.

Rebecca had only a second to glance at the article, a full page picture of Charles Morton smiling beneficently and holding his cowboy hat in one outstretched hand as if about to throw it. A headline on the opposing page read: *Time for a New Face in Congress?*

Jake urged her toward the receptionist who stood holding the door into the mayor's office.

Was Morton planning to run for Congress? She supposed that would be the next step up from mayor. If he was, he certainly wouldn't want an illegitimate daughter appearing on the scene. He'd likely do whatever it took to dissuade her from uncovering old secrets he'd prefer to keep buried. A man in his position would have no problem using his influence to get that daughter evicted from the only motel in town.

Rebecca crossed the threshold into the inner office on legs as shaky as if she'd run five miles.

Morton rose to greet them from behind a huge mahogany desk that dominated the room. The desk held the usual paraphernalia—a gold pen in a holder, papers stacked in boxes, a couple of files, a telephone, and a computer monitor. Plaques adorned the walls and a plant sat in one corner. A large tinted window behind Morton let in the afternoon light without glare. The office could not have been more ordinary, yet Rebecca felt as if she were walking straight into hell.

She clutched Jake's arm for support. Jake was a stranger, someone who'd come briefly into her life and would soon be gone from it. He'd made that very clear by his distance since they'd made love and by his lack of response to her announcement that she'd be leaving. But she had to have something to hold onto while she faced the possibility that the man smiling and offering to shake hands with her, the man who made her skin crawl could be the man who'd created her and regretted that accidental creation ever since.

Jake shook hands with him, but when Morton offered his hand to her, she could only stare at the broad fingers, the wide palm with no calluses, no signs of labor. An image flashed before her, the image of her father's hand—of Jerry Patterson's hand—with calluses from the hard work of maintaining a home and restaurant, with the puckered scar on one thumb from a grease spill when he'd been cooking, a white scar on the other from the time a knife slipped while he was slicing a roast. Those same hands had been gentle when they'd applied a bandage to her skinned knee or held her and stroked her hair when she cried.

A lump started in her throat then changed to bile and she felt certain that if she touched Charles, she would vomit.

He changed the outstretched hand into a motion toward the two burgundy leather chairs in front of his desk. "Have a seat. Sorry to keep you folks waiting so long. Being a public servant keeps you busy."

Reluctantly Rebecca let go of Jake's arm and sat gingerly on the edge of one of the chairs. Her revulsion to the inanimate object was, she knew, unwarranted, but the idea of sitting back in the chair was as abhorrent to her as shaking Charles' hand.

"What can I do for you folks today?" Morton asked, folding his uncalloused hands on the polished surface of the desk. Rebecca found herself examining her own hands, searching, against her will, for any resemblance.

"We thought we'd drop in before we left town," Jake said.

"Leaving town, are you? Well, I hope you enjoyed your stay."

Charles Morton is evil. Lorraine Griffin's words came back to her as the man sat before them, smiling and lying.

"It's been very educational," Jake said smoothly.

He was right. She had no place here. He was able to carry on a conversation with Morton, to do his job while she sat in silent shock.

"But, you know," Jake continued, "the damnedest thing happened. We've been kicked out of our rooms at the motel. Seems the whole place suddenly got booked up."

"Is that right?" Charles made no effort to sound or look surprised. "Well, once in a while that happens. Wilbur would go broke if he didn't have a full house every now and then. Probably a high school reunion or something."

"Probably. We thought you might be able to recommend a motel close to Edgewater. Something in a town twenty or thirty minutes away. Driving distance."

Charles' jaw muscles tightened, and his eyes hardened to chips of marble, the light blue color tinted with gray as if dirty. He bared his teeth in an imitation smile. "Don't know of any place like that until you get up close to Dallas. I have to say, I'm a little surprised that you folks are still digging around down here. I'd think by now you'd have realized you've come to the wrong place."

"We had begun to wonder, but then we talked to Lorraine Griffin."

Rebecca stole a glance at Jake as he dropped that potential bomb. He sat comfortably back, long, denim-clad legs stretched out in front of him, boots crossed, hands draped casually over the arms of the chair. His expression betrayed no hint of strain, concern or accusation. He might have been having a friendly chat. The detachment that kept her at arm's length served him well in his chosen profession.

"Lorraine Griffin is a very disturbed woman," Charles said coldly. "She lost her only daughter several years ago, and she never got over it. Of course, she always was kind of a fanatic. Her husband was the preacher at one of those extremist churches."

"I understand you were friendly with her daughter at one time."

Charles' knuckles whitened as he clenched his fingers more tightly about each other. Still his phony smile never wavered. "Of course I was friendly to her. I'm friendly to everybody. I'm a friendly guy."

231

"But you don't get engaged to everybody, do you?"

A sheen of perspiration glistened on Charles' upper lip. "I was never engaged to Janelle. She was a very sheltered, shy woman. Between the fact that she wasn't attractive and the strict way her parents raised her, she didn't get out much. Didn't date at all. Could be she took my friendliness the wrong way. If she ever told anybody we were engaged, I'm afraid that was just the fantasy of a lonely woman."

"I see."

Silence crowded around them as neither man spoke. The plush burgundy carpet beneath their feet swallowed even the sounds of breathing.

Rebecca knew what Jake was doing. It was a technique she'd often used in working with people. Refrain from speaking, and in the ensuing uncomfortable silence the other person would frequently say things he hadn't intended to say.

But this time Jake was wrong. Charles was proficient at his act. He was nervous but he wasn't going to say anything unguarded. He rose from his chair. "I hate to rush our little visit, but I do have another appointment. If there's nothing else I can help you folks with...?"

Jake stood and again shook Charles' hand. "You've been more help than you know."

Rebecca rose, and Jake wrapped one arm about her, supporting her. He propelled her toward the door, but before they could escape into fresh air, he stopped and turned back to Charles.

"Oh, by the way, good luck with your plans to run for Congress."

Charles hesitated only an instant before replying. "Thank you."

"Keep me in mind if you need a private investigator when campaign time gets here. You know, somebody to dig into the past of your opponent, haul out all his dirty little secrets, like they always do in those campaigns."

Blood suffused Charles' face. This time he couldn't hide his discomfort. His voice, however, was still smooth. "I'll be sure and do that."

Jake kept his arm about her all the way outside. If he hadn't, she wasn't sure she would have been able to stand.

"Breathe," he ordered when they stepped onto the sidewalk as the glass doors of the small building swung shut behind them, separating them from Charles. "Take a deep breath and don't you dare pass out on me."

"I'm fine," she said as firmly as she could.

He opened the passenger door of her car. "Get in. I'll drive."

She didn't argue. She certainly wasn't going to pass out, but so many images were swirling through her mind, she wasn't sure she could focus on driving.

Jake backed out of the parking spot, looked at where they'd been and frowned. "You definitely need to get your oil checked. There's another spot like the one at the park."

"I'll check the oil before I start back to Dallas." An oil leak was the least of her problems right then.

"Do you watch your gauges to be sure your car isn't overheating? Maybe I ought to check to see if that's antifreeze you're losing."

"No. Just drive. If you want me to breathe again, get away from this place. Anyway, that spot could be from the person who parked there before me."

With one last glance at the parking space, Jake put the car into gear and drove down the street.

"Where are we going?" she asked.

"We don't have a lot of options. It's either the park, the diner or we could run by Doris Jordan's. Get there a little early."

"Yes. Let's go to Doris' house." That was the only place she could think of at the moment that she really wanted to be.

***

The small white house with its medley of bright flowers belonged to a woman Rebecca hadn't known a week ago and would probably never see again after today, but as she and Jake drove up, she felt as if she'd come home.

Doris greeted them as though they were welcome guests, as though they hadn't arrived two hours early. "I was hoping we'd have some extra time to visit," she said graciously. "Would you like to sit out here? It's a bit warm inside, but the shade from the trees keeps it cool on the porch all day. Have a seat and I'll go get some iced tea."

The swing, hidden by the trellis of morning glory vines on one side of the porch, lured Rebecca with its seclusion and its promise of soothing, gentle motion. She took one side and Jake, after a moment's hesitation, took the other, beside her but not quite touching. No surprise there.

"You knew Morton was planning to run for Congress," she said, finally able to discuss the visit to his office now that she was in the safety of Doris' home. "That's what you were looking for in all those magazines."

"I didn't know. I suspected from something Lorraine Griffin said. *If somebody doesn't stop him, he's going to spread that dark evil of his over this entire country.*"

"I just thought she was being rhetorical."

"That was a possibility, but Morton has moved up from being a cop to being mayor. He strikes me as the type who'd like to go all the way to the top."

"That's a scary thought."

"Yeah, it is."

Doris came out with a tray holding tall glasses of amber tea.

Rebecca took a long sip of hers. The cool, clean liquid dissolved the lingering taste of slimy disgust that Morton had left with her. The fresh air, cooled by the shade of thousands of leaves, evaporated from her skin the last traces of the refrigerated, foul air of Morton's office.

"Did you know Charles Morton plans to run for Congress?" Jake asked.

Doris leaned back in one of the cushioned, wrought iron chairs. "There's been talk about it. He's a very ambitious man. If he'd had the charisma to match that ambition, he'd have been out of here and in Washington D.C. long ago."

"So you don't think he'll win the election?"

"I didn't say that. Charles may not have charisma, but he does manage to garner influence. I certainly won't vote for him. However, I imagine a lot of people will."

"You knew him when he was young," Rebecca said. "Do you—" She bit her lip then forced herself to continue. "Do you think I look like him?"

Doris set her glass of tea carefully on the porch beside her and folded her hands in her lap, her composure unbroken. "I gathered from all your questions about him yesterday that you were considering him as a possibility for your father. After you all left, I thought about it, about Janelle Griffin and him."

"An illegitimate daughter suddenly appearing out of nowhere, a former lover who committed suicide, those are things that wouldn't help his chances in a political race."

"No, they wouldn't." Doris studied her thoughtfully. "There's a sadness in your eyes that reminds me of Janelle."

The shade seemed to darken around them, and the image of Doris became a little fuzzy. Rebecca realized she was holding her breath. She made herself breathe deeply, bring the world back into focus.

Doris' expression softened, and she smiled. "But that doesn't mean anything. You also have a stubborn set to your jaw that reminds me of my daughter-in-law, Mary, and eyes the same color as Mabel Atherton, my best friend in grade school—we certainly know she wasn't your mother—and a nose that's straight like my Ben's was and hair like—" She frowned then shrugged. "The good news, for what it's worth, is that I don't see any of Charles' features in your face. But I don't like him and I do like you, so that may cloud my vision. Is it really so important to discover your heritage when you may be upset with your findings?"

"That's what I keep telling her," Jake said.

Rebecca drew a finger around the rim of her glass. "I've been thinking about that. In any event, I'm getting out of the middle of it. After dinner, I'll be heading back to Dallas."

Rebecca thought Doris looked disappointed but maybe she saw what she wanted to see in the older woman's expression. "Well, I feel privileged to be included in your last evening here. Any particular reason you decided to leave?"

"We got kicked out of our motel rooms. It seemed easier to go back to my condo rather than try to find a new place to stay." It was an adequate explanation, never mind that *easier* encompassed a world of meanings.

Doris scowled, a vertical line creasing her forehead between her brows. "Why would Wilbur kick you out? He gets so little business, he usually tolerates anything from his customers short of throwing the television sets in the swimming pool or not paying their bills."

Jake gave a short bark of laughter. "The reason he gave us was that he was all booked up for the next month."

"All booked up? Wilbur? Not in my lifetime!" Doris' gaze flickered from Jake to Rebecca. She lifted her glass of tea from the porch, sipped then tapped one side with an index finger. It was the first nervous or impatient gesture Rebecca had ever seen her make. "Then you'll both stay with me for as long as you want," she said decisively. "I have a guest room, and Edgar's office has a long sofa he used to nap on. Or you can both share the guest room if you like. I may be old, but I haven't forgotten what it was like to be young."

The almost imperceptible rocking of the swing increased. Rebecca wasn't sure if it was from her nervous movements or from Jake's. How on earth did everybody in town know they'd been intimate? Did it show on their faces? Was the old shed equipped with a video camera?

"We appreciate the offer," Jake said smoothly, "but we couldn't impose on you like that. Anyway, I've got to get back to Dallas and take care of some things, like getting that broken headlight repaired."

Jake was right, but Rebecca found herself desperately wanting to stay in Doris' house, to spend the night in a bed that probably had a floral spread, then wake in the morning to have coffee in Doris' sunlit kitchen from one of her flower garden cups, to immerse herself in the peaceful spirit Doris had found.

Not rational, she knew. She had to find her own peaceful spirit.

"You wouldn't be imposing at all," Doris said. "I'd love to have the company. I'll be upset if you refuse. If your car has a broken headlight, Jake, you shouldn't drive it tonight. You can stay here, get a good night's sleep, then tomorrow you can go back to Dallas or do whatever you need to do." She turned to look out to Rebecca's Volvo parked in the street. "Do you both have your luggage here?"

Jake shifted in the swing. "Well, uh, Rebecca's is, but mine's in my car at the park."

"Then why don't you get Rebecca's luggage now, and we can get yours after dinner."

He gave Rebecca a helpless look. She squelched a sudden urge to laugh. This man who maintained control of every situation, whether sparring with Charles Morton, extracting information from Lorraine Griffin, or making love with her, was out of his depth with the gentle Doris Jordan.

"My bag's in the trunk," she told him. "I believe you still have the keys."

Jake left the porch, and Doris leaned forward to pat Rebecca's hand. "Being a mother is a big responsibility. I remember when I brought Ben home from the hospital. That was absolutely the most terrifying experience of my life. I had no idea how I was ever going to take care of that baby by myself. If my mother hadn't been there with me, I might have been so terrified, I'd have refused to take him until he got a little bigger. Because your mother gave you up for adoption doesn't mean she didn't love you. It could mean she loved you enough to want somebody to take care of you at a time when she didn't think she'd be able to."

"What are you trying to say?" Had Doris figured out who her mother was?

"I'm not trying to say anything other than what I just said."

Jake returned with her suitcase, and Doris took them inside to show them the guest room. Rebecca smiled when she saw the bed spread and matching curtains with a soft floral print. Like the living room, the furniture, including a wooden bed frame with a tall, carved headboard, a small dresser and large chest of drawers, was old but well cared for. Pictures, music boxes and various paraphernalia were scattered about on every surface. It was part of Doris' home, part of Doris.

"This was Ben's room," Doris said. "I've changed the decorating scheme, of course. He had pictures of baseball players that he'd torn out of magazines and taped all over the walls, a carpet of dirty clothes on the hardwood floor, and he would never permit a spread on his bed. That might have meant he'd have to make it up occasionally. I'm sure you'll be quite comfortable in here. The bathroom is down the hall."

"Thank you. I'll just freshen up and be right out."

Jake and Doris left, and Rebecca stood for several moments absorbing the stability, the history of the room, of the entire house. The stability and history didn't belong to her, of course, but it was nice to borrow the feeling for a little while.

In a way it reminded her of the room she'd grown up in. Not that the appearance was the same or the feeling of history, but she had known stability, a sense of belonging...until that had all been yanked out from under her.

She grabbed her makeup bag and went down the hall to the bathroom.

***

Jake sat in the porch swing waiting for Rebecca to return. He couldn't believe he'd given in to Doris' request that they stay in her house. He wouldn't sleep a wink, wouldn't be comfortable in a place not his own whether by dint of ownership or renting a motel room.

He wasn't really sure why he'd given in so easily. Because Doris has been so insistent? Because he knew Rebecca wanted to stay there?

Or because he didn't want Rebecca to return to Dallas?

That couldn't be it. He had better sense than that. No matter how much he wanted her, he knew, when he consulted his rational mind and not his loins, that it was time for her to go. Past time.

Doris paused in her recitation of the various restaurants in the vicinity and turned to look toward the street. Her fact lit up suddenly, and she rose. "Mary! I'm so glad you dropped by."

"This book you've been wanting to read came in today so I thought I'd bring it over."

Mary? The woman from the library? Jake couldn't see her for the trellis of morning glory vines, but she certainly didn't sound the same. This woman's voice was soft and warm, a little tired but not low and hard.

241

"Why, thank you. You can stay a while, can't you? I'll get you a glass of tea."

"Do you have company? I saw the car in front."

"I do, but it's some people I'd like you to meet. Perhaps you could even join us for dinner."

Jake stood to greet Mary. She stepped onto the porch as the door behind him opened. Rebecca must be coming back out. Mary froze, eyes widening in horror, pupils shrinking to pinpoints, the blood draining from her face leaving her fair skin chalk white.

"Rebecca, you're just in time to meet my daughter-in-law," Doris said as if she hadn't noticed the odd reaction. "Mary Jordan, this is Rebecca Patterson and Jake Thornton. They're going to be my houseguests for a few days."

Before his eyes the caring daughter-in-law became the hard stranger they'd met in the library. Rebecca was right. She did have a haunted look about her.

But she wasn't normally a cold woman. Seeing Rebecca had sent her into shock. She knew something about Rebecca, and whatever it was, it upset her...a lot.

Rebecca stepped forward stiffly and offered her hand to Mary Jordan. "Nice to meet you, Mary," she said.

Mary stared at the outstretched hand as if it were covered in blood or horribly disfigured.

Then she lifted her chin, took the proffered hand and shook it once, briefly, before dropping it. "I'm pleased to meet you, Ms. Patterson." She nodded in

Jake's direction. "And you, Mr. Thornton. Doris, thank you for inviting me to stay, but I have plans. And I'm late. If you'll excuse me, I have to run."

"Of course. Perhaps another time." Doris was also watching Mary intently.

Mary turned and walked to her car, a small, rigid figure hurrying away.

"That woman hates me," Rebecca said softly when Mary had driven away.

Doris stared after the car. "That isn't like Mary. I actually thought—"

"What?" Jake demanded. "What did you think?" He was pretty sure he knew what Doris had thought and why she'd invited Rebecca and him to stay with her, but he asked anyway.

Doris smiled. "I thought we'd all get along famously, but apparently I was wrong. I'm getting quite hungry. I believe I'll go freshen up and then we can leave for the restaurant."

"While you're doing that, I think we should get my car and bring it over here," Jake said. "I really don't like the idea of driving it after dark with that broken headlight. If I was leaving town, it'd probably be all right, but I think Farley Gates would like nothing better than to give me another ticket if he catches me. He'd probably take great delight in running me in for being a repeat offender."

Doris smiled at Jake's absurdity. "Farley does get a little carried away sometimes. I'm sure I'll be ready by the time you get back." She disappeared into the house, and he and Rebecca walked down the sidewalk to the street.

"She thought Mary was my mother, didn't she?" Rebecca asked. "She thought Mary had a baby and gave it up because she was scared she couldn't raise it after her husband died. She thought I was her granddaughter."

He nodded. "I suspect that's what she thought."

He opened her car door for her to get in. She turned to him, pushing the hair back from her face and gazing directly into his eyes as if forcing both of them to confront what had just happened.

"Doris may be my grandmother, but Mary isn't my mother," she said. "The way Mary looked at me today, the way she acted at the library, Doris' comments about her reaction to Ben's death, they all fit your theory of Ben Jordan leaving behind a pregnant girlfriend. Mary learned about his indiscretion and became so upset she couldn't even attend Ben's funeral. Now, every time she sees me, she's faced with the reality of her husband's infidelity. She does hate me."

"It's possible, but we don't know that for sure."

Rebecca sighed, sliding into the front seat as if exhausted, and he realized how much it had cost her to confront Mary, to force the woman to acknowledge her and shake her hand. "We know that a woman I never met before yesterday hates me. She must have a reason."

"Worst case scenario, Doris would be your grandmother. Wouldn't you rather have her son for a father than Charles Morton?"

She managed a weak smile. "Yes, I definitely would."

244

They drove to the park and Jake got his car. As he pulled away with Rebecca following, Jake thought he saw Farley Gates on a side street in a nondescript black car.

You're getting paranoid, he told himself. Anyway, if it had been Gates, he'd probably have chased Jake down and written him a ticket...or worse. He could see Farley whacking himself in the eye with his stick just so he could swear that Jake had done it, providing him with an excuse to take him to jail for assaulting an officer.

The absurd thought brought a wry grin.

Of course, the whole situation in this town was absurd. He'd seen a lot of rude, callous people in his time including some who made it very clear they never wanted to meet the children they'd given up for adoption. But none of them had played with snakes or smashed out headlights or stolen evidence.

Rebecca's bonding with Doris Jordan was a very good thing whether or not Ben was her father. Doris was a caring, lonely woman. She'd cared about Rebecca from their first meeting even before she'd apparently spotted some resemblance to Ben and decided Rebecca could be her granddaughter. Maybe Rebecca would be satisfied with having a friendship with Doris. They could adopt each other as surrogate family, and Rebecca could give up her search for parents who made it clearer every day that they didn't want her.

Then he'd be off the case and back to Dallas and his life.

And in no time at all he'd forget about Rebecca and the way she'd felt in his arms, the way she could look so vulnerable one minute and strong the next. He'd even forget the twinge of...what? sadness? despair? loneliness?...that shot through him every time he thought of never seeing her again.

    ***

Following Jake back to Doris' house, Rebecca tried to focus on the evening ahead and forget about Mary Jordan. She'd been looking forward to dinner with Doris and, she had to admit, with Jake. After that she'd be spending the night in Doris' home, the first place where she'd felt comfortable in a long time.

But the image of Doris' daughter-in-law kept intruding. Mary had sounded glad to see Doris, but as soon as Rebecca appeared, her gaze had turned cold. No, not even cold. Blank. A curtain had fallen, cutting her off totally from Rebecca. When Rebecca had forced her to shake hands, the woman had dropped her hand as if she'd grasped a dead fish.

She'd made the right decision to go back home, to remove herself from direct contact with people like Mary Jordan and Charles Morton. She'd begun this quest searching for an identity, the place in the universe where she fit, and all she'd found so far was where she didn't fit.

Ahead of her, Jake slowed to turn the corner onto Doris' street. Rebecca attempted to follow suit, pushing gently on her brake pedal, then harder as her speed didn't abate. But no matter how hard she pushed, she got no results. Her car wasn't slowing.

She darted a quick glance to the dash and saw a red light blinking *Check Brakes, Check Brakes*. How long had it been blinking? Why hadn't she paid more attention?

Jake pulled up a little past Doris' house, leaving room for her...and she saw another of those spots of oil where she'd parked earlier.

Oil or brake fluid.

She slammed on her brakes, pumping desperately, pulling on the emergency brake...and slammed into the back of Jake's vehicle.

She scrambled out, her hands shaking and her heart pounding. Jake met her to survey the damage. "Jake, I'm sorry! My brakes went out!"

He wrapped an arm about her waist. "It's okay. Our bumpers locked, that's all. No real damage done. Thank goodness you weren't going very fast. What happened? When I drove your car earlier, the brakes were okay. Well, maybe a little spongy, but I just thought I wasn't used to your car."

She shook her head. "When we turned the corner up there, I noticed it didn't seem to slow the way it should and the brake light was blinking. Then—" She spread her hands helplessly. "I hit the brake pedal and nothing happened! Those spots it's been leaving must be brake fluid, not oil."

He nodded slowly. "You could have a small leak in one of the lines. Every time you used the brakes, you pushed out a little of the fluid until it was all gone. That would explain the spots when you parked."

"Damn! Why didn't they notice something like that the last time I had my car serviced?"

"It could be too small to find unless you're looking for it. Anyway, it probably just happened or you'd have lost your brakes on the drive down here."

"Just happened? How does a hole in my brake lines just happen?"

She looked at him. His dark blue eyes seemed gray in the shade from the tree overhead. He took his arms from about her, rubbed the back of his head and blew out a long sigh.

Surely he wasn't going to say what she thought he was.

"I'm no mechanic. There are probably a hundred ways it could have just happened. But taking into account everything else that's been going on, I think we need to consider the possibility that somebody tampered with your brakes last night, maybe cut a tiny slit in one of the lines, somebody who thought you'd be leaving the motel and going out on the highway before the problem was discovered."

"Somebody's trying to kill me?"

"Not necessarily. Even if this was deliberate— and we don't know that it was—it could be that somebody's trying to scare you. That would fit with everything else."

"Scare me? This isn't like the snake. If we'd left early this morning to find a new motel, the way we logically would have, I'd have been on the highway when this happened, probably going about seventy miles an hour. This could have killed me, couldn't it?"

"Yeah. It could have."

Her gaze locked with his as she tried to absorb the reality that somebody hated her so badly, that person actually wanted her dead. Or, at best, didn't care if his...or her...attempts to frighten her resulted in her death. Jake stared back, his expression grim, his eyes hard as if he would force her to accept that frightening truth.

"You warned me they might not want me." Rebecca's words came out in a whisper. She had no energy to speak louder. "You didn't warn me they might…" She swallowed, unable to continue.

His expression softened.

"What happened?"

Rebecca whirled around to see that Doris had come down the walk to join them.

"My brakes went out," she said dully.

Doris folded her arms in a self-protective, hugging gesture. As she looked from the cars to Rebecca then to Jake, Rebecca saw something she couldn't identify on Doris' face, in her eyes.

"Is your car drivable, Jake?" she asked.

"Yeah, Rebecca wasn't going fast enough to hurt it."

"Then you both need to get in that car and go back to Dallas tonight. Right now. You can send a tow truck for Rebecca's car tomorrow. I'm sorry, but you can't stay with me. I've brought Rebecca's luggage down." She gestured to the bags sitting behind her. "You must leave now."

The sting hit Rebecca with as much physical force as a slap in the face.

Doris turned and walked back to her house. She'd lost her relaxed posture. Now her walk reminded Rebecca of Mary Jordan's...rigid, stiff, unbending.

"What the hell?" Jake exclaimed.

Rebecca couldn't answer. If she opened her mouth, if she tried to speak, she'd burst into tears.

Doris had offered her kindness and caring and a place in her life then snatched it away.

It was eerily similar to discovering she was adopted.

Except her parents hadn't deliberately kicked her into the dark void of a black hole.

Doris Jordan had.

Chapter 18

November 5, 1979, Edgewater, Texas

Mary closed the door behind Clyde.

He had driven her by her bank, and she'd closed out Ben's and her account, taking the balance in cash. Then he'd brought her home, lingering on the porch, expressing his sympathy and urging her to let him know if he could do anything. She'd had to fight the urge to confess everything to him, beg for his help.

But she'd reminded herself not only that she could trust no one, but that if she did trust him, he might meet the same fate as Ben. She was on her own. It was the only way she could hope to get through this and save her baby.

She looked around her at the home she hadn't seen since the day Charles and Clyde had come to tell her about Ben. The sight of the familiar room, the blue sofa she and Ben had discovered in his parents' attic, the lamp they'd both fallen in love with the minute they saw it in the store...the home they'd created together...brought hot tears to her eyes. For a moment she wavered. For a moment she wasn't sure she had the strength to carry on.

Ben was gone. He wasn't coming back. He'd never walk through that door again, never sit on that sofa again, never wrap his big arms around her and hold her again.

Something fluttered beneath her breast like butterfly wings.

Her baby? Movement this soon?

It reminded her why she had to go on, why she couldn't even stop to cry.

She turned her back on the living room, ran upstairs to Ben's and her bedroom and yanked their big suitcase out of the closet.

For a moment she stood in the middle of the room with the suitcase open on the bed, paralyzed with thoughts of so much to do, where to start, what she ought to take with her.

She forced herself into action. Going by the bank, chatting with Clyde at the door, had cost her precious minutes. If she forgot something she needed, she'd have to replace it later or do without it.

Her purse still sat on the nightstand where she'd left it two weeks ago. That was a necessity. It had her driver's license.

Haphazardly she tossed clothes and toiletries into the suitcase, being certain to add the blue dress her mother-in-law had given her as a birthday gift. The dress, from Doris Jordan's shop, was the nicest one she owned, but, more importantly, Ben's mother, a woman she adored, had given it to her.

Finally she put in her wedding picture from the nightstand beside the bed.

With one last glance around the room where she and Ben had made wonderful love, where she'd thought they'd make love when they were old and wrinkled, she closed the suitcase and dragged it downstairs.

On the front porch she turned back for one last look, seeing the house the way she and Ben had seen it for the first time when they'd been full of love and hopes and dreams.

Lifting her chin, she turned away. If she let it, the sorrow would weigh her down, immobilize her, and she'd be lost. She locked the sorrow into a separate compartment of her heart, leaving the rest of her empty except for the fear that Charles would catch her.

She shoved the bag into the back seat of her car and drove away, telling herself she wouldn't look back ever again.

But she did. Every few seconds she checked her rearview mirror to see if Charles was following her.

What she saw was Ben's and her house receding into the past.

The sorrow threatened to escape, but a car turned the corner behind her and fear replaced everything until she saw that the driver wasn't Charles.

She made it to the edge of town and started to pull onto the highway.

No, that wasn't a good idea. That would be the first place he'd look for her. She'd take the old highway north.

She hesitated.

She'd gone south before when she ran to Sharon's place. Would he expect her to go north this time? Would he expect her to avoid the highway?

Panic gripped her with its jagged teeth. How could she possibly make the right decision when she didn't know how Charles would think?

She shook her head, clenched her jaw and shoved aside the panic. She could only make the best possible choice and go, drive as fast as legally permissible, focus on getting away.

North on the old highway.

***

Weaving through back roads, the three hour trip to Dallas took five. She reached the outskirts of the city and knew she had to get on the highway then decide at the downtown intersection whether to take Highway 30 east or west or Highway 75 north. Her entire trip so far had been consumed with driving to evade Charles, taking the least obvious route, checking the rearview mirror constantly, controlling her fear at every car that passed, keeping her runaway emotions in check and thinking logically. Now she would have another decision to make.

As she approached downtown Dallas, traffic became heavier. Rush hour. She'd heard talk about it on the Dallas radio stations but had never experienced it.

Cars—hundreds of cars—zipped past her, around her, pinning her in her lane. It was impossible to check all the drivers, to watch for Charles. Avoiding an accident became her primary concern as the bumper-to-bumper traffic slowed but still moved fast enough that, if anyone made a mistake, dozens of cars would crash into each other.

When she realized she had passed downtown Dallas without having a chance to choose an east or west route but had been funneled by the flow of traffic onto 75 north, she accepted that as her destination. It was as good a way to choose as any.

The traffic slowed to a maddening crawl. She consoled herself with the thought that Charles wouldn't be able to wedge his car into the solid wall of automobiles and catch her even if he knew exactly where she was. For the moment she was safe, but frustration at the delay kept her on edge.

The evening was warm, and she was perspiring from heat and anxiety. She rolled down her window and a popular song drifted from the radio in the car next to her. Then a traffic report.

"...five car pile-up on Central Expressway just north of the Walnut Hill exit has traffic backed up all the way from downtown. Expect about an hour delay as crews work to clean up the accidents."

Mary wanted to scream. Though she hadn't seen any signs, she'd be willing to bet Highway 75 was more commonly known as Central Expressway. She had to get off. She'd lost too much time already.

Almost thirty minutes later she finally made it off at Mockingbird Lane. All she had to do was continue northward, winding her way through the city, until she made it to the northern outskirts, then get back on the highway and head for...

Well, somewhere north. Oklahoma City, Tulsa, Kansas City. Even New York City was somewhere north.

***

Plano Diner, Serving Plain Ole Good Food

Mary almost burst into tears when she saw the sign two hours later. It was only advertising. She knew that. But the hominess of it lured her into the parking lot.

Since leaving the highway, she'd roamed through the Dallas area, becoming hopelessly lost. Streets were not straight. They changed names, dead ended, circled back on themselves, and with every wrong turn, the nightmare thickened around her. Panic beat at her with leathery bat wings. She felt trapped, an animal in a cage running in circles, unable to escape the hunter who could appear at any moment.

Fearful that someone might remember her or her license plate if she stopped to ask directions, she'd tried to make her own way. Finally she'd purchased a city map when she filled up with gas and was slowly, determinedly, making her way back to the highway. Plano was a suburb north of Dallas, so at least she was on the right track.

With her car door half open, she hesitated in the parking lot of the Plano Diner, afraid to stay and afraid to go.

Since she'd awakened in the back room of a strange woman's house, barely avoiding an unwanted abortion, faced with the news of her husband's death, her world had become shrouded in a perpetual fog of sorrow, fear and frustration. If not for the precious life she carried, she'd have given up long ago. If Charles wanted to kill her and only her, she'd have let him rather than continue on this way...rather than continue on without Ben.

But she had to continue. She had to go in the diner and eat. She hadn't had anything since breakfast at Sharon's. She wasn't hungry, but her baby would need the nourishment.

She got out of her car and headed for the diner, her gaze scanning every vehicle, every person. Logically she knew Charles couldn't possibly have followed her there. But logic and terror were incompatible companions.

The place was crowded so she'd be harder to remember if Charles came by looking for her after she left. And, paranoid as that sounded, she was unable to convince herself that it wasn't a very real possibility.

She slid into a booth in the back that allowed her a view of the door.

A waitress brought over a menu. She ordered the fried chicken then went back to studying every person who came in.

A woman strode purposefully toward her, blocking her view, and Mary froze. The woman, of medium height and weight, somehow projected an image of strength. Mary's heart pounded so hard and fast she expected it to push right out of her chest.

They made eye contact. The woman smiled, her brown eyes shining with kindness, then she looked away and slid into next booth over, and Mary released the breath she'd been holding.

"All right, Dorothy," she heard the woman say briskly, "you have George call this number and ask for Harry Pemberton. I just talked to him, and he said he can use a worker like your husband."

"Brenda, you're wonderful. I don't know how I can ever thank you."

"Seeing that happy look back on your face is enough. We've got pecan pie tonight, and I'm going to send over a piece for you and one to take home to George."

Mary lifted a shaky hand to her face. She had to get a grip on herself. Being careful was a necessity, but she couldn't go on being terrified of everything and everybody.

Her hand on her cheek was sticky with perspiration and grime from the steering wheel. The first thing she needed to do was find the bathroom, wash her hands, splash cold water on her face and try to think.

She rose from the booth, and the fog of fear thickened, turned black, swirled around her and completely enveloped her, pulling her into its inky depths.

***

Mary's head ached as she swam up from the bottom of a dark, viscous lake.

"I think she's coming around."

She bolted upright, panic knifing through her. Where was she? Had Charles brought her to another abortionist? She clutched her stomach, fighting the black, dizzying fog that tried to overwhelm her again.

"My baby! What did you do to my baby?"

A tall man grabbed her shoulder, and she flailed against him. "Easy! Easy! I'm a doctor. You're okay. You just fainted."

"My baby!" she shrieked, forcing her blurred mind and eyes to focus, to assess the situation...to figure out if it was too late.

The purposeful woman with kind brown eyes stepped forward and clutched Mary's hand. Mary felt peace flow from her. For an instant she was reminded of her mother-in-law, a woman she loved as much as if she'd been her own mother. Doris could soothe her with a touch.

But Doris was part of the past, someone she'd never see again. This woman was a stranger and not to be trusted.

"I'm Brenda Patterson," the stranger said, smiling and holding tightly to her hand. "The pudgy guy on your left is my husband, Jerry, and the tall character you tried to assault is a friend, Doctor Fred Wingfield. Jerry and I own this no-star restaurant where you passed out before you even ate any of the food. Most of our customers at least have one bite before it affects them that way."

Mary drew in a deep breath and looked around at the small room, apparently used as an office. It contained the sofa on which she lay, a filing cabinet and a desk littered with stacks of paper that almost hid a typewriter. The three people crowded around her, their faces etched with concern. None of them meant her any harm. They didn't even know who she was.

She longed to lie back on the sofa and rest, to take a break from the nightmare until she could gather the energy to fight again. To run again.

"You came in alone," Brenda said softly when she didn't respond. "You didn't have your baby with you."

Mary felt herself smiling as the horrible tension flowed away from her and her fingers traced the soft roundness of her stomach. *No,* she thought. *I didn't come in alone. I had my baby with me, and she's still here.*

Brenda's alert gaze dropped to the movement then returned to Mary's face. "Okay, guys," she said, briskly, "let's give the lady a little breathing room. Fred, I really appreciate your help. Sorry to interrupt your dinner. Tell Hazel to bring you dinner and a piece of pie, on the house. Jerry, honey, would you check on this lady's order—"

"I didn't order."

"Fried chicken and mashed potatoes okay?" Mary nodded. "Bring her a fried chicken dinner and a glass of milk."

"Sure, babe." He gave Mary's shoulder a comforting squeeze. "I hope you like milk because if Brenda's decided you need milk, you're gonna have milk!"

In the safe atmosphere, surrounded by the comfortable bantering of the Pattersons, Mary's eyes filled with the tears she'd held at bay for so long. "I love milk," she said.

The men left, closing the door behind them, and Brenda sat on the sofa beside her. "Got the little one tucked away, huh? When's it due?"

Don't tell! Don't admit it! Nobody can know! It's the only way to be safe!

"Mid-May," she heard herself say, then a sound that was somewhere between a laugh of joy and a sob of relief erupted from her throat, and she burst into unrestrained tears.

Brenda pulled Mary's head onto her competent shoulder and stroked her hair. Mary allowed herself a few moments of release, then bit back her sobs and pushed her hair off her face. "I'm sorry," she mumbled.

Brenda handed her a tissue. "For what? Everybody needs a good cry now and then."

Jerry appeared with Mary's purse and a tray of fried chicken, hot rolls, mashed potatoes, salad and a big glass of milk. "Everything okay?"

"Absolutely," Brenda assured him.

He set the purse and tray on the desk and left again.

"He's not pudgy," Mary said.

Brenda grinned. "You should see him with no clothes on."

Mary found herself returning the grin. "I'd rather not."

"A wise choice." Brenda winked, lifted the milk off the tray and handed it to Mary. "How long since you ate?"

Mary gulped half the cold milk before she answered. "This morning."

Brenda shoved aside a mound of papers and perched on a corner of the desk. "Not another word until you've finished every bite of food on this tray. Then you can tell me why you thought somebody wanted to hurt your baby."

Though she hadn't been hungry when she came in, Mary found herself ravenous now. She ate most of the food, determined to ignore Brenda's request to talk. She'd pay for her meal and leave. She couldn't tell Brenda what had happened. She could never tell anybody.

The heavy meal made her sleepy and languorous, but she set the tray on the desk and stood, retrieving her purse. "I need to pay and get back on the road," she said, fumbling for her wallet.

Brenda laid a firm hand over hers, halting her search for money. "Food's on the house. We never charge our customers who faint. Where do you have to go in such a hurry?"

"I'm not sure," she admitted. "North to a big city."

"Who are you running from?"

Mary gripped her purse tightly and refused to look at Brenda. "Nobody."

"This *nobody* sure has you scared. You can't just go running across the country, pregnant, without anyone to help you or a place to stay. You can stay here until you have your baby. We need another waitress, and Jerry and I both adore babies. We'd have a dozen if we could."

"I can't do that! I have to go farther away! He could find me here!"

"Who?"

Mary bit her tongue, realizing she'd said too much.

"Well, it doesn't matter who he is. Even if he does find you, he won't recognize you." Brenda leaned across the desk, opened a drawer and took out a pair of scissors. "We'll cut your hair and dye it dark brown and get you a pair of glasses. Hey, it worked for Superman, and Clark Kent didn't even change his hair."

The smile that crept over Mary's lips felt good, as good as the grin at Brenda's nonsense had a few minutes ago. It seemed like a lifetime since she'd done either. "Thank you. You have no idea how much I appreciate your offer to help, but I have to go. I have to get as far away as possible."

But, oh, how she wanted to stay with these people who made her feel safe and made her smile.

The door opened, and Jerry Patterson came in. "Feel better now?" he asked.

"Jerry, this is our new waitress, Jane, um, Clark. She's going to be staying in our spare room."

"Your spare room?" Mary gasped.

Jerry didn't bat an eye. He stepped forward and extended his hand. "Pleased to meet you, Jane Clark. Can you start tomorrow night? We're awfully short of help."

Mary shook her head in amazement. "You people don't even know me. You don't know what kind of problems I have, what kind of trouble I'm in. How can you offer me a job and a room in your home? How do you know I'm not a criminal?"

Jerry shrugged. "If you want to steal the television, go ahead. It's black and white, and the focus is really bad on it. And if you have any need for a really ugly orange sofa, we could work some kind of a deal where I pay you to take it."

"Jerry! He's kidding. He loves that sofa. His aunt gave it to us."

Jerry rolled his eyes. "Sure. I love a good case of the flu too."

"Hon, can you handle things the rest of the evening? Jane and I have to go home and do her hair. We'll take your car, Jane, put it in the garage and close the door so nobody can see it."

Mary couldn't agree to Brenda's plan, but she was too tired to argue and found herself swept along. It felt so good to have somebody else making the decisions, taking care of her. Maybe she could stay for a little while, just until she could come up with a better plan.

Chapter 19

Jake located a motel half an hour from Edgewater. Rebecca remained frustratingly silent the entire trip. At first he'd told himself he should leave her alone, let her work through this on her own. She was finally coming to grips with reality and, while it wasn't fun, it wasn't fatal either. She was building those muscles he'd told her about.

But he couldn't seem to do that. He felt her distress as if it were happening to him, as if he were once again a child being tossed from one family to another and unable to cope with the confusion and hurt. So he'd tried to talk to her, making conversation about inconsequential topics, avoiding the painful subject of Doris' rejection, unsure how to bring it up until she did.

She'd been unresponsive, answering in monosyllables or ignoring him completely.

They stopped at a drive-in for burgers, hardly the pleasant meal with Doris Jordan in the best restaurant in town that Rebecca had planned. She ate determinedly, as if the burger was an enemy to be vanquished. But at least she ate.

He checked them into the motel, relieved and disappointed that the place was full enough they couldn't have adjacent rooms. For the space of a heartbeat he'd considered asking for one room with a king size bed. What if the person who'd tampered with her brake lines tried to hurt her again? Shouldn't he be nearby to protect her?

If somebody <u>had</u> tampered with her brake lines. If it had been deliberate and not an accident. If he wasn't trying to find an excuse to spend the night with her.

He took the two rooms, returned to the car and drove around back. "You're in 145." He handed her the key. "You get the one with the patio door that opens onto the pool area."

She gave him an forced smile, took the key and got out.

He carried her luggage inside.

The rooms were nicer than the ones in Edgewater, but still institutional.

Rebecca stood beside the bed, gazing around the room. When she turned to him, he saw that she was wearing the haunted expression she'd ascribed to Mary Jordan.

"Thanks for bringing in the suitcase," she said.

He wanted to go to her, take her in his arms, comfort her, kiss her, make love to her, see passion sweep that haunted look from her eyes.

Instead he stood in the open doorway, one hand braced on the frame. He didn't dare close that door. No telling what stupid act he might commit if he did.

"Rebecca, while we were gone this evening, something happened to Doris to change her mind about us staying there. Who knows what it was? We could speculate all night and still not figure it out, but something did happen. She seemed confused, even a little scared. You can't take it personally."

She sank onto the bed and pulled one of the pillows into her lap, smoothing the white cotton case, avoiding his gaze. "My first guess would be that Mary told her I was Ben's illegitimate daughter."

"Which would still make you Doris' granddaughter so I wouldn't give that idea a number one rating. Hell, she could have received a phone call from an old boyfriend who wanted to spend the weekend with her."

Rebecca looked up and smiled wryly. "I wouldn't give that idea a number one rating."

"Okay, but you see my point. We don't know. Nobody can ever know what causes another person to act the way they do unless that person tells you. And even then you can't be sure they're telling the truth."

She tossed the pillow onto the bed and leaned back on her arms. "Thank you so much for sharing that bit of wisdom. Believe it or not, it comes as no surprise to learn that I don't know anything about anybody. I pretty much figured that out the day I discovered I was adopted."

Sarcasm was better than the withdrawn depression she'd exhibited during the entire trip.

"No, you didn't figure it out then. If you had, you wouldn't have come looking for answers and found only more questions. If you'd figured it out then, you'd have accepted that your real parents—the Pattersons—that's as real as you're going to get for parents—you'd have accepted that they loved you for a long time, longer than most people ever will, longer than most people are ever loved."

267

She flinched as if he'd struck her, but he'd said what she needed to hear. He wanted to shout at her, shake her until she accepted the truth, until she stopped letting people hurt her.

Then hold her until the wounds healed.

She stood abruptly and walked over to the dresser, her eyes meeting his in the mirror as if she couldn't talk to him directly. "I know my parents loved me." Her voice was soft but firm. "They loved the whole world. They were wonderful people, and I was damned lucky they took me in after my real mother tossed me aside. But that's what they did, took in outcasts. Our guest room was always full. A battered wife. A family out of work. If they had kids, the kids shared my room. I used to hate myself for being so petty about wishing those people were gone and I had Mom and Dad and our house all to myself. I realize now that I got more than I deserved."

"Rebecca, they loved you. That's more than a lot of people ever get. They only stopped loving you when they died, and their deaths don't change the past. They were there for you. They cared about you. Doris cared about you, and then she stopped though she didn't die. You don't know why she stopped, and you don't need to." He slapped the door frame. "Damn it, Rebecca, you've got to learn to love and let go. Enjoy it while it lasts and forget about it when it's over. Nothing lasts forever, especially something like love, an emotion that hinges on a thousand other factors, factors over which you have absolutely zero control. You need to live in the present and let go of the past."

"*Love and let go,*" she repeated. "*Enjoy it while it lasts.* Like you do?"

"Yeah, like I do." And then for some reason he could no longer bear to look into the reflected image of her smoky green gaze. He turned away. "I'm in room 287 if you need me."

He left, closing the door behind him.

***

Jake yanked the covers off his bed, stacked both pillows behind his head and stretched out, still wearing his jeans. He wasn't sleepy and, though he was exhausted, he was too wired to think about resting.

This case, a simple matter of locating Rebecca Patterson's parents, had turned into one of the most complicated and most frustrating cases he'd ever taken on.

Something was definitely going on with Doris Jordan, and he wasn't basing that solely on his impression of her state of mind when she'd sent them packing. She wasn't the type to turn against someone because of that person's heredity. No, it would have to be something pretty big to make Doris act the way she had, to cause such a well-adjusted, self-confident woman to become confused, frightened and rude.

Nothing in this case made sense.

Especially not his reactions to his client.

Rebecca was fragile and vulnerable and had just received from Doris one of the many blows he'd warned her to expect. That should reinforce her decision to return home tomorrow as soon as she could make arrangements for her car. Her leaving would solve a lot of his problems.

His head would clear when she was gone. She had a way of keeping his hormones stirred up, his mind in a fog, going off in directions that made no sense, constantly thinking about her, unable to focus on what he needed to focus on.

A knock sounded at the door.

He knew it was Rebecca before he opened it. He could feel the energy, the tension of her nearness the way he'd felt the approaching electricity in that storm.

She wore a white satin robe, belted at the waist. Her skin glowed and her hair was damp at her cheekbones as if she'd just showered. She looked up at him, and in the glare of the outside light, the sadness and vulnerability that had been a part of her expression since the first time he'd seen her appeared to have been replaced by a brittle hardness. "Make love to me," she said.

He gulped, not quite certain he'd really heard her. "What?"

"Make love. Have sex. Do it. Whatever phrase you want to use. Tonight. The last time I'll ever see you. For an hour, let's be lovers or sex partners, if you prefer that terminology. In the morning we'll let go and be on our separate ways. Like you said."

He stared at her, trying to determine if she was serious...afraid to believe she was serious.

For a moment her expression faltered. "Don't you want to make love to me?"

He stepped back and allowed her to enter then closed the door and turned to face her. She stood two inches away, so close he caught her scent of honeysuckle and roses and summer, felt the current that sparked between them, so close he had only to reach for her and pull her into his arms. He held his hands rigidly at his sides.

"God, yes, I want to make love to you. I wanted you the first time I saw you. Since that day in the park, I haven't been able to think about you without wanting you."

So why was he hesitating? Because suddenly he wasn't sure he could love and let go?

Because suddenly he was afraid she could?

Where the hell did he come up with such strange stuff? Of course he could love and let go. And if Rebecca could too, that was what he wanted. He could make love to her without worrying about anybody getting hurt when it was over.

He drew her into his arms and kissed her. She returned the kiss with an intensity that amazed him even after their lovemaking in the park.

Suddenly his desire blazed beyond control. He deepened the kiss, holding her tightly with one hand, unwilling to break the contact even as he fumbled with the tie of her robe. Her fingers joined his, tugging at the knot as her mouth clung to his and her tongue danced with his, moving in and out, back and forth, in pale imitation of the dance that was to come.

She hadn't been shy last time, but tonight she was bold, voracious, meeting him on an equal footing.

The knot loosened, the sash fell away, and her robe opened. His hand touched bare, satiny skin at her waist. He slid his hand upward, around her breast, over the swollen nipple. She'd worn nothing beneath the robe, not even the skimpy gown he'd seen her in the first night. A minute ago he'd have sworn he couldn't become more aroused, but he was.

She tangled her fingers in the hair on his chest then slid them down, stroked the bulge in his jeans and struggled with the zipper. Unable to stand the pressure any longer, he moved away from her, yanked off his jeans and shorts, and pulled her onto the bed with him.

He could wait no longer to bury himself inside her, to be joined with her, to feel her hot slickness, to relieve the tension and ride again that storm of ecstasy, arriving at the peak with her around him and beside him.

As he entered her, the single thought shot through his mind that this was even more incredible than the first time. After that, all thought processes became lost completely in overpowering sensation.

He thrust hard, almost angrily, and she met him in the same fashion. Together they raced to that white-hot pinnacle. He cried out as he exploded over the top and heard her do the same. The aftershocks seemed almost as potent as the initial quake, and for a moment he thought they might go on like that all night.

Finally he calmed and rolled over, pulling her on top of him, unwilling to break the connection. For a few moments they lay still, her heart pounding against his, the rhythm gradually slowing.

He pushed her hair back from her face and kissed her forehead gently, the storm abated for the moment.

"Rebecca," he whispered.

"Hmm?"

He had no idea what he wanted to say. *That was incredible. That was the best. You're the best. We're the best.* It all sounded so inane, so inadequate. And it wasn't really what he wanted to say anyway.

She pushed upward, and his arms tightened around her reflexively. "Don't go," he heard himself say and was astonished at the edge of panic in his voice. No sex could possibly be that good.

"I need a drink of water."

He released her and allowed her to leave him. Sitting up, he watched her walk across the room, recalling his first impression of her as willowy. She was. Tall and sleek with flowing curves and an easy, elegant grace as she moved, barefoot, totally nude, to the bathroom.

At the sink she ran water, tilted her head back and drank, then refilled the glass. She returned with the tap water and sat on the bed beside him, offering it to him.

"Thanks." He took the glass from her and drank. The water was tepid and flat but the act of drinking from the same glass she'd placed between her lips was inexplicably erotic.

"Well," she said, and he knew from the single word, from the way she held her head, from a thousand little things about her, that she was suddenly uncomfortable. "I guess I'll see you in the morning." She stood then bent to retrieve her robe from the floor.

"You're leaving already?" There it was again. That trace of alarm in his voice. What the hell? He smiled lazily and reached a hand toward her. "That was just the appetizer. You can't go before the main course."

She hesitated then dropped the robe, returned his smile and came back to him. As she slid into his arms, Jake marveled at how perfectly she fit there, how good she felt. This time when they made love, he was able to restrain himself, to go slowly and tantalizingly, inflicting exquisite torture on both of them, caressing every inch of her delectable body, bringing her to the summit again and again until he finally joined her.

Afterward he turned off the light and held her. Her body against his still felt good even when they were both satiated, so good it was almost frightening.

But she was leaving in the morning. They could share a night of pleasure then move on. He'd done it plenty of times before.

Though he couldn't remember that any woman had given him so much pleasure, was still giving it just by lying next to him in his embrace.

Tomorrow. She was leaving tomorrow.

Enjoy it while it lasts.

Love and let go.

His arms tightened about her and he drifted into a deep sleep.

***

274

Rebecca disentangled herself from Jake's embrace and slipped out of his bed.

She wanted to spend the night with him, wake in the morning and make love again, have breakfast together, smile at each other over their scrambled eggs. But she knew that wasn't the way things worked with Jake...or, it appeared, with anybody she was involved with. He was right. She had to learn to love and let go.

Fumbling in the dark, she found her robe, put it on and left, closing the door quietly behind her.

Back in her room, the still-made bed mocked her with its emptiness and sterility. The sheets on Jake's bed had become soft and crumpled, scented from their lovemaking.

She changed to a pair of shorts and a T-shirt then went out to the pool. It was small and square, functional rather than aesthetic, but the quiet water tempted her. A late night swim, gliding through the water silently, would have been wonderful, but she hadn't brought a suit.

Instead she sat on the concrete at the deep end and dangled her bare feet. It was almost two in the morning. The sun's warmth had long since dissipated leaving the water cool, even a little chilly.

All around the pool, all around her, doors were closed with people sleeping behind them. She was alone...at the pool, in her life. Jake slept in a room on the other side of the complex. They'd made incredible love, their very souls had seemed to touch. And then it was over.

Love and let go.

Some people were able to hold on. Like her parents. Their love for each other had always been obvious. They'd had so much, it had spilled over to encompass everyone.

After this past week of experiences with Jake and people who might be her blood relatives, she needed to reassess her outlook. Perhaps she'd been wrong in thinking she wasn't special to Brenda and Jerry Patterson. True, everyone was special to them, but that didn't negate her relationship with the two of them. It just meant they'd been unusual people, people with enough love to go around.

Not everybody had their ability. Her biological parents had apparently been lacking. They hadn't even had enough for their own daughter.

She'd felt close to Doris and to Jake, but some element had been missing there too.

Rather than bemoaning her lack of natural parents, she should feel grateful for people who'd started out as strangers and then became parents who'd possessed the ability to care for her.

She began this search to find her identity, her past, to find her life and take control of it. Doris and Jake had both told her the past wasn't important, only the present and the future.

She needed to go home. Be glad she'd had her parents to care for her but realize they were gone. Find her own future, turn loose of the past. Tell Jake to stop searching for her biological parents. Judging from what she'd found so far, she was better off not knowing.

For the first time, she felt as if she really was taking charge of her life, making decisions, not being swept along by circumstances.

Nobody was going to fill the empty spot inside her, give her an identity. Nobody but herself. She'd counted on Jake, on Doris, on parents she'd never met, and all had failed her. The only person she could count on was herself.

Tomorrow she still had to deal with getting her car towed from Doris' house. She would probably have to face Doris one more time, and that would hurt.

She'd have to face Jake, too. Just like after the first time they'd made love, he'd undoubtedly be cool and impersonal, as though the events of the night had never happened. And that would definitely hurt.

Love and let go.

From the strength given to her by Brenda and Jerry Patterson, from the core of genuine love they'd shown her, she'd have to find the courage to do that.

As she stood, ready to go back to her room and try to get some sleep, an eerie sensation darted down her spine, as if she wasn't alone, as if somebody was watching her. She froze, poised on the edge of the pool.

A shadow moved over by the stairs on the second floor.

A shadow. That's all. She was imagining things.

From behind her she thought she heard something, a faint movement of the air. She started to turn in that direction but a weight shoved against her back, sending her splashing into the pool.

She gasped in surprise, swallowing some of the chemically treated water that engulfed her. For an instant she was a kid again, being pushed into the community pool by one of the boys.

Instinctively she held her breath and pushed upward. Through the distortion of the water, she saw someone in black kneeling over the pool, reaching for her.

Jake? Had he pushed her in? Surely that's all it was. No reason to worry. Jake had followed her, playfully pushed her in the pool. Now he was going to help her out.

She reached upward, planning to grab his hands and pull him in with her.

But the hands eluded her, grasping her hair near the scalp and pushing down, holding her head underwater, and suddenly she realized this was no rough-housing event. She could drown.

Someone was trying to kill her.

She fought against the hands, trying to pry up the fingers. Big fingers. Strong fingers.

Every movement yanked her hair and increased the pain. She needed to breathe, hadn't been prepared to stay down this long, hadn't had time to take a deep breath.

Panic seized her, threatening to steal any chance she might have.

She refused to give in, resisted the urge to flail wildly, forced herself to think. She couldn't free herself from the grip of steel. Instead she focused on the little finger of one hand, on using both her hands to bend back that little finger, as far back as she could, to break it.

Suddenly the pressure on her hair released and she surged upward, gasping for air.

Something hit the side of her head and she heard a loud explosion. A shot? Was she dying?

At least she'd made love with Jake one more time.

Cold darkness rose up to swallow her.

Chapter 20

Jake halted with his fist in mid-air, poised to knock on Rebecca's door, when he heard the gunshot.

It came from somewhere close, the sound bouncing and echoing until he couldn't be sure of the source, whether it came from inside her room or outside.

"Rebecca!" An image of her bleeding, dying, burst into his head. Without a second thought, he kicked down the door and charged inside, his gaze sweeping the empty room. Her bed hadn't been slept in.

Come to the pool, she'd said on the phone.

He sprinted across to the patio door, found it unlocked and shoved it open.

A few people had stepped out of their rooms and were looking around curiously, apparently roused by the noise, but he didn't see Rebecca.

Until he checked the pool.

At the deep end a body floated near the bottom, blond hair swirling in the still-moving water.

Rebecca!

Oh, God! She couldn't be dead!

The waves and ripples told him she hadn't been down there long. There was still hope. There had to be hope!

His heart clenched painfully as he dove into the water, but he ignored the sensation, ignored the fear that threatened to paralyze him. Emotions would hamper his efforts, could cost Rebecca her life. He fell back on his police training, focused on dealing with the emergency, assessing the situation and taking appropriate action to guarantee the best possible outcome.

He grabbed her about the waist, one part of his mind noting that he saw no blood staining the water, no evidence of a gunshot wound, while the other part did something he hadn't done since he was a child...prayed to a God he'd given up on years ago.

He dragged her onto the rough concrete, checked for pulse and breathing, found none and began CPR, concentrating on the action, trying not to think about the fact that this was no stranger, this was Rebecca, the woman he'd made love to and held in his arms a short time ago.

He knew how to do this. He'd done it before...saved drowning victims, lost drowning victims.

He couldn't lose Rebecca!

Forget it's Rebecca. Concentrate!

"Is she okay?" someone asked, and in his peripheral vision he saw that a small group of people in their night clothes had begun to gather around them.

Useless fools. Couldn't they see she wasn't okay? And they weren't doing a damned thing to help.

He ignored them.

And Rebecca coughed.

The cap on his emotions blew then, and intense relief burst over him like hot lava exploding from a volcano. Only then did he allow himself to realize how terrified he'd been, how devastated he would have been if Rebecca hadn't survived. But he didn't have time to think about the implications of that right now.

He turned her on her side and held her hair back while she coughed and choked and vomited chlorine water, took in deep, gasping, beautiful gulps of air, then coughed and choked some more.

He looked up at the fascinated bystanders. "Can anybody stop gawking long enough to call 911?"

A couple of people moved away, and he could only hope they would make the phone call.

Rebecca lifted a hand to the side of her head. "Hurts," she rasped.

He moved her hand and looked at the spot. An angry red welt was already forming. "What happened?"

She shook her head and coughed some more.

He rose, lifted her into his arms and carried her back into her room.

She moaned when he laid her on the bed. She was shivering, from shock and from being wet in the air conditioned room.

He stripped off her soggy clothes, pulled the covers from under her and threw them over her then went to turn off the air, close the broken door and get a towel for her hair.

When he came back, she'd curled into a ball and her teeth were chattering. He dried her hair as best he could, flinching with her pain when he hit the sore spot on the side of her head and caused her to wince and groan.

She was still shivering when he finished. He could think of only one way to warm her.

If somebody had called 911 as he asked, an ambulance, police, firemen...maybe half the town...were on their way. But Rebecca's well-being was what mattered.

He tossed the towel onto the floor, pulled off his own wet clothes and crawled in bed with her, holding her body against his, trying to infuse her with his warmth.

She no longer smelled like summer flowers. Now they both reeked of chlorine and fear and dampness and because it was a part of Rebecca, he drank it all in as greedily as if it were expensive perfume.

She was alive. She was still with him, solid and real and breathing.

She burrowed her head against his chest, and he was amazed at the surge of protectiveness that swept over him. When she'd come to his room earlier, she hadn't seemed vulnerable anymore. She'd been strong, giving and taking in equal proportions, and he'd told himself that was what he wanted.

Now she needed him, and he desperately wanted to take care of her, so desperately it scared him. Just as his terror at the thought of her not emerging from that pool alive scared him.

Of course he didn't want anyone to drown, but his distress had gone beyond that.

He didn't want to lose Rebecca. He cared about her.

He groaned at his own stupidity. How the hell had he let that happen? Over the years he'd known plenty of women, liked them, enjoyed being with them, then one or the other of them had moved on, and he had never given it a second thought.

Tomorrow Rebecca would be moving on, and he had a horrible feeling he was going to be having lots of second thoughts about her. Third, fourth and fifth thoughts, for that matter.

Well, he'd just have to deal with it. It wasn't like he hadn't had plenty of practice in getting over people who came into his life long enough to make him care then left. But all that had been years ago when he was young and dumb and still believed that love was forever. He knew better than that now.

So how come he'd let himself get emotionally entangled?

A loud knock came from the broken front door. "Police!"

"Coming!" he shouted. "I'll be right back," he assured Rebecca as he slipped out of bed and struggled into his wet jeans.

She looked up at him and gave him a weak smile. Something inside him spilled over, warm and sweet and wonderful...and damned scary.

The knock came again, louder this time.

Jake opened the door to find two police officers and two paramedics.

He pointed to Rebecca. "She almost drowned, and she took some kind of a hit on the side of her head."

While the paramedics checked her over, Jake talked to the officers, Johnson and Turner. Both were young, couldn't have been out of the academy more than a year.

"I heard a gunshot, kicked down her door, ran out to the pool and found her. She'll have to tell you the rest."

"Do you know who fired the shot?"

"I have no idea. You might ask some of those people in rooms around the pool if they saw anybody. A bunch of them came out."

Turner left to take care of that part of the investigation.

"What were you doing at her door at this time of the night?" Johnson asked.

"She called and asked me to meet her at the pool."

Johnson lifted an eyebrow. "I see. Did she say why?"

"No. She just said, *This is Rebecca. Come to the pool.* I figured she'd tell me why when I got here."

"When had you last talked to her?"

Before Jake could ask the kid why he was asking stupid questions instead of getting to the bottom of things, one of the paramedics left Rebecca's side and came over to where he and the officer stood.

"As far as we can tell, she's all right," he said. "She's got a trauma to the head that we'd like to

285

check for possible concussion, but she refuses to go to the hospital."

Jake turned to see Rebecca propped up in bed, clutching the covers to her breast. Her face was the color of the sheet, her eyes dark by contrast, but she seemed alert. "I'm okay," she croaked.

"It won't hurt you to go to the hospital and at least spend the rest of the night," Jake urged.

"I'm okay," she repeated, her tone weak but firm.

"She's probably fine," the second paramedic said. "But she shouldn't be left alone tonight. If you can't wake her up, if she gets dizzy or disoriented, if her pupils become fixed and dilated, if anything changes, you get her to emergency right away."

Jake nodded. The paramedics left and Johnson pulled the chair over to sit beside the bed. "You feel good enough to tell us what happened?"

She nodded. "I was sitting at the pool. Something—somebody—pushed me in."

"Somebody pushed you?" Jake exclaimed, let loose a string of swear words, strode across the room and back then sat on the bed beside her, resisting the impulse to pull her into his arms. "Who?"

Johnson glanced at him, unperturbed, then returned his attention to Rebecca. "Who pushed you, Ms. Patterson?"

"I don't know. It happened so fast. I thought it was—I thought I was a kid—I mean, it was like when I was a kid." She paused to cough again.

"You thought you were a kid," Johnson repeated. "Do you often think that?"

Jake couldn't believe the man was asking such asinine questions.

"I didn't think that, not really. Just for a minute. Then I thought it was Jake."

"You thought Mr. Thornton pushed you into the water?"

She lifted a shaky hand to her face. "At first. But then he grabbed my hair and held me under."

"Mr. Thornton?"

She scowled. "No. Not Jake. The man."

"So you saw him, you can describe him."

"He was wearing black. That's all I know. His face was distorted by the water."

"Then how do you know it was a man?"

"Big hands. Strong fingers. I couldn't get them off. I bent his little finger back."

"I see. And then what happened?"

"I must have hurt him. He let go for a second. I came up and heard a noise and something hit my head. I thought I'd been shot."

"No, ma'am. You weren't shot."

She touched the place on her forehead that was already beginning to swell then looked at her hand. "No blood. I wasn't shot."

"No, ma'am. Did you hit your head when you fell in the pool?"

Jake clenched his teeth and his fists. The man was an idiot. Wasn't he listening to anything she told him?

"No, the bullet hit me." She shook her head. "No, it didn't, did it? Something hit me. The man. His fist. I don't know."

287

"You sound like you're a little confused about what actually happened, Ms. Patterson."

"Damn it," Jake said, "of course she's confused! She almost drowned. Somebody tried to kill her. Wouldn't you be a little confused?"

Johnson stared coldly at Jake. "We understand Ms. Patterson has been under a lot of stress lately."

"Yeah, I'd classify attempted murder as pretty damned stressful."

"I mean before that."

"What, exactly, do you mean?" Jake asked slowly. Something wasn't right. "Where did you get the idea that Ms. Patterson has been under a lot of stress?"

Johnson gave Rebecca a look of pity then turned back to Jake. "The Edgewater police department called to tell us you two were headed our way."

Jake shot up, looming over the officer. The man flinched and eased one hand toward his gun. "Why?" Jake demanded. "What do you care if we come to town? We haven't broken any laws. What did the police in Edgewater tell you about us?"

"As a professional courtesy, they thought we ought to know that the motel owner down there had to evict Ms. Patterson after her suicide attempt."

"Suicide?" Rebecca squeaked.

Jake clenched his fists. If he could get hold of Charles Morton or Farley Gates right now, he'd smash their lying heads together until they cracked like Humpty Dumpty. "There was no suicide attempt in Edgewater, and there hasn't been one here. Is that what you think happened? That Rebecca hit herself on the head then held herself under water? And let's not forget the shot. How did she manage to fire a gun at the same time?"

"Do you own a gun, Mr. Thornton?"

"Sure I do. And I've got a permit to carry it."

"Where is that gun right now?"

"In Dallas. I don't normally bring along a weapon when I'm investigating a civil matter." Though he was beginning to think he should have this time.

"Everything all right in here?"

Jake turned to see that Officer Turner had come back in through the patio door. "Yeah, it's fine." He sank onto the bed. No point in losing his temper with these guys. Of course they'd believe another police officer rather than him. The Brotherhood of Blue.

"Someone tried to kill me," Rebecca insisted, her voice sounding more normal though still pretty hoarse. She was starting to regain a little color.

"Did you find anything?" Johnson asked his partner.

"Nothing. A loud noise woke up some of the people. They said it could have been a shot, but nobody was certain."

"I'm certain," Jake said. "You don't mistake that sound when you've heard as many as I have."

"Where did you hear all these shots, Mr. Thornton?" Johnson asked.

"I used to be a cop in Dallas."

Turner shrugged. "I didn't find any evidence of a shot. Nobody hurt. Nothing broken. Several of them saw Thornton run out of this room, haul Rebecca out of the pool and resuscitate her. That's all they know."

The officers stayed for a few minutes longer, asking more inane questions, but Jake could tell they thought Rebecca had tried to kill herself. There'd be no investigation.

Finally they left.

Jake stood for a moment leaning against the door, wanting to kick it, to smash his fist through the wall, do something to vent his anger...and knowing all that would be pointless.

Rebecca could see the anger in Jake's posture, in the bunched muscles of his shirtless back, of his forearms, in the way the cords in his neck stood out. She could feel it in the vibrations that came from him.

He was angry on her behalf, and that aroused odd feelings in her. In fact, this entire experience had her completely confused about Jake Thornton just when she'd thought she had her feelings for him all straight and nonthreatening.

He'd saved her life. Though she didn't remember him pulling her from the pool, his recitation of events to the police officers had painted such a clear picture of his breaking down her door, diving into the pool and rescuing her that she almost thought she'd seen it. She did remember him carrying her into the room, tucking her in bed, towel drying her hair, then crawling in with her and sharing his own body heat. This was not the cynical Jake Thornton who'd warned her not to expect too much from people.

Ironic that she'd see that side of him just when she'd accepted that he was right, at least about most people with Jake definitely included on that list.

Ironic that he was angrier than she about this latest incident. Maybe tomorrow she'd be more upset. Maybe her lack of reaction came from the fact that she was completely exhausted, drained from her physical ordeal as well as the reality that somebody wanted her dead. Unlike the brake line incident which could have been an accident, this time there could be no doubt that someone had tried to kill her.

Or maybe she wouldn't be angry tomorrow. Maybe she had become numb from so much rejection that even the ultimate rejection...attempted murder...had no effect on her.

But one part of Jake's story bothered her.

"Why did you tell him I called you and asked you to come to the pool?" she asked. Had he found her missing from his bed and come after her then lied to preserve her reputation or was there something else going on?

He turned to look at her, a frown creasing his forehead. "Because you did."

"No, I didn't."

He came back to sit in the chair beside her bed. "Sure you did. Don't be concerned. Lots of times people forget things that happen just before an accident. You called me and you said, *This is Rebecca. Come to the pool.*"

"I did not call you."

He smiled and took her hand. "Relax. You've been through a lot and you're a little confused."

291

She pulled her hand away from him. "Don't patronize me. I remember distinctly what I was doing before somebody pushed me into that pool, and I wasn't calling you or even thinking about calling you."

Jake stared at her silently for a moment. Slowly the implications dawned on her and, apparently, on him too.

"Somebody called me," he amended quietly. "I thought it was you."

"So it was a woman."

"I don't know. I was asleep. She—the person— was talking softly, almost in a whisper. It could have been a man."

"Whoever it was got you down here and saved my life."

"And shot at you."

"Or shot at the man trying to drown me. There must have been at least two people. The one who called you and the one trying to drown me. My attacker couldn't have made that call or fired a gun. He had both hands in my hair."

"You're right. Guess that means we're back to the two person conspiracy theory." He grinned without humor.

"One trying to kill me and one trying to scare off my attacker or maybe scare me with a shot? Then it must have been dear old dad doing the drowning and mom or grandmother with the gun. Gee, I can't wait for the family reunion."

Jake blew out a long breath and ran his fingers through his hair, looked at her then looked away.

"Why don't you get that white robe you had on earlier and let's go up to my room?" His tone was soft with an edge of forced teasing.

"Why don't I not?" She'd already let go of that element, left his arms and walked away from him. She didn't want to have to do it again, wasn't sure she had the strength to do it again, not after tonight, after he'd held her naked body against his, comforting and soothing her with no sexual intent, after he'd shown her another facet of himself and added another level to her desire for him.

He stood, his eyes darkening, his brow furrowing in irritation. "Fine. Why don't you stay here in this room with a broken front door so the guy with the big, strong hands can get to you easily and finish you off tonight?"

He turned away, took two steps toward the door, then strode back, leaned down, yanked the covers off her, slid his arms under her and lifted her off the bed. "Or why don't I just carry you, buck naked, up to my room? Give everybody here a little more entertainment."

The way he looked at her, with a combination of hunger, gentleness and anger, tugged at her, made her want to wrap her arms about his neck and let him carry her away. The anticipation of having Jake's arms wrapped around her, holding her securely all night, with or without sexual context, was entirely too tempting.

"Why don't you put me down and let me get on my clothes then I'll ask the manager to move me to another room." She forced herself to retreat, to make her voice cold.

Jake's eyes went as cold as her voice, and he deposited her back onto the bed. "In case you've forgotten what the paramedic said, you can't be alone tonight. So it's either me or the emergency room."

She pulled the sheet around her. "I'll get my robe."

If only she wasn't so pleased about losing the argument. If only she didn't remember quite distinctly that her last thought, when she'd believed she was dying, had been thankfulness that she'd made love with Jake.

Love and let go.

An easy resolution to make and such a hard one to keep.

But she would.

She would spend the night with Jake, face Doris Jordan tomorrow and let go of both of them, then get on with the rest of her life.

"After I have my car towed, I'm going home," she said.

"I know."

"And your job is ended. I don't want to find out any more about these people. I want to forget them entirely."

He gazed down at her for a long moment, his eyes black as the darkness that had enveloped her in the pool. Finally he nodded. "Wise decision. I'll wait outside while you put your robe on."

The distance between them gaped wide and deep. She would spend the night in his bed, but she might as well be back in Dallas. Jake had already let go.

Chapter 21

Rebecca stared unseeing out the car window as she and Jake crossed the city limits sign into Edgewater the next morning.

She'd been so exhausted when they got to Jake's room the night before, she'd slept soundly and awakened in his arms, the thing she'd both wanted and feared. For one luxurious, shining moment, she'd reveled in the feeling before she came completely awake and remembered all the circumstances, the temporary nature of everything with Jake.

Jake had awakened when she'd tried to move away from him, and they'd shared a tense breakfast then called a towing service to meet them at Doris' house.

Tonight she'd be back in her condo, ready to begin sorting things out, trying to find herself and create her place in the world rather than searching futilely for one that didn't exist.

At least at home she wouldn't have to worry about snakes in her bathtub or men in black trying to drown her.

"I keep expecting Farley Gates to show up and slap me with a ticket or haul me off to jail," Jake said, turning onto a residential street, a deceitfully peaceful street. The whole town was deceitfully peaceful.

"Or worse," Rebecca added.

"Yeah. You think that might have been him last night?"

Though she'd like to forget the episode entirely, Rebecca thought back to the steely fingers in her hair, to their strength as she'd tried to pry them loose. "No, I don't think so. Gates is pudgy and has small hands. Charles Morton has big hands, and he looks like he works out regularly. But I guess it doesn't matter. By this afternoon I'll be home and all this will seem like a crazy dream. A nightmare."

As they turned onto Doris' street, a block ahead of them Doris and Mary Jordan appeared to be involved in a heated discussion as they moved down the walk toward Mary's car.

Jake stopped and backed up a few feet. They'd still be visible if either Doris or Mary looked up, but that seemed unlikely. The two women stopped at the curb and Doris held one hand toward Mary beseechingly. Mary shook her head and yanked open her car door. Doris went around and got in the other side, and they drove away.

"Something's going on," Jake said. "We have about an hour before the towing service should be here. Why don't we just ease along behind those two, see what they're up to?"

"No. Let's park behind my car and wait. I don't want to know. I told you, I'm through with this whole thing."

Jake stole a quick glance at her. "You're lying. And you don't even do it very well. I can hear it in your voice and see it on your face."

He was right. In spite of all her good resolutions, she did want to know. Obviously she hadn't honed either of her newly sought skills—lying or letting go.

They followed Mary and Doris across town, never losing sight but always staying a careful distance behind.

"This is easier when there's a little more traffic and when I'm not driving a car with a broken headlight which makes me easily identifiable," he grumbled, but he was successful in tracking them to their destination.

The Edgewater Cemetery.

"This could prove interesting," he said as he parked behind a large tree. He opened his door and turned to her. Rebecca sat frozen even as the oppressive heat invaded the air conditioned vehicle.

"Might be better if you wait here."

His comment galvanized her into action. "No. I'm going with you. You were right. I don't care about these people, I don't care who my mother was, but I want to know why they're acting this way. I want to know why somebody wants me dead." Her lethargy of the night before had passed, and she found herself developing a righteous anger. Searching for her birth parents might be misguided, but it shouldn't be a fatal offense.

She slid out of the car and was already crossing the cemetery in hurried strides, determined to do this before she lost her nerve, when Jake caught up to her.

"You might try walking a little more slowly and quietly unless you want them to know we're coming."

She slowed her steps just as they spotted Mary and Doris up ahead. Doris sat on the ground beside a grave and Mary stood next to her.

In the summer morning the cemetery stretched around them, peaceful with its collection of softly weathered old stones and sharply cut new ones, its recently-mown grass, the stately trees adding the deeper hues of their shade to patches of grass, birds chirping in the background. But the air around Doris and Mary seemed darker and roiling with disturbances.

Doris rose slowly and spoke quietly, embracing Mary who shook her head again as she stood rigid, arms folded, refusing the comfort offered.

Jake held out a restraining arm, trying to halt Rebecca while they were still some distance away, but she brushed past him. If she ever stopped, she'd turn around and run back the other direction, all the way to Dallas and out of this nightmare.

"It's got to stop." Rebecca heard Doris' tense words just before the older woman, apparently sensing or hearing their approach, turned to face them. "Good morning, Rebecca," she said. "And Jake."

Mary whirled toward them, a horrified expression draining what little color she had left in her pale features, leaving only the dark circles beneath her eyes. Immediately a curtain fell, cutting off any hint of a discernible emotion in the haunted depths of those black-ringed eyes.

"Good morning, Doris, Mary," Jake replied.

Mary turned wordlessly and walked a few steps away.

Rebecca greeted Doris but ignored the younger woman who so obviously disliked her.

As she and Jake approached, she could see tear stains on Doris' lined face. Her usual tranquility had been replaced by a deep sadness. In spite of the recent rejection, Rebecca wanted to go to Doris, wrap her arms about her, soothe away that sadness.

She glanced at the stones and noticed that the graves Doris stood between were those of Edgar and Ben Jordan. Her husband and son. Father-in-law and husband of the stoic Mary.

Rebecca wanted to march over to Mary, grab her shoulder, force her to look into her eyes, shake her and demand to know how she could be so cold, how she could refuse her mother-in-law's comfort. Yet for all her irritation, there was something indefinable about Mary Jordan that tugged at her heart and kept her from completely hating the woman who was consistently rude to her.

"We came to get Rebecca's car and saw you leaving," Jake said. "We were afraid you wouldn't get back before the tow truck arrived, and we wanted to talk to you."

Doris cast an anxious glance in Mary's direction. "I apologize for last night, but something's come up. You have to leave. Please."

Jake folded his arms, making his spraddle-legged stance even more formidable. "We're leaving as soon as we get Rebecca's car. She's given up, decided finding parents who don't want to be found isn't worth risking her life."

Doris' gaze darted to Mary then back to them.

Rebecca thought Mary stiffened, but her small body was already so stiff, it was hard to tell. For a fleeting moment, Rebecca considered that Mary was the right size to have worn the blue dress.

But surely a mother couldn't hate her own child the way Mary hated her.

Surely.

Anyway, that made no sense. Mary had been married. Though she might not have wanted a child, it wouldn't be something shameful, something to hide and run away from. Mary in the role of her mother didn't fit with any of the data they had accumulated.

"What did the police say?" Doris asked. "Did they find any clues? Did they see anybody leaving the pool area?"

It was Rebecca's turn to stiffen. How had Doris known about the incident last night?

Jake's arm slid around her waist as if to caution her to be silent.

"No," he said. "Nobody suspicious was seen and the police don't think there's anything to investigate. Seems they'd already had a call from the Edgewater Police telling them Rebecca was suicidal. They think Rebecca tried to drown herself. Hit herself on the head too. You know how cops are. They stick together."

Doris' eyes flared wide, her pupils shrinking to pinpoints, then she turned away and sank to the ground as if she no longer had the strength to stand. Her long fingers traced the name of her son carved into the cold, lifeless stone. "Yes," she whispered. "I know about the brotherhood of police."

"Doris," Jake said softly, "how did you find out about what happened to Rebecca last night?"

Doris froze then shook her head. "It doesn't matter. All that matters is that you need to get out of this town and never come back."

"We're both getting out of here as fast as we can," Rebecca assured her. Yet none of her determined resolutions of the night before prevented her from feeling empty and desolate. Easy to say she was going to forget about people who didn't want her, but not so easy to do.

"Let's go, Jake," she said. Only by getting away from Edgewater, from Doris, from all the pain that seethed just beneath the surface, could she make good on those resolutions.

As Jake walked beside her, close but not touching, never touching in any real sense of the word, she reminded herself that he was one of the things she had to get away from.

Go home and forget about it. That was the advice he'd given her the first time she walked into his office. If she'd only taken it then, she could have saved herself a lot of heartache.

But then she'd never have made love with Jake, never have felt him slide into bed next to her to warm her body with his after saving her life.

Love and let go.

As she slid into Jake's car and he closed the door behind her, she resolved that she would take that last piece of advice.

Let go of her parents, natural and adopted. Never think again about the woman in the blue dress. Reclaim the beautiful memories she had of Brenda and Jerry.

Let go of Jake and sometime in the future when it didn't hurt so badly, she could take out the memories of him and revel in them.

***

As he drove back toward Doris' house, Jake cast a surreptitious glance at Rebecca. Her lips were compressed into a thin line and she was a little pale, but other than that, she appeared to be dealing pretty well with this latest rejection. She was acquiring those emotional muscles fast, growing stronger.

She wasn't going to have any problem walking away from Doris and Mary...and from him.

Which was the way he wanted it, the best possible outcome. If her walking away from him caused a ripple of unease, he just needed to flex his own emotional muscles.

"Doris and Mary are somehow involved in what happened last night," he said, changing the direction of his problematical thoughts. "Otherwise they wouldn't know about it."

"I don't care. We shouldn't have followed them. I shouldn't have come here. You were right all along. This whole thing has been a mistake."

First time being told he was right had made him feel lousy.

He didn't say anything else until they got back to Doris' house. The tow truck had already arrived and was hooking up Rebecca's car.

"I'll be right back," she said.

He got out and waited as she walked over to the man, spoke briefly to him then returned.

"Would you get my suitcase for me?" she asked.

"Get your suitcase? Why?"

"I'm going to ride back to Dallas with this gentleman."

"But...I thought you were going with me. I mean, I'm going anyway. There's no point in your riding in that thing. It's uncomfortable. That's a long ride."

"I expect I'll survive. There's a car rental place next door to the garage. This will be more practical than to have you go out of your way."

"I see. Okay, sure. I'll get your bag." Of course she was right. Practical. What difference did it make whether or not he got to spend the next three hours with her? After that, she'd be just as gone. Three hours one way or the other was inconsequential.

He carried the suitcase over and loaded it in the tow truck.

"Okay, Ms. Patterson, I think we're ready to go." The operator climbed up in the driver's seat.

Rebecca turned to Jake, squinting into the sun and shading her eyes with one hand. "Send me your bill and I'll put a check in the mail. I appreciate all the work you've done, and I certainly appreciate your saving my life last night."

She sounded so formal. The green slits of her eyes revealed no clue as to what might be going on inside. He could only accept the stiffness of her voice and her posture.

They'd made wild, passionate love three times and yet it all came down to this.

He rubbed the back of his neck to give his hand something to do other than reaching for her and pulling her to him for one final kiss. Suddenly he felt an overpowering need to have one more kiss, to touch her lips one more time.

As if a last kiss would make any more difference in the overall scheme of things than the three hour ride to Dallas would have.

"So long, Rebecca. Saving your life was my pleasure. Well, have a good one. Life, that is."

He grinned, spun on his heel, shoved his hands into his pockets and walked back to his car.

This was the way relationships always ended. He knew that. He'd never expected anything different. They'd had some really good times together, shared fantastic sex, and now it was over.

So maybe he cared for her more than he should. Maybe he even loved her a little. So? Nothing lasted forever, certainly not love.

A week from now he wouldn't even remember the way Rebecca had felt in his arms.

Or maybe a month from now.

He got in his car and peeled off, determined to get far ahead of them on the highway to Dallas, to avoid any accidental glimpses of Rebecca, to speed up the forgetting process.

Chapter 22

May 3, 1980, Plano, Texas

In the small office in the back of the Plano Diner, Mary finished typing a letter, stretching to reach the typewriter over her enormous stomach. With a sigh she leaned back and spread her hands over the bulge.

"Soon, baby," she promised. "Any day now you'll be in my arms instead of my stomach, and I'll be able to see my feet again." She flinched then smiled as one side of her stomach bulged outward. "And we'll see if you're Sharise or Ben. With a kick like that, you could be a great football player."

She looked around the room and again blessed the Pattersons for helping her, taking her in, accepting her without question, and for insisting she do book work this last month when she'd become too unwieldy to wait tables.

They didn't want her to leave even after the baby came. Brenda, unable to have children, insisted Mary couldn't take away her God-child.

With all the horrible things that had happened over the past year, Brenda and Jerry Patterson were the rainbow after the storm.

Almost they'd convinced her that the storm was over. She listened to their reassurances and wanted to believe that Charles couldn't find her this far away, separated from Edgewater by four hours and the sprawling, growing cities of Dallas and Fort Worth with a Metroplex population of over six million. In spite of niggling doubts, she desperately wanted to believe that her baby was safe and she could start her new life there with those caring people who'd so rapidly become her surrogate family. She'd lost so many people she loved...her mother and father, Ben and, by the necessity of her leaving, Doris and Edgar Jordan. She didn't want to lose Brenda and Jerry.

But Brenda and Jerry didn't know Charles Morton. They'd never looked into those icy blue eyes and seen the madness there.

As if summoned from her thoughts, Brenda came in, concern marring her normally smiling features. When she carefully closed the door behind her, Mary's heart began to pound even as she told herself to relax, that Brenda was undoubtedly worried about some problem with the new waitress.

"What's the matter?" she asked.

Brenda slid onto the desktop, dangled her feet and tried to smile. "Nothing. Not really. It's just—" She stopped and bit her lip. "We've never asked who you were running from or why. Not even who you are."

"I know. I appreciate that." Mary's mouth went dry and her words came out stiffly.

"There's a police officer out there with a picture of you, of the way you looked before your makeover." She gave a weak half-grin.

Mary felt the blood drain from her face as a whirling tornado of panic swept over her, fogging her senses and blurring Brenda's image. She clutched the edge of the desk. "What…?" She swallowed and licked her lips. "What does he want?"

Brenda laid her own hands over Mary's fingers where they gripped the desk. "Jane, it's okay. Relax. Take a deep breath. Do you want a glass of water?"

Mary shook her head, clutching at Brenda's words—*It's okay*. How she wanted to believe that.

"This man is saying the police in Edgewater, a little town about 200 miles from here, are looking for a pregnant woman named Mary Jordan, that she's unstable and could harm herself or the baby if she's not taken into protective custody."

"Oh, God! It's Charles!" She tried to get to her feet but fell back.

Brenda slid off the desk and grasped Mary's shoulders, forcing her to look into her eyes, to focus. "Jane! Mary! Stop it! You're safe! I swear!"

Mary pressed her hands to her cheeks. "I should have known I could never hide from him. The police stick together. They'll do anything for a fellow officer. Does he know I'm here?"

"No, nobody knows you're here. This officer was checking because he'd heard we had a pregnant waitress but nobody could identify you from the picture he had. See, I told you the disguise would work." She grinned, but for the first time since they'd met, Brenda's gift of happiness didn't transmit to Mary. "I told him you were my cousin," Brenda continued, "and I knew for a fact you'd never been to Edgewater. When he asked if he could speak to you, I told him the father of your child had shown up yesterday and you'd left this morning for Oklahoma to marry him."

Mary broke into hysterical giggles. "You lied! The most honest person I've ever met and because of me you've turned into a liar."

Brenda laughed softly. "And a darned good one, if I do say so myself. I was pretty impressed that I came up with all that stuff!"

"What am I going to do?"

"Just off hand, I'd say you're going to have a baby, and pretty quick now. Beyond that, if you want to tell Jerry and me what's going on, maybe we can help you decide how to handle it."

Mary leaned back in the uncomfortable chair, trying to find a position that didn't make her back hurt. "I can't tell you. I told someone and now he's dead."

Brenda squatted beside the chair. "That's not going to happen to Jerry and me. A psychic assured me once that I'm going to be very wealthy before I die, and we're pretty broke right now, so I figure I have a lot of years to go."

Mary found herself smiling in spite of everything. Brenda could always make her or anyone else smile. But even as her lips curved upward, tears sprang to her eyes. "You are rich, Brenda. You have a beautiful spirit, a wonderful husband, lots of people who love you. I can't put you in danger."

"Jane...or is it Mary?"

"It's Mary." The pain in her back increased, tensing the muscles in her stomach.

"Mary, do you really think this Charles person is going to believe you've lived with us all this time and not told us the whole story? He'll assume we know, so you might as well tell us. That way we can be prepared."

Whether she knew what Brenda said was true or whether she couldn't stand the stress any longer, Mary heaved a long sigh then began to talk, at first hesitantly, then faster and faster, hurrying past the worst parts, not wanting to relive them.

When she finished, she was out of breath, and tears streamed down Brenda's ashen face.

"Mary, you have to tell the authorities. Charles has to be stopped!"

Pain, from the memories, from her back, from all over her body, rolled around and through her, stabbing, squeezing, obscuring her vision. "Charles *is* the authority. I'm telling you, police stick together. They uphold each other, no matter what. You just saw that! That officer who doesn't even know him is helping him. You can never tell anyone. Swear!" The last word ended on a note that came perilously close to being a scream.

Brenda sprang to her feet. "Omigosh! You're in labor!"

"No, it's not time yet. I have to…" She didn't know what it was she had to do.

Get away from Charles. But she didn't know how.

"Time or not, you're having our baby right now! Stay there! I'll get Jerry!"

"I need to get up. I need to go." She pushed halfway to her feet, but the pain slammed her back.

Brenda disappeared for an indefinite period of time, a minute or an hour. Mary couldn't be certain. Pain rushing over her, receding then returning, was the only certain thing in her life right then.

Finally Brenda returned with Jerry. He leaned over her. "How you doing, kid?"

She gritted her teeth until the pain receded and she could breathe. "I'm okay," she said, trying to sound as if she meant it.

"You'll have to carry her!" Brenda exclaimed. "She can't get up."

"Of course I can."

But Jerry scooped Mary up in his arms. "No problem. She and the baby together don't weigh as much as that furniture you've always got me moving around."

He carried her out to their old station wagon and settled her in the back seat.

Brenda climbed in beside her. "Mary, listen to me. Everything's going to be fine. The bad stuff is over. You're having a baby, and that's a beautiful miracle. Jerry and I will be right here. We'll raise this baby, the three of us." She smiled and patted Mary's hand. "They've been doing it in communes for years, having lots of parents for each child. So we'll just have our very own mini hippie commune. Or maybe that's hippie mini commune. Otherwise it sounds like a tiny little hippie with his own commune."

Mary tried to laugh but another pain turned it into a groan.

"I'm being funny but I'm not joking," Brenda said quietly. "You know we want you and your baby to stay with us. You know we're as excited about this baby as you are. This kid's got it made with all of us just waiting to spoil it rotten!"

"Her," Mary said. "It's a girl. Ben said it's a girl. He said he knows these things and she's a girl."

With Ben's eyes and nose and dark hair, please God.

***

The love inside so fierce it made her dizzy, Mary lay on her side in the hospital bed, curled around her baby, around Rebecca. She'd been reluctant to name her Sharise, reluctant to leave any possible links Charles might pick up on.

"Rebecca," she whispered, touching the soft blond fuzz, marveling again at the tiny hands and feet, the wonder of this precious child who almost hadn't been allowed to survive. "If only your daddy could be here to see you." She bit back the tears that still came when she thought of Ben.

"But your daddy's not here. Because of what I did, he's not here. He was trying to protect us. Your daddy's a hero."

As if she knew what was being said, Rebecca opened her unfocused blue eyes and waved her fists.

"Hi, sweet girl. Are you waking up?"

Rebecca pursed her miniature lips, sighed and settled back to sleep.

Mary tried to stop herself from searching Rebecca's features for Ben. A three-day old baby

looked like other three-day old babies, not like her
mother or her father.

*This baby is ours. I don't care whose eyes or
hair she has, who started the process. I don't care
who planted the seed. It's our baby*. One of the last
things Ben had said to her.

"I don't care, either, Rebecca," she whispered. "I
loved you from the time you were a cluster of cells,
multiplying hourly and making me throw up every
morning. I loved you so much then, I thought I
couldn't possibly love you more. Then you started to
move, like butterfly wings beneath my heart, and I
did love you more. Every day my love for you grew
as you grew, but I never knew how much I could love
until the first time I held you in my arms." She kissed
the soft cheek. "I failed your daddy but I won't fail
you, no matter what it takes. I'll move heaven and
earth for you, sweetheart. I promise."

The door flew open and Brenda charged in
carrying a huge purple teddy bear. Jerry followed
with Mary's suitcase.

"How are both our girls? We're here to take you
home! Look what I brought for Rebecca!"

"And I brought her mommy some clothes so she
doesn't have to leave here in that awful hospital
gown." Jerry set the bag beside the bathroom door.

Mary sat up in bed, holding her child against her
breast. "Has he been back?" she asked, as she'd
asked every time Brenda had come to see her.
Rebecca whimpered, and Mary realized she was
holding her too tightly.

"No, the officer hasn't been back. The other girls at the diner can hardly wait to see the baby! Come to Aunt Brenda while your mommy gets dressed."

Though Mary hated to turn loose of her daughter for even a moment, she relinquished her to Brenda. At least she could still see Rebecca, not like when the infant was out of her sight in the nursery. During those agonizing hours, she spent most of her time going up and down the hall to check on Rebecca, reassure herself that her baby was still there, still all right.

Brenda cuddled Rebecca and cooed over her while Mary took the suitcase and went into the bathroom to change.

"Look at that," she heard Jerry say, "she has knuckles! And fingernails."

"She has everything. She's perfect," Brenda told him. "Here. You hold her."

Mary walked out in time to see Jerry take the small bundle tentatively, as if accepting a priceless, fragile piece of crystal. Not too far off, she thought.

He studied the baby intently then touched her smooth forehead with one big finger. "Hey, Rebecca! This is your Uncle Jerry. Can you say Uncle Jerry?" He looked up, a wide grin stretching his lips, his eyes full of wonder. "She's beautiful, Mary! You got everything just right."

"Of course she's beautiful," Brenda agreed. "My turn to hold her again."

"You've had lots of turns. This is only the second time I've been here," Jerry protested. "You know what? She looks just like my grandfather."

314

"Your grandfather?" Brenda exclaimed. "Oh, she most certainly does not!"

"Sure she does. Bald head, no teeth, wrinkled red face. Uh, oh. She's leaking. You're right. Your turn."

"Come on, I'll show you how to change a diaper."

Mary sat on the edge of the bed, smiling as she watched Brenda and Jerry fuss over Rebecca. If only things weren't so crazy and she could settle down in Plano, near the Pattersons, let them be Rebecca's surrogate aunt and uncle.

But for the rest of her life, she'd be running, looking over her shoulder. Her child would never know a stable home life.

Unless—

The idea punched her in the gut with the force of a sledgehammer...excruciating pain that knocked the breath from her.

No, she couldn't do it, couldn't give up her daughter, couldn't live without her.

But her daughter might not be able to live with her. How far would Charles go to destroy any possible evidence of what he'd done? He'd murdered Ben and tried to murder Rebecca before she was born. There was no reason to think he'd stop just because she was no longer in a womb.

At best, Rebecca would have an erratic existence.

Filled with love! Nobody could love her daughter as much as she did.

Brenda and Jerry loved her baby. Brenda and Jerry Patterson had enough love for everybody, even a stranger who came to their restaurant and fainted.

If she went back to Edgewater, told Charles she'd lost the baby and stayed always in his sight, deliberately led him away from her baby like the killdeer bird who pretended to have a broken wing and lured predators away from her nest, then Charles would stop looking for her child. He'd believe he was safe.

And Rebecca would be safe.

She looked at her daughter, kicking chubby legs as Brenda and Jerry struggled to get the bulky diaper in place.

Did she love her enough to walk away from her, to place her in the care of others to insure that she'd have a good life...that she'd have a life?

Mary licked her dry lips and swallowed around the lump in her throat.

If Brenda and Jerry were willing, she had to do it. She had to leave her child without a backward glance, knowing she'd never see her again, never see her first tooth or her first step, never bake a cake for her birthday or see the wonder on her face at Christmas. If she did this, she could never have any contact with her daughter as long as Charles Morton lived.

Pain, greater than any of her labor pains, knifed through every cell of her body and soul.

She sent the pain away, knowing she couldn't do this if she allowed herself to feel. She'd have to turn her heart to granite, never permit herself any emotion except relief that her daughter was safe and happy.

She walked over to Brenda and took her baby, holding the tiny person, savoring the feel of her soft skin, the blond fuzz on her head, the scent of her, memorizing her perfect features, storing it all away for the empty years ahead.

Rebecca, my precious daughter, I won't be around to watch you grow up and celebrate a good report card or cry with you when you fall and skin your knee, but deep in your heart, in the blood we share, in your blue eyes and blond hair that came from me, in every cell of your body that developed from mine, I'll always be there and I'll always love you.

Chapter 23

Back in Dallas, Rebecca drove from the car rental place to her condo, pulling into the covered parking area behind the units. The complex, a small, quiet one comprised of renovated two-story apartments in the older Oak Lawn area close to downtown Dallas, had a dignified, gracious feel. Large live oak and magnolia trees provided privacy as well as shade.

Moving slowly, as if uncertain of where she was going, she entered her unit through the kitchen door. Though she'd left the air conditioning set on low, the place had a closed-up, uninhabited odor. The familiar two-bedroom dwelling, decorated in subdued southwest style, seemed large, empty and unfamiliar. The silence rang loudly in her ears.

Upstairs in her bedroom, she tossed her suitcase onto the king size bed which seemed to mock her with the huge, unused spaciousness. The motel bed she and Jake had shared had been a small double and more than big enough for the two of them.

The ache she'd been fighting ever since she'd left Jake in Edgewater threatened to overpower her. If her world had crashed around her before, now that crash was doubled.

She'd give anything to have her parents back, to run to Plano and have the man and woman who'd raised her comfort her and make her laugh. To love her and always be there for her.

Leaving the suitcase unopened on her bed, she pulled an overnight bag from the closet and filled it with clean clothes. She couldn't stay there that night, couldn't sleep in that large, sterile bed or go downstairs to that subdued, sterile living area. She'd spend the weekend in Plano, reestablish contact with all the years she'd become detached from, get a firm footing in the past and then maybe she could go on to the future.

   ***

Rebecca woke Monday morning in her old room. She'd spent the weekend regaining her parents then grieving for their loss and searching for a core of peace within herself.

It was time to leave.

She rose and made her bed, smoothing the faded spread with its floral pattern. Odd that she'd yearned to sleep beneath Doris Jordan's floral spread, completely forgetting that she had her own.

Not really forgetting, she corrected. She'd just seen it so many times that she had ceased to really see it.

She moved about the room, looking carefully at all the familiar, forgotten objects, storing them away to keep as a part of her...the lamp with a cola stain on the side of the shade that was always carefully turned to the wall, the battered chest of drawers, the durable white-painted iron bed frame where she'd gotten her head caught between the bars and screamed bloody murder until her mother had raced in to rescue her.

She touched the cold metal and smiled, remembering how Brenda Patterson had made her laugh with her threats to pour cooking oil in her hair if her head didn't slip through, then had gently maneuvered that head safely to freedom.

"I'm sorry I doubted you, Mom and Dad," she whispered. "I know you loved me, and I love you. And I miss you something awful. If only you were here, you'd know the exactly right thing to say to explain why those people acted so strange, why the woman who gave me to you didn't want me."

They'd even be able to explain Jake.

Not that she needed to have Jake explained. She understood him only too well. He'd been upfront with her from the beginning, never pretended to be anything other than what he was, never pretended that their relationship was anything other than temporary.

She smiled as she imagined the way Brenda would come up with something witty and off-the-wall that would somehow put Jake in perspective.

Her parents—Brenda and Jerry—had been very special people. She'd been lucky to have them. Whether her birth mother knew it or not, whether she cared or not, she'd done her daughter a favor by turning her over to people who had the ability to love.

Had her birth mother passed to her the same defective gene that had prevented her from wanting her own child? Would Rebecca be forever looking for love where it couldn't be found? That's what she'd been doing when she'd started searching for her biological parents. That's what she'd been doing when she got involved with Jake. Both were futile endeavors, best forgotten and relegated to the past.

She left the house just before noon.

One day soon she'd have to go through and sort out the furnishings and personal items, decide what to keep and what to give away, finish the job she'd started the day she found the blue dress and the note.

Someday but not today.

***

As she approached her condo, she noticed in dismay that a fire truck was parked in the street. Had someone had a fire or was it a medical emergency? The building appeared intact so it couldn't have been a major blaze. She hoped it was a grease fire or something minor, that one of the complex's elderly residents hadn't had a heart attack or worse.

The front door to her unit stood open while firemen milled about.

She came to a screeching halt in the street, got out and ran over.

"What's going on?" she asked the first fireman she saw.

Jake appeared out of nowhere before the man could answer. Such a surge of ecstasy swept over her at the sight of him that she had to blink twice to assure herself it wasn't a fantasy or a case of mistaken identity, of her eyes seeing what her heart wanted.

He strode up to her, anger flushing his face but not before she'd seen the concern and fear. He clutched her shoulders and she thought for one soaring moment that he was going to embrace her.

With a sinking feeling, she realized that she hadn't progressed very far in getting him out of her system, relegating him to the past.

"Where have you been?" he demanded.

She shook off his grasp. "What are you doing here? Why is my door open? What's going on?"

"This your place, lady?" the fireman asked.

"Yes, it is. Will somebody please tell me what's going on?"

"Place was full of gas. You left a burner on your stove going and the flame went out. I think we've about got it cleared, but you ought to leave all the doors and windows open and your fan going the rest of the day. Might even want to sleep downstairs tonight. Gas rises. And in the future you sure need to be more careful, ma'am. If you'd been home, you'd be dead."

The fireman walked away, and Rebecca looked at Jake as horror slowly spread over her. "I didn't turn on my stove," she said, her mouth dry.

Jake nodded. "I know. Let's go inside. We've got some things we need to talk about."

Jake knew he had to sit down soon. He'd never before realized that it was possible to become physically weak from emotional overload.

Saturday night when he couldn't reach Rebecca, he hadn't been overly concerned. But by Sunday he'd become worried, then frantic. He'd driven across town to her condo, rung the bell, pounded on the door and broken it down when she didn't answer.

Finding her home full of gas had sent him into complete panic. He'd raced from room to room looking for her but found only the unopened suitcase on her bed. That had brought up the fear that Charles had kidnapped her.

Now he had to force himself to turn from her, from drinking in the sight of her in hungry gulps, reassuring himself that she was there, alive and safe.

He stepped into her condo, not because he had any reason to go in but simply to try to get away from his own feelings.

She followed. He could feel her presence behind him as if she were physically touching him. As he stepped inside her living room, the scent of summer flowers trailed in and out of the lingering foul odor of natural gas.

"This is getting to be a habit with you," Rebecca said, and he turned to see her examining the splintered frame where he'd kicked in the front door.

"I'll fix it. Won't take an hour."

She wrinkled her nose. "Let's sit out on the step for a while. It smells awful in here."

"Nothing like what it was when I got here a couple of hours ago." He walked back outside, sank down on the concrete step beside her and plucked a blade of grass. Folding the grass, unfolding it, rolling it up and unrolling it, gave him something to do with his hands rather than pulling her to him and touching every inch of her body to reassure himself she was still alive the way he'd been able to do after she'd nearly drowned.

"Where were you this morning?" he demanded. "Where have you been all weekend? I called several

323

times trying to get hold of you to tell you about Charles."

"I went to my parents' house in Plano. What about Charles?"

That was good, referring to the Pattersons as her parents. That meant she really was over her obsession to find her birth parents. She'd slipped back into her slot, would carry on as though the past week had never happened. And so would he.

As soon as he figured out how to end what they'd stirred up in Edgewater, as soon as he knew for sure she was safe.

"I think we may have some major problems, Rebecca."

"You mean like the nest of hornets I disturbed in Edgewater that seems to have followed me back here?" She picked up a pebble from the small flower bed of marigolds beside her front step and flung it across the lawn. "Damn every one of them! What did I do to them? Why are they doing this to me?"

He could tell it hurt, but her anger was a shield against the pain. She'd learned a lot, come a long way from that vulnerable, fragile woman who'd walked into his office.

"I have some more information, Rebecca. But I think it's going to bring up more questions than it's going to answer."

She looked at him a long time, her eyes shifting from green to blue and back again as the shadows from the live oak blowing in the breeze shifted. Finally she exhaled in a long sigh, drew her knees up, wrapped her arms around them and looked away. "I probably don't need to know, but go ahead and tell me."

"Actually, you do need to know. You need to know who you're up against." What the man who could be her father was capable of. "When I got back up here Saturday and checked with my office, I had a message from my buddy on the force that I asked to run a check on Charles."

She flinched but remained stoically silent.

"Using the official information my friend got, I made a few phone calls and came up with a fairly well rounded picture of Charles. Seems His Honor the Mayor got off to a rocky start in life. His parents were religious fanatics. His dad wanted to be a preacher, but he was so far off center that no legitimate church would take him. So he formed his own little cult, *little* being the operative word here. He was zealous enough but lacked the charisma of a cult leader. Nobody wanted to follow him."

Rebecca nodded. "Doris mentioned that Charles would be president except he didn't have the charisma. Guess he inherited that from his father."

"Apparently. Anyway, a few misfits came out to their farm from time to time but nobody stayed for long. The only congregation the old man could count on was his wife and son. According to the people I talked to who remembered that far back, the dad spent a lot of time trying to beat the devil out of his wife and Charles, literally, and the mother then passed her frustration along by abusing the boy, physically and verbally."

"Nice family."

He hesitated, knowing she had to be considering the fact that they could be discussing her own grandparents. And the worst was yet to come. But she had to know. Her life depended on it.

"Charles seemed determined to pull himself up by the bootstrap. In spite of everything, he did well in school, played football, made decent grades, went to college. He wasn't a popular kid, too much of a bully, but he did some things right. He had plans to be a lawyer."

He studied the firm set of her slender shoulders, determined but too narrow to carry what he was about to tell her. That was why he'd decided to deliver the news in person, so he could be there for her.

"The summer before he was to leave for college, the teenage daughter of the Baptist preacher accused him of rape."

Rebecca sat up straight and whirled around to face him, her eyes wide, the pupils pinpoints.

"It never went to trial. In those days the attitude toward rape was different, something to be shoved under the carpet and ignored. The girl didn't even tell anybody until she turned up pregnant. Charles denied it, of course. Accused the girl of trying to ruin his life, making up lies. Then two more girls came forth to accuse him of the same thing, both of them good church-going, God-fearing kids."

"Janelle Griffin," she whispered, the sound so soft he read her lips more than heard her words. "That describes her perfectly. She was the daughter of a minister. He took advantage of her naiveté, got

326

her to trust him, and then he raped her and she killed herself."

"That's pretty much the way I have it figured. Anyway, Charles was persuaded to join the army and serve his country in lieu of embarrassing the girls by having a messy trial. By all reports, he was pretty upset about being forced out of school and into the Army. Blamed the poor pregnant girl, of course. Swore up until the time the kid was born that it wasn't his, but the baby had his blood type, B negative, rare enough there wasn't much doubt. He never went back to Williford. Met Ben Jordan in the Army and made his way to Edgewater."

Rebecca drew a shaky hand over her face. "My blood type is A positive." Her voice was as shaky as her hand.

He didn't say anything, couldn't bear to destroy her single ray of hope.

"Which doesn't prove anything, does it?" she went on, shooting herself down. "Not until we know what my mother's blood type is."

"Yeah. You can inherit your blood type from either parent. Today we have DNA testing. That's the only way to be positive."

She emitted a choking sound somewhere between a hysterical laugh and a sob. "So we just go up to Charles and ask for some of his blood to match to my DNA. Or, better yet, we find his latest rape victim and get a sample of his sperm. Then we dig up Janelle Griffin's body and take a sample of her bones."

He grabbed her shoulders. "Stop it! Don't do this to yourself!"

She twisted away from him and shot to her feet. Feverish spots of pink burned on each pale cheek. "At least we know why dear old Dad wants me gone. DNA testing would prove he's been up to his old tricks." She leaned her head back and closed her eyes. "God, I wish I'd never found that note or that blue dress! I wish I'd never thought I needed to know my roots. My father's a rapist who wants to kill me, and my mother committed suicide rather than live with the guilt of my birth. And both sets of grandparents are religious fanatics. Some roots. Thank goodness I've never had children. What a set of genes to pass on!"

A blinding flash of jealousy shot through Jake as he thought of Rebecca's potential children...of the father of those children.

He stood, wanting to put his arms around her and crush her to him, though the desire came as much from a need to hold her as from a need to comfort. So he didn't dare indulge. "In the first place, you still don't know for sure that Charles and Janelle are your parents, and in the second, you've turned out pretty damned good. I don't think you need to worry about the fate of your children."

He walked down the steps, away from her, trying to escape the unsettling picture that frightening flash of jealousy had illuminated. Incorporated in the fear he'd had for Rebecca's safety when she didn't return his phone calls had been his own fear of rejection...that she was at home and avoiding his calls, avoiding him.

What the hell was going on with him? The master of loving and letting go, the man who knew the ropes, understood the rules, lived for the thrill of the moment and didn't indulge in impossible romantic fantasies. Was it possible he'd fallen in love?

While Rebecca had been learning the temporary nature of love, the need to live in the present only, he'd been losing his mind.

No matter. Whatever it was, it wouldn't last. All he had to do was keep his mouth shut, not do anything dumb, ride this out and wait for the feeling to go away.

She came to stand beside him, tall and willowy and unbowed. In spite of the tough blow she'd just received, a blow that would have been fatal only a few days ago, she wasn't breaking. She was upset, her features ashen and drawn. But she hadn't gone under. She was a survivor after all.

That only reinforced the feeling he had for her. Whatever that feeling was, it was only getting stronger, showed no signs of going away any time soon.

"What do I do now?" she asked, her voice unsteady yet determined. "I have to do something. I can't spend the rest of my life waiting for my father to kill me."

"I don't know. I've been thinking about it ever since I got this report, and I haven't come up with any answers. If it is Charles Morton who's doing these things, we're going to have a hard time getting the authorities to listen. He's got the Edgewater Police Department in his back pocket, and there is an unwritten loyalty between policemen everywhere. Most of the time, it's a good thing, something that has to be there when you're putting your life on the line every day. But that loyalty has been known to cause them to be blind to the faults of fellow officers."

"Like the officers who came to the motel Friday night."

"Yeah, like them."

She wrapped her arms about herself. "So we need tangible evidence, and what we have is a phone call in the middle of the night, a broken headlight, a missing dress, a harmless snake, a near drowning and my gas left on. Threatening, near-fatal, but nothing solid."

"Afraid so. If the motel owner in Edgewater is willing to corroborate the story that you tried to commit suicide, and I'm betting he will, then we don't have much. I called the Dallas police this morning when I couldn't find any sign of you, told them the whole story, and they weren't too concerned. Told me I'd have to wait twenty-four hours to file a missing persons report. None of my former buddies work this area, so I was just your ordinary over-wrought..." He hesitated, the word *lover* poised on his lips. "Caller," he finished.

Rebecca nodded. "If I hadn't gone to my parents' house, I'd be dead and it would have looked like a suicide."

330

"I'm sure that was the whole idea."

She smiled wryly. "Even now, my parents—Brenda and Jerry, that is—are still taking care of me."

"Yeah, it looks like they are."

Rebecca was definitely getting her head on straight, getting things worked out.

"I'm going to call Lorraine Griffin and confront her," she said with that same reluctant but determined tone.

"It's a place to start." He turned and started back inside.

She took his arm, halting him in place.

"I'll do it," she said. "You don't work for me anymore. Remember?"

He wanted to shake off her grasp, tell her to stop being silly and let him make the phone call. But the bare skin below his shirt sleeve where her fingers wrapped gently around his arm didn't want to shake her off. Her touch, even under these circumstances, was like spring sunshine after a hard, cold winter.

Hard, cold winter? It had only been two days since he'd seen her, two days and two nights since he'd made love to her and held her in his arms. Did that constitute a hard, cold winter?

Apparently it did.

Her eyes darkened as if she could read his distress, and she dropped her fingers.

"I remember that I got a lot more out of Lorraine Griffin last time than you did," he countered, the edges of his words rough and grating. "If I don't work for you anymore, then you can't give the orders. I'll call Lorraine Griffin."

She stared at him for a moment, and he opened his mouth to apologize, to explain that he was irritated with himself, not with her. But he didn't have a chance.

"You can get on the extension if you want, but I'm doing the talking. I don't take orders either, and this is something I need to do." She brushed past him, walked inside, and picked up the phone.

She turned and looked at him. "I have nineteen messages!"

He tried to smile and make light of something that was far from light. "Most came from me. I got worried when you didn't answer my calls. That's why I came over and broke down your door."

"Oh." She smiled. "Thank you, Jake. For rescuing me again. Or at least trying to." She was so damned tantalizing standing there in the smelly condo, wearing a pair of faded cutoffs and a white shirt, looking vulnerable and strong and fragile and tough.

She's getting it together, you jerk. Don't mess her up.

"Any time." He took out his small notebook, flipped through a couple of pages and handed it to her. "Here's Lorraine's number."

She punched in the numbers. "It's ringing."

He stepped into the kitchen, picked up the portable phone and returned to stand behind her.

"Hello?"

"Mrs. Griffin, this is Rebecca Patterson." She hesitated for only a heartbeat. "Am I your granddaughter?"

For a moment electronic silence hummed over the phone line.

"How dare you suggest something like that!" Lorraine Griffin's voice exploded. "My Janelle went to her grave pure as the day she was born!"

"Did she? Or did Charles Morton rape her?" Rebecca wasn't pulling any punches.

"What do you want, coming around and trying to stir up things best left buried?"

"I want to live, that's what I want. Somebody's trying to kill me because of all those shameful little secrets you people have buried in your shameful little town."

"I'd be careful about looking for those buried secrets if I was you. You may not like what you find."

"I'm sure I won't like it, but I don't have much choice as it stands right now. I seem to have started a chain reaction. One way or the other, those secrets are going to rise up out of the muck, into the light. Don't you think it would be best if that could happen before they harm any more people?"

"Janelle had nothing to do with you. If my girl had a baby, bastard or not, she wouldn't have thrown it away. You're no kin to me, and you'd better not go around saying you are." Rebecca flinched as the receiver on the other end was slammed down.

Jake placed a hand on her shoulder. "You okay?"

She nodded then turned to look at him. "I believe the part about her not being my grandmother." One corner of her mouth quirked upward in a half-hearted, wry smile. "But maybe just because I want to believe it."

"I think she believes it. But I'm not so sure about the rest. She didn't deny that Charles raped Janelle. Lord only knows how many other defenseless women he's attacked. Doris said he goes to Dallas and Fort Worth a lot. Maybe that's so he can keep his misdeeds away from his own back door."

Her unwavering gaze held his. "Maybe. And maybe we're not completely off base about him. Maybe my mother was one of his victims, and that's why she didn't want me, the child of a rape."

Suddenly Rebecca was ready to take on the world, face her greatest fears, stand alone. Suddenly she was the type woman he could have an affair with, not worry about hurting her because she didn't need him or anyone else.

He was happy for her.

So why couldn't he be happy for himself too? Wasn't this what he wanted, this tantalizing woman he couldn't resist, strong enough to handle a no-commitments-given-none-expected fling?

"Doris Jordan knows something," she continued. "Do you have her number?"

"Flip back a couple of pages in my notebook," he told her. "It's in there."

Doris answered on the first ring.
"This is Rebecca. I—"

"Please don't call me again, Rebecca. You've got to forget about everything and everybody down here."

"She'd like to do that," Jake interjected, "but something she unearthed has followed her home. There's been another attempt on Rebecca's life."

Doris' gasp was soft but quite distinct.

"Somebody broke into her condo and turned on the gas. Fortunately Rebecca wasn't home, but we can't count on that kind of luck the next time. Unless you want to be a party to her murder," Jake continued, pushing his advantage relentlessly, "you're going to have to tell us what you know. We can't fight an invisible enemy."

"Doris," Rebecca said when the older woman didn't answer, "I need your help. Please."

"Yes," Doris replied quietly. "Something has to be done. Can the two of you come to my house today?"

"We'll leave right now," Jake said.

"It's time to make things right," Doris said. "It's time, Rebecca, for you to meet your mother."

Chapter 24

"Mary, what's going on?"

Mary looked up from her desk to see David standing in the doorway of her office at the library. She smiled as if nothing was wrong and waved a hand at the scattered papers. "I'm working."

He shut the door behind him then walked around to put his hands on her shoulders and gently massage her neck. "Your muscles are even tighter than usual. Yesterday in church you were so distracted you'd have left after communion if I hadn't stopped you. Then I had to nudge you to get moving after the recessional. Now you're working on your day off, and Eunice called to tell me to get you out of here."

"Eunice called you?"

"Yes, she's worried about you. So am I." His gentle fingers continued to work on her neck muscles, but she knew his efforts were futile. Those muscles weren't going to unknot. Not for a while. A long while. Not until she knew for certain that her daughter was safe.

She patted David's hand. "I'm fine. Do you want to come over for dinner tonight?"

Socializing was the last thing in the world she wanted to do right then, but she had to act as if nothing was wrong, she had to continue with her twenty-nine year charade.

He moved around to sit on the desk and face her. "I'd love to come for dinner," he said softly. "For dinner and the rest of your life."

She turned away, back to her work.

He took her left hand, his fingers rubbing the golden band she hadn't taken off since Ben placed it there. She tried to pull away, but his grip was surprisingly firm.

"I don't expect you to stop loving him," he said, "but surely you have room in your heart to love more than one person."

She looked up at his concerned, familiar features. "David, you know how I feel about you."

"No, I don't. For six years we've been together almost constantly, but we never talk about us."

"When we first started seeing each other, we agreed that neither of us wanted anything but companionship, no involvement."

"That was right after my wife died. Things change." He stood, a scowl wrinkling his brow. "I still love my wife. I'll never forget her, and I don't expect you to stop loving Ben or to forget him, but they're both dead and we're alive. Why shouldn't we continue to live?"

"You don't understand."

He threw his hands into the air. "Of course I don't! You won't give me the chance to understand. You've always kept a part of you secret from me, and now something's going on and you won't let me be a part of that, either. Mary, I love you, but I'm getting tired of waiting, of only having half a person."

For a moment panic surged over Mary, fear that she'd lose David, a sudden realization of how much he meant to her. But she shoved that fear aside. "I'm sorry. That's all I have to give. I don't want to lose you, but I can't—" She shook her head. "I can't do what you're asking."

She couldn't open her heart to him anymore than she could open it to the tall blond woman who'd come into the library last week, who'd walked out of Doris' house to meet her and later confronted them at the cemetery.

Though Mary hadn't wanted to, she'd taken in every detail of her daughter at those three beautiful, scary, sad meetings. She knew the exact shade of Rebecca's hair, the way it swung about her face, the arch of her eyebrows, the single vertical line that appeared between them when she frowned, the curve of her cheeks, the length of her slender fingers, could probably even guess her shoe size.

But if she ever let herself dwell on those details, on how she'd felt when she'd seen Rebecca, if she ever relaxed and turned loose of one hair's breadth of control, the entire structure of her soul would collapse. She wouldn't be able to bear the loss of her daughter, her husband, her world.

If she turned loose of that control she'd take Ben's gun—the one she'd fired to frighten Charles away from drowning her daughter—and she'd march over to the mayor's office, and this time she wouldn't aim above Charles' head. She'd aim right at his black heart and squeeze the trigger until the gun was empty, until Charles was dead, until Rebecca was safe and—

"Mary!"

"What?"

David shook his head and ran his fingers through his hair. "You did it again, went completely away from me, off into another world."

The phone on her desk rang, and Mary's heart sprinted into overdrive, the way it had done with every phone call since Doris had casually, innocently mentioned the detective who wanted to talk to her about the blue dress and the woman who was searching for her mother.

She lifted the receiver. "Mary Jordan."

"Mary, this is Doris. You need to come to my house as soon as you can. We have to talk. Rebecca and Jake will be here in about three hours."

"No! They returned to Dallas!"

"I asked them to come."

"But I told you…" She looked up at David. He stood with his back toward her, but she knew he was listening. "Just a minute, Doris." She covered the mouthpiece of the phone. "I need to take this call."

He turned and nodded, his expression strained. "I'll see you at your house later."

She gazed at him, unable to take in what he was saying, unable to think about anything except the fact that her daughter was returning to danger.

"For dinner," he said.

"Oh. Dinner. I don't know. I'll call you."

"Right." He walked out, closing the door behind him.

"David, wait!" She stood, wanting to go after him, call him back, then she remembered the phone in her hand. "Doris, we agreed that we had to get her out of town. I told you the whole story and you agreed to help me."

"Things have changed. There's been an attempt on Rebecca's life all the way up in Dallas."

Mary's stomach clenched into a knot. "Oh, no! Is she all right?"

"For the moment. Someone broke into her condo and turned on the gas, thinking she was sleeping upstairs. She wasn't. She spent the weekend at the Pattersons' old house in Plano. But we're going to have to tell her. We're going to have to do something about Charles. We've got to stop running and fight back."

Mary searched the corners of her mind for an answer, a way to guarantee Rebecca's safety now that Charles knew about her. With a sinking feeling, she realized the time to run and hide was over. Doris was right. They had no choice but to fight. "Yes," she assented quietly. "It's time."

"Mary," Doris said, her voice softer, "it's also time you met your daughter."

"I met her at the library and at your house and at the cemetery. I can't bear to see her again. It's too hard." Mary spoke the words through numb lips, her mind already leaping ahead to what had to be done.

"I mean really meet her. Tell her who you are." Doris paused. When she spoke again, her words were even softer. "Take her in your arms and tell her you love her. She needs that very badly, and so do you.

All these years I've known something was eating away at you. I thought it was because you couldn't accept Ben's death. Now that I know the truth, I don't see how you've managed. This can't go on any longer."

Mary couldn't think about what Doris was suggesting. It could never happen, and to even consider it then let it slip away would be too painful.

"I'll come by your house when I get through here," she promised. "I have some things to finish."

"All right, sweetheart. Get here as soon as you can."

Mary depressed the button, breaking the connection but still holding the receiver. Without hesitation, she dialed another number.

"City of Edgewater. How may I direct your call?"

"Mayor Charles Morton's office, please."

Charles had all his calls screened, but she knew he'd talk to her. And he did.

"Mary, to what do I owe the pleasure of this call?"

"I need to see you."

"Come on by my office any time you want. I'm always here for you."

"No. You come to that old farmhouse where you killed Ben."

He clicked his tongue a couple of times. "Mary, Mary. You shouldn't make such accusations. Bad things happen to people who talk too much."

"You be at that house in two hours or I'm going to talk about a lot more than Ben's death."

He chuckled. "Are you threatening me? That's not a smart thing to do. Much as I'd enjoy seeing you again, I'm a busy man. Afraid I can't make your little rendezvous."

She lied without the slightest hesitation. "Rebecca Patterson is going to be there with me. She has evidence about her birth that either you or the media is going to be very interested in. I don't think she much cares who has the story first. It's your choice."

She slammed down the phone and turned to her typewriter.

My dearest Rebecca, she typed. *I'm not sure if I'll be dead or in jail when you read this. Probably the former. But one thing I promise you, you'll finally be truly safe.*

The phone rang but she ignored it.

Chapter 25

It's time for you to meet your mother.

Over and over the words echoed through Rebecca's mind as she rode beside Jake, hands clenched in her lap, while they sped toward the small town she'd come to hate and fear. The town and the mother she'd vowed to put behind her.

"You sure you're ready for this?" Jake asked as they passed the city limits sign a scant two hours after they left her condo.

No, I'm not ready!

"Yes."

"You're a tough lady."

"Yes." Her second lie in less than a minute. She didn't feel tough at all right now.

Only this morning she'd told herself that her birth parents didn't matter, that Jake didn't matter. What a cruel twist of fate that, her rational decision made, she wasn't allowed time to implement it before being thrust into the company of the very people she needed to forget.

Jake had barely spoken the entire trip as he sat hunched over the steering wheel, glaring at the road ahead, watching for radar traps. Those flickers of caring and concern that she'd thought she'd seen when she'd arrived home a few hours ago had obviously been her overactive, needy imagination. Even if he had been concerned about her welfare, now that she was safe...for the moment...that concern was gone.

She was grateful, however, for his silence. She didn't want to think about what awaited her in Edgewater, speculate on who her mother might be. If she was going to be able to meet her, she assumed that ruled out Janelle Griffin. The alternatives would seem to be Ben Jordan's mistress, a complete stranger they knew nothing about or Mary Jordan.

Surely even the cruelest fate wouldn't stick her with the cold Mary Jordan for a mother, a woman who so obviously disliked her, and crazy Charles Morton for a father, a man who was probably trying to kill her.

Focusing on the dotted white line of the highway as it marched before them then disappeared beneath Jake's car, she forced her thoughts to Brenda and Jerry, to the happy times of her life, to the strength and love they'd given her. It would be enough to get her through this and out the other side. It had to be enough. It was all she had.

Jake turned onto Doris Jordan's street and recalled how innocent the neighborhood had seemed the first time she'd seen it, how innocent she'd been. If anything, Brenda and Jerry had loved her too much, protected her too much. While she'd been living in the safe cocoon they'd provided, selfishly wanting to be the only special person in their lives, an entire world of pain and loneliness and evil had been going on outside.

Jake parked in front of Doris' cozy white house with the colorful splash of flowers.

"Rebecca, I—" Jake compressed his lips, twisted his hands on the steering wheel, looked away from her then back. "You fired me. I don't work for you now. I'm here solely in the capacity of friend. I'm here because I...I care about what happens to you."

The kind comment was like a knife through her heart. Better he should turn and walk away than offer to be just her friend after the passion they'd shared, the passion that had meant so much to her and so little to him.

"Thank you," she said. "I appreciate that." She had become an accomplished liar.

She looked up to see Doris hurrying down the walk toward them, her peaceful features contorted with worry and fear.

"Jake, did you bring a gun?" Doris asked as soon as she reached them.

Rebecca's blood froze.

"Yes, I did," Jake replied. "It's in the glove box."

"We're probably going to need it." Doris yanked open the back door and slid in. "We've got to get out to the old house where my son was killed. It may already be too late. Turn left at the next street and I'll direct you. It's about five miles out of town. Don't worry about speed limits. The entire police force is about to be turned upside down."

Jake pulled away with a screeching of tires.

"What's going on?" Rebecca's lips seemed to crack as she spoke.

"Mary—your mother—"

"My mother?" Rebecca gasped in dismay, whirling around to look over the seat at Doris.

345

"Mary Jordan?" Jake exclaimed in disbelief.

"Mary Jordan, your mother," Doris continued evenly. "She's going to kill Charles Morton and probably get herself killed. Turn right at the top of that hill."

"My mother?" Rebecca repeated, unable to comprehend Doris' second statement about Charles Morton until she could grasp the concept of Mary Jordan as her mother. "Mary hates me! She won't even speak to me or shake my hand!"

Doris smiled sadly. "Your mother loves you very much, enough to give you up so you'd be safe. She's spent the last twenty-nine years thinking of you and missing you and living in constant fear trying to protect you."

"Trying to protect me? What are you talking about?"

"From Charles Morton. He wants you dead."

Rebecca's heart clenched painfully as if it would shrink to a hard, shriveled hickory nut. "So he is my father," she said dully.

"We can't be sure, but he thinks he is and as long as you're alive, you could prove he raped your mother. You could end his career." Doris spoke briskly and without emotion as though she could thus make her words less painful. "After I talked to you, I called Mary and told her what happened in Dallas. I told her it was time to stop running and fight back. She agreed, but when she got to my house, she gave me two letters, one for you and one for the authorities. She told me not to open either of them until she got back, but I opened the one for the police as soon as she was out the door."

She handed two envelopes to Rebecca who took them with fingers so numb she feared the paper rectangles would slip through.

"It's the whole story," Doris went on, "including the fact that after I called her, she called Charles and told him to meet her at that old house. She lied to him and said you'd be there too so she could get him out there. She knows you'll never be safe as long as he's alive. She has Ben's revolver. It's the gun she used to scare off Charles the night he pushed you into the swimming pool."

"She—" Rebecca licked her dry lips, but her tongue was dry, too. Sandpaper on sandpaper. Confusion swirled around and through her at this new picture of her mother and the confirmation that the man who might be her father was trying to kill her.

"Mary was there," Jake said. "That's how you already knew about the incident the next day."

"She was there. She called your room to get you down to the pool when she saw Rebecca sitting alone. She was afraid Charles would try something, and he did. All these years she's devoted her life to making Charles believe you were dead, Rebecca, and then you two showed up asking questions. She tried to warn you off the first day with that phone call, but you're as stubborn as she is."

"The snake?" Rebecca asked, barely able to squeeze out the two words.

Doris nodded. "She had Lucinda do that. They've known each other all their lives. She also

347

had Lucinda steal the dress because she was afraid I'd remember it. But nothing worked. You wouldn't leave. When she found out you were going to stay with me, she told me the whole story. I'll tell you as much as I can on the way, but if I don't finish or if anything happens to me, the rest is in those envelopes."

Between giving directions to Jake, Doris told Rebecca an unbelievable horror story of Mary's rape, her husband's death and Charles' determination that Rebecca was his daughter and that he had to kill her to protect himself.

As Rebecca listened, her stomach tightened and she thought she was going to be sick. The nightmare Mary Jordan had suffered, the inhuman cruelty of Charles, all the things that had gone on around her without her ever knowing. She had, indeed, led a sheltered life.

"There's the place," Doris said grimly. "Or what's left of it after so many years, and there's Mary's car."

Jake swung his car into the weeds that surrounded the ruins of the old house. He leaned over, opened the glove compartment and took out a holster then deftly extracted the black revolver. "Stay here," he ordered, opening his door.

For an instant Rebecca sat paralyzed, but then she scrambled out, too. She had to meet the mother who'd loved her so much after all, so much she was ready to sacrifice her own life. And she wanted to see Charles Morton again, to scratch out his pale eyes, to slap his arrogant face, to cut off his testicles for what he'd done to so many women.

Jake shot her a scowling glance.

"I told you, I don't take orders," she said.

The tall weeds scratched at her bare legs and hampered her progress, but she pushed forward determinedly, reaching the ramshackle porch at almost the same time as Jake.

She entered the open doorway beside him.

"Oh, my God! What are you doing here?" Mary stepped from the shadows in a back corner of the room, one hand clutching her throat, the other behind her...holding Ben's gun, no doubt. Late afternoon sun streamed through a hole in the roof, illuminating her light hair and horror stricken face. "Get out of here! Doris, what have you done? Charles will be here any minute!"

Doris moved in front of them, stepping carefully over the broken boards in the floor. "What have I done? Brought your daughter to you. Come and meet her, talk to her. Hold her for the first time in twenty-nine years."

Mary moved sideways, away from Doris. A tear rolled down her cheek as the horror in her eyes turned to yearning. "Please leave. Now. Before he gets here."

"We'll face him together, Mary, contact the authorities, make him pay for what he's done."

"The authorities?" Mary gave a quick, sharp imitation of a laugh. "Which authorities shall we contact, Doris? The police? He has something on at least half the force, maybe more. Farley's been solidly behind him ever since he made the evidence against Farley's son disappear in that drug case a few years ago."

"Farley hates him. Everybody does. Somebody has to be the first to speak up, and that somebody needs to be you."

"Farley may hate him, but I'm sure Charles still has that evidence. Even Lucinda was terrified to help me at the motel because Charles keeps her in line by threatening to send her mother back to Mexico. Farley won't say anything. He'll look out for his son, and you can't blame him for that." She darted a quick glance at Rebecca, then focused on Jake. "If you care anything about my daughter, you've got to get her out of here!"

"Not without you." Rebecca finally found her voice.

Mary wavered and took a step toward Rebecca.

"Isn't this just too cozy? The whole family's here."

Rebecca whirled to see Charles standing in the open doorway.

A loud explosion burst through the house followed by five more.

Charles stumbled, pushed backward by each shot, until he fell onto the porch.

Rebecca whirled toward Mary in time to see her lower the gun to her side and heave a sigh of relief. Doris rushed to her daughter-in-law, supporting her as she sagged.

Jake shoved his own gun into his belt and sprinted toward Charles.

"Stop right there." Farley Gates, clutching an automatic in both hands, stood behind Charles who was, amazingly, struggling to his feet.

Jake came to a halt, one hand reaching for his weapon.

"Don't even think about it unless you want to die," Charles advised, rubbing his chest as he eased forward and yanked Jake's gun out of his belt. "As I was saying, the whole family's here, except you're not really family, Doris. Don't you know that Mary's bastard is no relation to you?"

"Dear God," Mary exclaimed. "You really are a monster. How can anybody survive six bullets?"

Charles smiled. "Mary, Mary, Mary. Did you really think I'd come here unprotected after you tried to shoot me at the swimming pool?" He thumped his chest. "Bullet-proof vest. The policeman's best friend. Those bullets packed quite a wallop. I'll be bruised and sore for days, but no real harm done. You always have been naive. That's how you got to me that day your little bastard was created." He nodded toward Rebecca. "I gave her life and it's my right to end it. Charles Morton giveth and Charles Morton taketh away."

Mary, Jake and Doris moved as a unit to stand in front of Rebecca.

"Oh, stop the heroics," Charles ordered. "You're all going to die in an unexplained fire so what difference does it make who goes first? Farley, where's that gasoline?"

They were all going to die. Somehow the threat didn't hold the power it might have. If this man was her father, Rebecca didn't care if she died.

But Mary was her mother. Mary had given her up to save her life, had tried to commit murder for her. That courageous blood ran through her own veins, and she wasn't going to surrender easily. There had to be something she could do.

"How long do you think you can get away with this?" Jake demanded. "How long is it going to be before somebody takes you down? You can't control people with threats forever."

"Sure I can."

Rebecca pushed between Jake and Mary even as Jake tried to restrain her. "I'm not your daughter," she said quietly. "I couldn't be. I'm nothing like you."

"She's not your daughter," Mary echoed. "Look at her. Look at Doris. She has Doris' eyes, Ben's nose. She's Ben's daughter!"

"Mary, what was Ben's blood type?" Jake asked.

"A positive," Doris answered for her. "I just realized who you reminded me of the first time I met you, Rebecca. Myself when I was young."

"Mary? Blood type?" Jake continued.

"O positive," Mary said.

"Rebecca's A positive, Charles." Jake wrapped his arm tightly about her waist. "Like her father. Her mother's O positive, and you're B negative. No way can she be your daughter. Why don't you just turn around and walk out of here before you do something you'll regret?"

Farley Gates came back with a large red can and began to splash liquid around the floor and walls. The acrid smell of gasoline permeated the air.

"Regrets are a waste of time and energy. I don't regret our afternoon together, Mary, not even considering all the problems it's caused me. The only thing I regret is not doing away with another idiot woman back in Ohio. She did what you tried to do to me. Her brat ruined my life. I'd be president now if not for that bitch. I had to start all over and do it the hard way, but I'll still get there in spite of you fools. And, believe me, I damn sure won't regret getting rid of any of you."

Jake folded his arms across his chest and looked down at the floor. "I'll take Charles, you get Gates," he whispered.

She gave a single, brief nod. As if she could read his mind, she knew exactly what Jake wanted. Charles had backed him into a corner, told him they were going to die no matter what. When Jake went for Charles, she was to tackle Gates, an easier target since both of his hands were occupied with the can of gasoline while his gun hung in a holster at his side.

"At least let Doris go." Jake moved forward a step, gesturing with one hand toward Doris. "She has nothing to do with any of this. Your problem is with Mary and Rebecca and now with me."

"I'm sick of all of you." Charles cocked the hammer of Jake's revolver, and Jake lunged forward, tackling the mad man and throwing him to the floor just as the gun went off.

A loud whoosh sounded from across the room as Rebecca charged Gates. He dropped the can, staring toward the column of flames sparked by Charles' bullet.

Ignoring the burst of searing heat, Rebecca flew into him, adrenaline lending her strength as she scratched his fleshy face with one hand and fumbled for his pistol with the other.

"I've got his gun." Doris stood beside her, calm voice audible above the steadily increasing roar of the fire.

Rebecca stumbled backward, away from Gates. Heat scorching her face and arms, smoke searing her lungs, she spun around to see if Jake was all right.

Against the backdrop of the flames greedily devouring the dry wood of the old house, Jake stumbled to his feet clutching his gun in one hand. Morton lay groaning on the floor.

Mary kicked Charles' shoulder. "Damn you!" She kicked his head as he folded himself into a ball, his hands grasping his ankles, tugging at one of his pant legs. "Damn you, damn you, damn you! All these years separated from my daughter because you're a crazy, mean bastard! Damn you!"

"Get out!" Rebecca yelled, grabbing her hand. "This whole place is going to collapse on us any minute now!"

"I ought to let you burn in your own hell, Morton!" Jake leaned down, reaching a hand toward the man on the floor.

Charles yanked a small automatic from a holster on his leg and came to his feet in a single motion, knocking Jake backward and spinning toward Mary.

Rebecca grabbed her mother, stopping her frantic lunge toward Charles.

Doris screamed.

Jake took aim.

A bullet shrieked through the room from the front door, straight to Charles' head.

He crumpled silently into the fire.

Jake grabbed Rebecca's arm and pulled Mary and her out the door as the roof behind them toppled with a crash, sending a burst of searing heat over them with leaping flames right behind.

They sprinted across the porch, toward Doris and Gates who were already outside.

Doris must have shot Charles, Rebecca thought.

The five of them ran through the weeds until they were far enough away from the fire to be able to breathe again. When Rebecca turned to look, all that remained of the house where Ben had died was a raging orange inferno. Her father's murder had been avenged.

"It's over. He's really gone," Mary whispered. "Isn't he?"

"Yeah," Gates said, his voice tired. For the first time Rebecca noticed that the chief of police had his gun back. He held it up and studied it. "The bastard's really gone. Even a monster can't survive a head shot from a .45 and a fire like that. And you were right. He was a monster."

"You shot him?" Jake asked and placed a hand on his gun where he'd again stuck it into his belt.

Farley nodded and offered his weapon, butt first. Jake took it.

"Yeah, I shot him. To protect my son, I did a lot of things for Morton. I thought I could do this, help him commit murder, to protect my son." He shook his head and looked toward the fire. "But it was all so pointless, everything he did. You're not even his daughter."

He turned away, his shoulders slumped, walked slowly toward his squad car, then stopped and looked back. "I'm going to his office before word gets out that he's dead. I found the combination to his safe a few months ago, and I've just been waiting for my chance. I'm going to clean it out and burn everything in there, and a whole lot of people will sleep a whole lot better tonight. If you folks could give me about an hour before you report this, I'd sure appreciate it."

Jake nodded. "I don't think an hour's going to make any difference one way or the other. You file the report and call us when you need us. If you need us."

Gates nodded. "Sorry about the headlight."

"Did you cut Rebecca's brake line?"

"No. I didn't stop Charles from doing it, but I followed you." He shrugged, looking at the ground. "I guess I thought I could pick up some of the pieces when you crashed. I'm sorry. He didn't give me much choice."

"We always have a choice. At least you made the right one in the end." Jake lifted the hand that held

Gates' gun. "Here. You don't want to have to explain how you lost this." Jake tossed Gates his gun.

"Thanks." Gates got in his car and drove away.

Mary dropped her face into her hands and began to sob.

Doris laid one arm about Mary's shoulders and the other about Rebecca's. "Mary, I'd like you to meet your daughter. Rebecca, this is your mother."

Mary looked up. "My baby." Timidly she touched Rebecca's face, drawing her fingers along her daughter's chin, then smiled shyly, her eyes shiny with tears and wonder. "You have my chin and your father's mouth." She reached down and took Rebecca's hands in hers, touching each finger in turn, then raised her eyes again. "Ten. I counted them over and over when you were a baby. I couldn't believe you were so perfect. You still are."

Rebecca opened her mouth to speak, to say something though she had no idea exactly what, but all that came out was a sob. And then she was in her mother's arms as they both laughed and cried.

"We need to get out of here," Jake said. "It's going to be dark soon."

Mary stepped back but kept hold of her daughter's hand. "Will you ride with me, Rebecca?"

"I'll drive Mary's car," Doris said, "and Jake can take you two with him."

Jake shook his head. "No. You take the two of them in Mary's car, Doris. You all need to be together right now."

Though Rebecca's heart was full, she felt a slight twinge at Jake's words, at the coldness in his tone.

"All right," Doris replied. "We'll meet you back at my house."

He shook his head. "I have some things to take care of."

He wasn't going to Doris' house.

Love and let go.

She was safe. Her case was closed. He was walking away.

She should have been prepared, but she wasn't. The bleak shadow of sadness, of loneliness, fell over her happiness. She had made peace with her feelings for Brenda and Jerry and now she'd found the birth mother that a part of her heart must have remembered and loved all these years.

But it wasn't enough. Jake had become a part of her life, had stolen a place in her heart even though he'd never intended to.

If she'd never stopped loving her mother even when she couldn't remember her on a conscious level, how much harder would it be to stop loving Jake when she'd remember him every day for the rest of her life?

"You will come by when you're finished, won't you?" Mary asked Jake, and Rebecca knew that her mother had guessed how she felt. Just as she'd known Jake's thoughts when he'd wanted her to tackle Gates, so her mother knew her thoughts. Through the telepathic bonding of love.

"It'll be too late," Jake replied.

"We'll be up very late." Mary smiled at Rebecca. "We have a lot of years to catch up on."

Jake shoved his hands in his pockets, turned and walked away.

He was gone. He wouldn't be back.

"It's all right, baby," Mary soothed. "He'll be back if I have to hunt him down and drag him to you."

They both laughed, and Rebecca reminded herself that she should be grateful for the love she'd found and not grieve for what she'd lost.

Jake heard the soft laughter of mother and daughter as he yanked open his car door. Rebecca had found what she'd set out to find...a mother who loved her beyond all reason. Though her father was dead, at least she knew who he was, and Mary and Doris would tell her all about him. They'd make him real for her. She had a family.

No wonder she and Doris had bonded so instantly. Grandmother and granddaughter. Blood calling to blood after all.

So what if it hadn't worked that way in his family. Obviously it did in some families.

He drove out to the road, refusing to look back at the three generations of women.

Some people did, after all, love forever. All those years Mary had stayed away from the child she loved because she loved her. That was a forever kind of love.

Rebecca didn't need him anymore. He'd helped her find that love, and now he was free to be on his way, back to his real life. Back to being free.

The loving was over. Now it was time for the letting go.

Chapter 26

The square ivory envelope, hand addressed, came to Jake's office, mixed in with bills and solicitations.

Noreen laid it on his desk in front of him. "Sorry," she said. "I didn't know it was personal. I opened it with the rest of the mail. It's just a wedding invitation, not a letter or anything."

"No problem."

A wedding invitation?

He recognized the neat, precise handwriting instantly. It was the same as he'd seen two months ago on the faded note Rebecca Patterson had handed him. Mary Jordan's handwriting.

He heard the door close quietly and knew Noreen was gone, but he didn't look up. He couldn't seem to tear his gaze away from that ivory envelope.

Was Mary inviting him to her daughter's wedding?

And if she was? What did he care? Why had his gut suddenly clenched into a knot? Why was perspiration breaking out on his upper lip? Why did his chest feel empty and hollow?

He'd almost forgotten about Rebecca.

Well, maybe he hadn't actually almost forgotten about her. The truth was, she'd been in his thoughts pretty often. Constantly, actually. But he hadn't seen her since the night of the fire that killed Charles Morton.

After an off-the-record conversation with Gates, he'd given his statement concerning the events of that night over the phone. He'd corroborated Gates' story detailing how Gates had followed Charles to the old farmhouse, overheard him threaten to kill Mary and Rebecca, then shot Charles before he could shoot Mary. The story was factual; it just left out a few things, like Mary's attempt to kill Charles and Gates' initial complicity with Charles. Jake had no problem with that. Gates had redeemed himself in the end. It was a fair trade-off, to cover Gates' actions in return for covering Mary's.

So it hadn't been necessary to see or talk to Rebecca again. She'd called his office once asking for her bill, but he'd been out and Noreen had taken the call. He'd sent a bill and she'd paid it. End of story.

He tapped the envelope on his desk. It was already open. All he had to do was take out the invitation and read it.

Maybe it wasn't a wedding invitation at all. Maybe Noreen was wrong.

With clumsy, sweaty fingers, he reached in and pulled out the card with wedding bells embossed at the top.

Pain ripped through his gut, and his vision blurred at the verification of Noreen's comment. It was a wedding invitation.

How could Rebecca find somebody so quickly? Had all they'd shared meant nothing to her?

He tossed the card onto his desk and swore under his breath.

What the hell was the matter with him? What he and Rebecca had shared had been wonderful...at the time. But that time was past. It was over.

Love and let go.

He stared down at the printed script, forcing himself to read it, to prove that it didn't bother him that Rebecca was going to marry somebody else.

Mary Elizabeth Jordan and David Carl Baldwin request the honor of your presence at the celebration of their marriage on October 14.

Mary and David's marriage?

Not Rebecca's marriage, but her mother's?

Jake smiled.

He laughed.

He scowled. There was no reason for him to be this relieved and delighted that Rebecca wasn't getting married.

But he was.

He stood, shoved his hands into his pockets and strode over to look out the window. In his mind's eye he saw Rebecca walking across the parking lot the way she had the first day she'd come to his office three months ago—fragile, vulnerable, needy. He'd thought of her then as bent to the ground like a willow branch. But like the willow, she'd proved amazingly tough. She'd withstood attacks on her life as well as on her emotions and emerged a stronger person.

A stronger person who didn't need him.

But he needed her.

Try as he might, he hadn't been able to forget about her. For the first time in his life, he remembered every detail of a woman's face, of her walk, of her touch, of the scent of summer flowers that surrounded her, her blue-green eyes. Every minute of every day since he'd walked away from her at the fire, he'd thought about her and missed her.

The way he'd felt when he'd thought it was Rebecca getting married had forced him to confront that fact, to stop lying and trying to tell himself he was going to forget about her any day now.

He'd fallen in love with Rebecca, and that love wasn't going away.

He sat down at his desk again and picked up the invitation. Mary had probably sent it as a courtesy. She probably didn't expect him to attend the wedding.

But he was going.

He'd done his best to get Rebecca out of his mind and out of his heart, and he'd failed miserably. There was only one thing he could do now.

He had to confront Rebecca.

He had to tell her he loved her.

The very thought sent a shiver down his spine.

If he did that, he ran the risk that she would reject him.

If he never confronted her, she couldn't reject him.

He turned from the window and went back to his chair. His legs had gone strangely shaky.

In a painful burst of self-revelation, he recognized what he was doing. What he'd been doing for years. He'd learned early in life the necessity of maintaining his emotions in a temporary mode. As an adult, he'd left people before they could leave him. Just the way he'd left Rebecca. Only it hadn't worked this time. He'd left her physically, but his heart had stayed with her.

Love and let go.

What self-delusionary crap.

However fragile Rebecca had been when she'd come to his office, she'd had the strength to institute a search for her birth parents, to confront them no matter how things turned out, and for a while it had seemed they were going to turn out pretty bad.

Now he, a cynical, worldly-wise, battle-scarred veteran of life had to dig way down deep inside and find the strength Rebecca had had all along, even when neither she nor he had realized it.

Without the risk of rejection, he had no chance for happiness.

***

Rebecca fluffed her mother's hair and gave it a final spritz of hair spray. "You look beautiful," she said. "Just like a bride."

Mary stood and smoothed the slim skirt of her ivory suit. "I'm so nervous. I can't believe this is really happening. I never thought I'd marry again, and I certainly never thought my daughter would be my maid of honor."

Rebecca smiled and squeezed her mother's hand. "I'm still having a hard time believing any of this myself, but that doesn't stop me from being thrilled about all of it."

Doris entered the small room in the back of the chapel carrying a bouquet of chrysanthemums and other late-blooming flowers from her garden. "How lovely you both are," she said, then handed the bouquet to Mary. "Are you ready? Your groom is waiting."

Mary accepted the flowers. "Thank you, Doris. I guess I'm ready." She looked from Rebecca to Doris. "You both know I wouldn't be doing this without your blessing."

"And you know you have it, from both of us," Doris assured her. "David's a wonderful man."

"He loves you," Rebecca added. "He makes you happy and that makes us happy." In the two months she'd known the quiet professor, she'd come to care for him and to respect him for the kindness he showed her mother.

"Okay," Mary said, squaring her shoulders. "I guess I'm ready." She took a step toward the door, but Doris stopped her with one hand on her arm.

"Mary," she said softly. "Ben's ring. You'll have to take it off."

Mary lifted her left hand, and tears filled her eyes. "I don't think I can. I'll always love Ben."

"Of course you will. But you're marrying David and you'll wear his ring on that finger. Maybe you could move Ben's ring to your other hand."

Mary gave her flowers to Doris and tugged the ring from her finger. "Or," she said, turning to Rebecca, "I could give it to his daughter."

Rebecca's vision blurred as tears welled in her own eyes. "Are you sure?"

"I'm sure. Wearing or not wearing his ring won't change how much I love him. I'll always have him in my heart, right beside you and David and Doris."

"Do you love David more than you loved my father?" Rebecca asked the question she'd wanted to ask for some time.

Mary smiled. "No. I could never love anybody more than I loved Ben. I love David in a different way, with a different part of my heart." She pressed the ring into Rebecca's hand and closed her daughter's fingers around it. "Oh, sweetheart, I spent so many years trying not to love, having you and David is like a banquet after a starvation diet! The more you love, the more you're able to love."

Rebecca nodded. "My parents—I mean—" She stopped herself, not wanting to hurt her mother, to remind her that she still thought of Brenda and Jerry as her parents.

"It's okay. You can have more than one set of parents just like I can have more than one husband. I'm glad the Pattersons were good to you. I knew they would be. They adored you from the minute you were born. Brenda even made them let her into the delivery room."

Rebecca pressed her lips together, blinking rapidly.

"Don't you dare cry!" Mary said with a soft smile. "I don't want my maid of honor to have raccoon eyes."

Rebecca pressed a finger to the corner of each eye to blot the moisture before it could spill. "I can see my mother pushing into the delivery room! I'll bet she had everybody laughing while you were in labor."

"Even me. I'd laugh and then I'd scream. She and Jerry had a rare gift of love."

"Yes, they did. I'd give anything if you could have been with me all those years, but I wouldn't trade the life I had with them. I'd want you both there. You're right. The more you love, the more you're able to love."

Finally she understood that she had been special to her parents, that their love for others had in no way diminished their love for her any more than her love for her mother diminished her love for them.

Rebecca opened her hand and looked at her mother's wedding band, tried it on her ring finger then placed it on her little finger. "Your hands are smaller than mine," she whispered, her voice shaky.

"That's where you should wear it. Someday soon a man you love with all your heart will be placing another ring on your finger."

In the midst of all her happiness, Rebecca felt a stab of sadness. Her mother was wrong about that last. In spite of determined efforts to forget Jake the way he'd forgotten her, he was the man she loved with all her heart, but he'd never put a ring on her finger, never promise to love, honor and cherish for the rest of their lives.

He hadn't lied to her, hadn't promised anything beyond the brief, intense encounters. It was entirely her fault that she couldn't forget him.

Perhaps someday she'd find her David, someone she could love in a different way than she loved Jake, but right now that didn't even seem a possibility.

Over the last two months she'd been forced to admit to herself that she did love Jake in an elemental, forever kind of way. It wasn't that she needed him because she had no one. She had others to love...her mother and her grandmother...and that love should have filled her heart, yet still there was an empty spot.

Each love was, indeed, special and precious.

Mary took her flowers from Doris. "I'm ready now."

Rebecca walked down the aisle of the small chapel to take her place at the front, and the wedding march began.

The simple ceremony was beautiful and moving.

When it was over, Mary and David walked back down the aisle, pausing to greet some of the small gathering of guests. It was then that she thought she saw Jake in the middle of the third row from the back.

Her heart fluttered though she told herself it was only a tall man with dark hair, a case of mistaken identity, something that had happened to her more than once over the last couple of months.

Mary turned at the church door, lifted her bouquet and tossed it straight toward Rebecca. She'd have had to jump aside to miss catching it.

The thirty or so guests broke into noisy confusion, laughing and talking and milling about as they left the chapel to go to the reception at Doris' house.

Jake caught her eye and pushed against the flow of traffic, slowly but determinedly making his way to her.

She wanted to run to him, throw herself into his arms.

She wanted to run from him, hang onto any infinitesimal ground she'd gained in forgetting him.

She stood rooted in place.

"How've you been?" he asked. He looked essentially the same but different in a suit. His hair was still a bit too long and still shaggy and his eyes were still the shade of the midnight sky in summer. She yearned to touch him, to tangle her fingers in his hair, to kiss his lips, to feel his arms around her.

"Good," she answered, clasping both hands firmly about the bouquet to keep them from doing anything stupid like touching him. "How about you?"

"Good. Fine." He shifted from one foot to the other. "Your mother invited me."

"I see." How strange that her mother would have done that and not mentioned it. "Are you going to the reception at Doris' house?"

"Yes. I don't know. Maybe." He glanced around at the almost-empty church. "It was a nice ceremony. Your mother looks happy, not like the first time we saw her."

"She is happy."

"This is a nice chapel."

"Nice chapel, nice ceremony, nice day outside, and you look very nice. Guess that takes care of all the niceties." She gave him a brittle smile. Now he could leave, having satisfied the requirements of etiquette, or he could ask her to spend another night with him if that was what he wanted, and suddenly she thought it might be. His gaze was heated as it stroked over her.

She had no idea what she'd say if he asked. Her arms ached to be around him again, her body yearned for him. The leaving had been so hard before and would be hard again. But she didn't regret one second of their time together.

If he wanted to be with her again, she'd say yes, she decided abruptly. She knew her mother didn't regret loving her father, no matter how short their happiness had been.

If Jake wanted her to go with him for a weekend, a night, an hour, she'd say yes.

He expelled a long breath. "This isn't easy for me. I don't have your courage."

She blinked at the strange comment. "My courage? When I first came to you, I was an emotional wreck."

"You'd been dealt some pretty hard blows, but you had the strength to go on, the courage to want to find your birth parents no matter what the consequences. I've spent my entire adult life running."

"I don't understand what you're saying."

"I didn't understand it either until recently. All this business about *love and let go* was just cowardice. I was afraid to stay around long enough to let myself care about somebody for fear they'd leave me. So I left first. Or at least I tried to. I can't leave you, Rebecca. You've become a part of me. You're everywhere I go. I can't get away from you. I don't want to get away from you."

"I know. I feel the same way. I'm here, Jake. For however long it lasts, I'm here."

One corner of his mouth quirked up in a half grin. "Are you sure you mean that?"

She took a deep breath, ordering herself to think about the present, the immediate future, about being with Jake and the wonderful, soaring way that always made her feel, not to think about the eventual pain of parting.

"I'm sure," she said.

He reached in the pocket of his jacket with one hand then extended the other toward her. She placed hers in it and her soul seemed to lighten at his touch. She'd made the right decision. Whatever bits of love they shared would be worth the price.

"I love you, Rebecca." He opened his other hand to expose a sparkling diamond ring. "I want you to marry me and stay with me always."

Rebecca opened her mouth to say yes to the question she'd expected from him, the request to spend the night or the day together. It was, after all, what she'd already told herself she'd say no matter what Jake asked of her.

But his words registered and she heard what he'd really said.

Not an hour, not even the entire weekend, but the rest of their lives.

She must have misunderstood. How many times had he told her that nothing lasted forever, that *love and let go* was the wisdom of the ages?

"Marry?"

"Yeah, like your mother and David just did, in a nice ceremony in a nice little chapel. This one, if you'd like."

"Marry? For always?"

"Forever. It has to be forever. I'll never be able to get up the courage to do this again."

Forever? Going to sleep in Jake's arms and waking beside him? Having breakfast together, coming home at the end of a hard day to veg in front of the television together? The possibility of more than a weekend had never even crossed her mind.

"Do you need some time to think about this?" Jake asked as she hesitated, and she was amazed at the uncertainty in his voice. "Or if you're afraid to say no, to tell me you don't love me, don't sweat it. I've had plenty of experience with moving on, though I gotta admit, it's going to be pretty tough this time. I never loved anybody before."

"Not love you? Of course I do! I love you so much, Jake, I was ready to face loneliness the rest of my life in exchange for one more night with you. And now you're offering me a lifetime of nights with you. *Yes* seems an inadequate answer."

"It's all the answer I need." Jake's smile stretched from one side of his face to the other. He slid the diamond ring onto her finger, pulled her into his arms and kissed her.

Rebecca reveled in the delicious sensations of his lips on hers, his body pressed against hers, sensations she'd thought she'd never experience again. Now she not only had them for the moment but a promise of a lifetime of ecstasy, of loving Jake.

A few minutes later when they walked out of the church, arms wrapped around each other, Mary and David were waiting beside the door.

Mary introduced Jake and David then looked up at her daughter expectantly. Rebecca knew she was beaming, knew her happiness showed on her face.

Silently she lifted her left hand to show her mother the ring.

"Congratulations!" Mary hugged Rebecca then Jake. "Welcome to the family!"

"Thank you for inviting him," Rebecca said.

"I've missed twenty-nine birthdays and Christmases," Mary said. "Do you think getting him here is a start on all those gifts I didn't give you?"

Jake's arm slid around Rebecca. "I can't speak for your daughter, but as for me, you're caught up on birthday, Christmas and everyday gifts for the rest of my life."

The End

About the Author:

I grew up in a small rural town in southeastern Oklahoma where our favorite entertainment on summer evenings was to sit outside under the stars and tell stories. When I went to bed at night, instead of a lullaby, I got a story. That could be due to the fact that everybody in my family has a singing voice like a bullfrog with laryngitis, but they sure could tell stories—ghost stories, funny stories, happy stories, scary stories.

For as long as I can remember I've been a storyteller. Thank goodness for computers so I can write down my stories. It's hard to make listeners sit still for the length of a book! Like my family's tales, my stories are funny, scary, dramatic, romantic, paranormal, magic.

Besides writing, my interests are reading, eating chocolate and riding my Harley.

Contact information is available on my website. I love to talk to readers! And writers. And riders. And computer programmers. And poets and pirates and paupers and pawns and kings and cats and dogs. Okay, I just plain love to talk!

http://www.sallyberneathy.com